ISBN-13:978-0692692882 (Black Phoenix, Vol I: Intersection)
ISBN-10:0692692886
ASIN: B01E99N5WW

BLACK PHOENIX I: INTERSECTION

BY

MATTHEW TREADSTONE

PRELUDE: WOMAN OF IRON

Dawn sunlight spread across rolling peaks of the Hindu-Kush. Clouds turned blood red, crowned in gold against stark blue sky. Low mist blanketed peaks and valleys like a cotton laced embrace.

Chief Petty Officer Jordan "Cooper" DeBlanc looked down upon it from her high overwatch position, situated between two faces of rock on the rolling descent beneath the summit at eight thousand feet. She'd observed the village all night through her Barrett M82 50-cal's thermal scope.

The village sat there, as it had, probably since the days of the Khans. Grids of low, craggy stone-mason walls interlocked with mud-brick, thatch-roofed hovels tucked into corners. An ancient tractor with no wheels, and some other broken up vehicles, probably "gifts" from past Soviet PR actions, rusted around the near side of the village.

"What's it been, Cooper?" asked Ramon, her partner. "Anything new?"

"Village is starting to stir. No movement at all overnight," she reported.

Her headset crackled to life, though she heard her team leader's voice anyway from his position twenty feet up the hill.

"AQ's probably moved out in the night," said Bossman.

"Negative," Cooper countered. "I would've seen them. Nothing's been in or out in the last ten hours. I have a full field of view."

"It's possible you might have missed something," Bossman replied.

Cooper's jaw shifted. "No, I don't believe so, sir, not from this angle. The thermals would have lit up anyone moving over that cold surface like a flare."

"I know how thermals work, Cooper." He stood up and came down, stirring the rest of the team, HK416 in hand. "Get ready to move then. Pack up the Barret."

"Roger."

Another voice crackled into her headset, one that sent shivers up her spine and rankled her neck hairs with anger, "Compensating for something, Coop? Got to up the boss?"

A jackal like chuckle followed, while Cooper grit her teeth.

"Call it like I see it, Lenny," she almost whispered.

"They call me Hardknox, remember?"

She didn't reply. Cooper got out from behind the massive sniper rifle, unloaded the box magazine and cleared the chamber. She loaded the round from the weapon back into the magazine and packed it. Ramon covered her. When done, she covered him with her small MP7 back-up while he broke down his position.

"Don't let them get to you," Ramon whispered to her, "not here. They'd want you to fuck up."

"Don't worry," she replied. "I won't."

6

The forty SEALs, two platoons from Team 4, moved down from the summit in a wedge formation, pushing forward at an even pace, weapons at the alert positions. An Apache gunship passed over the crests a mile away, little more than a dark speck. Bossman kept on the radio with the attack helicopter while it observed the village for threats.

"Gunship reporting anything?" she asked to Sparky, their radio operator.

"Hillsides to the north are clear," he replied.

The villagers watched their approach. Cooper wanted to know what they were thinking. She tried to imagine what it would be like back in San Francisco, watching armed, uniformed soldiers walking up the streets to her parents' house.

They seem a lot calmer than I would be, Cooper thought. *Must not be the first time for them.*

"They're not closing up their windows and doors," said Ramon. "That's good."

"Means they're not expecting a fight?"

"Yeah, that's a plus. They're not throwing roses or opening up, though. You can smell the tension. Something's been here recently."

Cooper and Ramon had been in the same BUD/S class, been in the SEAL teams as long as each other. Ramon, however, had started as an intel specialist with Naval Special Warfare. It hadn't been as a trigger puller, but with one deployment under his belt he at least knew what to expect more than her.

"Maybe the HUMINT we got this time was right. AQ or Taliban been here recently?" she asked.

"Bossman'll find out. Trust me, he's not good with women in uniform, but he knows how to work the locals."

"That's a plus," Cooper said under her breath. "Just don't mind him as much as the others. Can't believe they're still in my shadow."

"That's where Lenny and Scotty will always be," Ramon said. "They got nothing on you."

She smiled slightly sideways at him, gave him a warm thump on the shoulder with a gloved fist. The next couple of hours passed on their search of the village. Their attached interpreter worked with Bossman to gather information out of the villagers. Cooper and Ramon took a rest near a sheep enclosure at the edge of the village. They looked out to green-brown hills rolling towards craggy bluffs half a mile away.

"Bossman been eating at you, Coop?" asked Ramon.

She shook her tired head and sat against the wooden fence. "That short little shit," Cooper growled. "Telling me if I might have missed anything. The village is smaller than a football field, it's well within my scope's range and inclined toward my position. There was no path in or out that I couldn't cover. All night watching this place, no food or sleep."

"Speaking of which." Ramon broke up a piece of local, unleavened brick-oven bread and handed it to her.

"Thanks, Ramon." She munched it down and drank from the bite valve of her camelbak. "I can take a little FNG bullshit. I'd prefer it to this, actually. Been in Team 4 almost a year, and it hasn't escaped my attention I've never been hazed."

"Never got the treatment?" he chuckled. "If you want I'll tie you to a chair with duct tape and perform an interrogation for your last lesbian experience."

"Just wish he'd get over it. And I wish Lenny and Scotty wouldn't have to echo everything he says with their own bullshit. Next overwatch, I'd like to put 661-grains through one ear and out the other, in both of their heads."

"Couldn't be any worse than BUD/S, could it? I remember you being pretty stoic about it back then. Instructors really tried to drill the woman angle in your head."

"It's different. Instructors were doing what they needed to, to shape me. Those two are different. They mean it. They keep looking at me with that same goddamn stare. The harder I try, the harder they push. Just like Annapolis."

"They'll never try that again, Cooper. You know they won't." He nudged her shoulder with his knuckles. "But doesn't make up for Annapolis does it?"

She stared up into his dark eyes and huffed, her voice almost croaked out the words, "How could it? The only uniforms Lenny and Scotty should wear are prison orange."

He pursed his lips. "Yeah, for sure. You got your hits in though. Bet that felt good."

"Not enough," she said, staring out. Then went quiet for a long pause, then said again, "not enough."

"Does it affect what the others guys say? Like the Boss?"

"I always expected it. I wasn't naïve about this. Back in BUD/S they were trying to break us down, get in our heads any way they could, race, religion, gender, height. I still didn't think I'd hear that shit when downrange in the goddamn Afghan of all places. Sandwich jokes too? Really? Get a new schtick, already."

Ramon patted her shoulder. "I wouldn't sweat it. Bet your sandwiches taste like shit anyway."

"I didn't join the Navy to be a cook."

He chuckled. "What about your husband?"

"He's a worse chef than me." She smiled. "You'd think biologists would know more about flavors."

She pulled out a locket attached to the dog tags about her neck, opening it to see her four year old son's smiling face, born a year after she left Annapolis. "Maybe our son will take it up."

Her headset crackled. "Cooper, Bossman." She nearly rolled her eyes, but then keyed her mike.

"Cooper, here."

"Need you at the north corner of the village, ASAP."

"Roger that, oscar mike." Cooper rechecked her MP7, resettled the Barrett on her back, and headed towards Bossman's position.

The tight "tanker" style jump suit beneath her gear betrayed the femininity of her curves, revealing what her tall stature and short hair hid. Her helmet and Oakleys concealed her features, but still left her full lips on display, something the local males picked up on, especially since she was the only member of the team without a beard. They looked at her with a mix of abject fear and disgust.

She towered over them, and they probably didn't appreciate the way her jump suit showed the sway of her hips. Her own disgust at their veiled and sequestered women she had to hide.

In this Taliban-influenced part of the country, women couldn't go to school, drive, or hold a job. They couldn't be anything but their husband's or father's property. Seeing a tall woman warrior with guns strutting between their hovels must have been a shock.

She made the sixty yards to Bossman's position without incident, from the locals, at least. Then Lenny Knox and Scotty Chambers stood at the corners of two buildings in front of the alley she needed to go into.

Their eyes hit like a wall, stopped her dead in her tracks. That same gaze, the ones they always had. Even before. She didn't understand those gazes until it happened. Now, those predatory looks, those hungry breaths fogging into the cold mountain air. Lenny dropped his shades over pale blue eyes, but still smiled slightly from the center of his blond beard.

Scotty Chambers left his shades up, brown eyes cold beneath an ebony brow. Bright, perfect teeth grimaced at her while chomping the end of a licorice. He loved those things. He'd had it on his breath.

"Sup, Coop?" Scotty asked. "Boss is waiting."

She stepped forward, Oakleys down, and murmured. "You were waiting too?"

"Where's the Chief, Chief?" Lenny asked, referring to Ramon.

The bulk of their equipment in the narrow alley made it difficult to pass, but she forced through. Lenny lost balance, and her packed Barret barrel tapped against Scotty's rifle. They just cooed and huffed.

"Be that way, damn Shorty," one of them said. She couldn't tell which. Didn't care. They were practically one. Still calling her "Shorty," an ironic nick name she picked up from her fellow cadets. Only *they* still called her that.

She reached the end of the alley, her destination. Bossman looked up at her, short even by Afghan standards.

"Reporting, Boss," she said. "You needed me?"

"Got a piece of intel, thought you might be best to handle it."

"Me?" she asked.

Bossman stepped up to the nearest hovel and opened up the cloth entrance, allowing her to peek through. A woman sat in the corner among the hay-thatch floor. Young, with a cute face looking out from a baby blue hijab. Bossman moved the curtain back down.

"She speaks some English," he said, craning his neck to look up at her. At 6' even, she towered over the stocky 5'6" commander. Probably another reason he could not often hide his disdain. "She doesn't seem very interested in talking to us."

"But she'll talk to me, sir?"

He shrugged. "Said she wanted the woman with the gun. Says she knows the whereabouts of the Taliban. Don't know why, but she doesn't want to talk to a man."

Cooper nodded, but her understanding of the notion couldn't help but put an assured smirk on her lips. "I'll find out what I can."

She pushed the cloth opening aside, but then Bossman grabbed her wrist. "Oh, and, don't get too emotional in there."

She scowled at him beneath her Oakleys. "I'll try not to get all gushy, Boss."

"That a girl."

Cooper moved into the hovel and murmured, "Homegrown Taliban."

"Hom...?" the girl asked. "Grown?"

She smiled slightly and took off her helmet, then her Oakleys. The girl grinned softly and gazed toward her with innocent, almond eyes. Her beauty struck Cooper in the chest, elevating her heart rate a little. A sudden, giddy nervousness filled her limbs.

“Hi....” she said, trailing off.

“Hello,” she said back.

Cooper set the massive, 30 pound M82 Barrett against the wall. The tall female warrior sat down next to her, leaning forward after drawing off her combat vest and gear to sit only in her uilities.

“You know English?”

“Yes...som. I learn in Kandahar.”

“Kandahar?” she asked. “You’re a long way from there.”

“Hm?” the girl asked, then shook her head.

“Oh, um, very far away. Far. And, I’m Cooper.”

“Oh, yes. Very Far. My name Malala. My father come, eh, move us here for husband.”

“Your husband? You?”

“Yes, my father...betroth me.”

Cooper nodded. “Ah, okay. Your father not like Kandahar?”

Malala shook her head. “In Kandahar, he see Imam. Imam say, girls, no school. Girls in school bad for Muslim. Haram. Eh, forbidden.”

“Mm,” Cooper sounded, moving in closer to talk quieter. “And this Imam...Taliban?”

“Yes. And my husband...Taliban.”

“So your father got radicalized in Kandahar and moved out here to get you a proper Taliban husband?”

“Em....” She shook her head. “No understand. Too much word.”

“Sorry,” Cooper said and shook her head. “Sorry, I forgot—”

She stopped when she looked down at Malala’s hand, and the marks on her wrist peeking out from beneath those substantial sleeves. Cooper slipped her fingers under the other woman’s and gently lifted back the fabric.

“Ehh,” Malala sounded and winced.

“Sorry,” Cooper whispered, but saw the burn marks, shaped in parallel bars, like a grill. Cooper looked over to see a skillet set up over a fire pit a few feet away. The crossbars looked about the same distance apart as the burns on Malala’s arm.

Cooper swallowed, lips tight, to contain herself. She reached to her gear and pulled out bandages from her first aid kit.

“No,” Malala said. “Is not....”

“Shhh,” Cooper whispered. “Your father or husband? Which one did this?”

“Both...both burn me. I shame them...say I have jinn...eh, demon.”

She sucked in a breath. The girl smiled at her, then bit her lip. She let Cooper wrap up her arm once she dabbed rubbing alcohol on the dirty, jagged burns. The female SEAL kept her jaw tight, grinding her molars together, thinking about a father dragging his own daughter’s arm onto a hot skillet.

“Your father did this....” Cooper trailed off and shook her head, “because he thought you had a demon?”

Her face contorted in fear and pain while Cooper tightened down the last of the bandage, now covering almost her entire forearm.

“Yes,” she said. A tear fell from Malala’s eye.

Cooper nodded. "It's okay. I can't believe a man could do this to his own daughter. And you're so pretty, it's just...and, I have a son. If someone ever harmed him, I don't know how I would control myself."

She placed her palm on Malala's face, then lowered it to her shoulder. "Why? Why did your father do this? What demon is he talking about?"

She looked into Cooper's gaze then, cinnamon eyes so gentle, yet eager. "I not want man. I not want husband."

"No husband. Don't want one?"

"I not want...not like...men."

Cooper gulped. Malala's look burnt into her, and a slight upturn at the corner of the girl's lip signified a delightfully mischievious intent.

"Yeah," Cooper whispered. "I got you."

Malala smiled. "In Kandahar, I met woman at school. We become friends. We...em, we..."

"It's okay," Cooper said. "You can tell me."

Malala's hand fell on Cooper's, fingers gripping tight. A fire set off in her belly, warm chills shooting up her torso. She closed her eyes and let out a breath.

"She like you," Malala continued. "Very strong. I go with her. She a belly dancer from Egypt, teach music and dance."

Cooper looked into Malala's pained, yet enchanted eyes. In that gaze she gained a familiarity, one she felt herself. A caged desire, a restrained passion.

"You loved her, didn't you?" Cooper asked.

"Yes." Tears fell from her eye, but she locked her teeth together. "I shame my father. He take me away, take me here to punish. Marry old Taliban. I want to go city, study, make music. I dream to go Egypt, be belly dancer." She chuckled then.

Cooper smiled. "Yes, I saw them. Sharm el-Sheik resort. I saw belly dancers. Very beautiful...so seductive."

Malala touched Cooper's face with the other hand. Fingers locked into Cooper's short, scruffy hair, teasing at her ear. Her fingertips felt like bolts of lightning.

Still, she resisted, as much as she wanted to feel Malala's warmth and softness. *Michael*, she thought of her husband. *My son. My family. My career. How can I seek this? Why do I have to want it so badly? Why did I let them chain me like this, never to even tell anyone? Never to love like I used to.*

Lenny and Scotty stood over every intimate feeling she ever felt since that day, like dark specters forever laughing and taunting. They'd always talked about how she wore her uniform skirt too tight, their voices menacing, not playful. Their eyes looked on her like she was their property.

She liked the tight skirts, body proud from a lifetime of freediving and swimming, riding bikes, running, and hiking, talents that led her to join the Navy. Tight clothes and short shorts had been her favorite adornments, her body the envy of her peers. Throughout high school and her sexual awakening, Cooper sought whatever girl or boy she wanted. She dared the same in the Academy despite their oppressive ethics rules.

In one fell swoop, Lenny and Scotty stole her power and free sensuality, shamed her for it with their aggression, thrusting while she bled from their hits to her face. Worse, they escaped the justice she deserved. And she wondered about where the Academy's ethics rules were then.

Still did.

Cooper regretted letting them dominate her even now, eager to get back what she had lost. What they had taken.

If I was half the woman I used to be, I'd have Malala stripped and naked under me right this second. Writhing and sweating and kissing and licking. But I can't.

Her free ranging spirit to love as she wanted, trapped, beaten, and chained within her like she had been bound by their grips against the shower room floor while her blood trailed into the drain. Trained to face down implacable enemies, having overcome so much, still she cowered from her own needs and the consequences her culture might drop upon her again.

"I not want husband...." Malala whispered and gently rubbed Cooper's cheek.

"I can't...I can't let them control me. Why'd they do it? Why'd they have to do that to me? Why can't I just be? Why can't you just be?"

"You talk much," Malala hissed, fingers gripping the front of Cooper's zippered utilities and pulling them open. Her good hand cupped Cooper's breast while the other wrapped her around the waist.

Cooper gasped, looked deep into her eyes then. Malala gripped and owned her the way Cooper had so many uncertain girls before. She moved forward. Lips gently met. Malala's kiss felt so soft, her skin so smooth. Pain and fear vanished as if it were never there. Within Cooper an eternal darkness flared to life.

Malala pressed like a Taliban spring offensive made of tongue and fire. As much as Cooper felt herself reignited, she needed to stop. She resisted her urges, asking between kisses.

"Where are they? Your husband? Your father?"

"Mountains north," she said softly. "Trail for goat north of village, take you to old place for water."

"A spring?" she asked. "Where they can rest and gather water and food."

"Yes, many gun."

"I've got plenty of gun for them."

Cooper pulled back, zipped her utilities back up.

"No go," Malala pleaded, but Cooper stayed her.

"It's okay," she said. "How many fighters? How many Taliban?"

"Fifty. Maybe some more."

She stood and recovered her weapons, helmet, and Oakleys. She stroked Malala's cheek and turned to walk away when she clasped Cooper's wrist.

"You come back?"

"No," she said, then smiled, ran her fingers along Malala's jaw line and chin. "Go back to Kandahar. Get out of here. Your father and husband will not find you. Find your girlfriend."

Malala stood and hugged her. They kissed again. For the first time in years, Cooper felt so alive. So ready, thankful that nothing happening between them could get beyond these mudbrick walls.

The Team's vehicles arrived from further down the mountain, a column of mine-re-

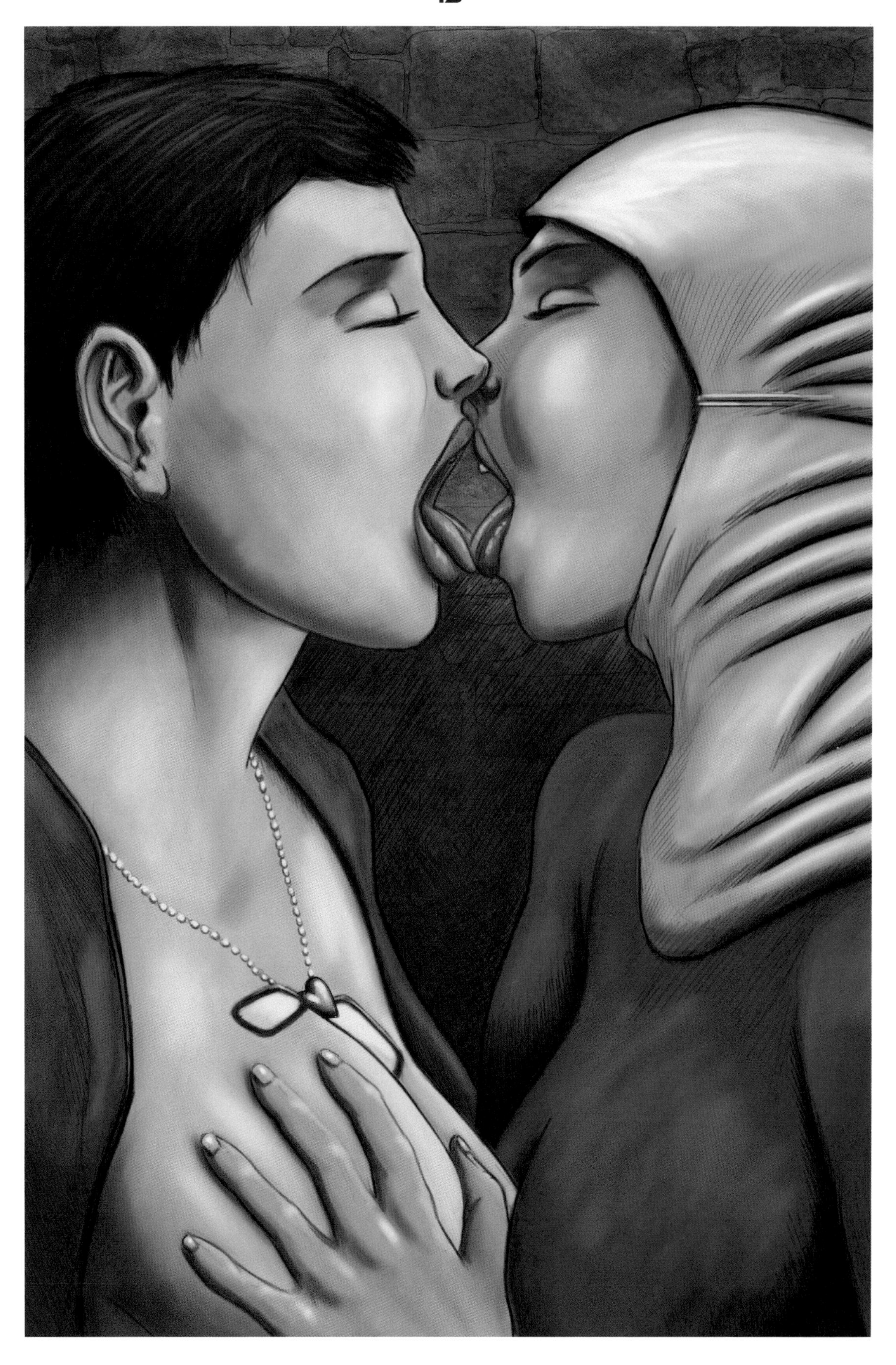

sistant Chargers and armored Humvees with MK-19 automatic grenade launchers, M2 .50-cal's, and M240B machine guns. They rolled out to follow the goat trail up to a point, then dismounted.

Cooper and Ramon studied their maps as they got their orders from Bossman.

"If we keep going with the vehicles, they'll no doubt spot us," said Bossman. "Reapers have confirmed sighting of thermal contacts ahead. Looks like the girl's intel was right."

"I'm pretty certain they already know we're here, Boss," said Ramon. "I wouldn't doubt if they've been observing us from that bluff all morning."

"You thinking ambush?" asked Bossman.

"Certain of it," answered Ramon.

"We need to find it first," said Cooper. "Ramon and I will take those rocks up, find a perch for the Barrett. We'll find them first and turn their ambush in on them."

A snicker from above rankled the hairs on the back of her neck. Scotty stood behind a .50 cal machine gun in the turret of a Charger.

"I'm sure Cooper can sniff out an ambush by now," he said, smiling wide while chewing on a piece of licorice.

"Shut the fuck up, cabron," Ramon spat.

"You're talking to an officer," Bossman quietly admonished. He never yelled. Never laid his hands on anyone. Low and quiet meant something bad. Ramon's lips tightened, knew he'd just signed a virtual death warrant to be meted out when the operation ended.

Scotty just smirked down, cocked the large handle on the powerful machine gun. Cooper ignored him, looked at her team leader.

Bossman cocked his head. "You've cleared a village by observation, and gotten intel out of a frightened young girl. You've been right twice, Cooper."

"Third time's the charm," she said, smiling slightly.

"Yeah, if you can pull the trigger on a live target. Ramon'll take it from you and finish the job if you can't."

Scotty quietly "ooooohhh'd" from above. Cooper didn't even look. "Shall we go then, Commander?"

Bossman licked the inside of his lip, then spat some chaw onto the dirt. "Do it."

Ramon and Cooper returned to their vehicle and prepped, leaving behind their packs. Cooper strapped the Barrett to her back, cushioned against her full camelback. They double-checked all magazines for the sniper rifle and personal weapons.

Ramon situated the radio into his assault pack. They removed excess warming gear, performed a comms check, then stepped off from the vehicles. They reached the bluff in ten minutes and began their ascent, zig-zagging from one available path to the next.

"Apaches scanning the rocks above you," came Bossman's voice into their headsets. "You look clear."

"Roger that," said Cooper. "Strobes on." They activated the infrared strobes on their shoulders to keep from being lit up by friendly aircraft.

The burn in her muscles only fueled her. The Barrett never seemed so light. Her anger defied gravity. Anger at the Taliban for what they did to Malala, anger at the men of similar caliber behind her. Ramon growled and heaved to keep up.

"Fucking that's the last time," she spat. "If I can't take the shot, you have to take it? You're as new as me, Ramon."

"Hey, it was his idea," he replied. "And keep your voice down. We got haji's up there."

"I hope so." *For Malala's sake.*

They reached the top in twenty minutes. Cooper helped Ramon haul himself up. They took a knee and looked ahead.

"Cooper, Bossman. Vehicles moving out. Keep calling out your position so we don't light you up."

"Roger," she replied. "We're atop the bluff, moving forward, due north."

The two of them kept their weapons at the ready, staying low on their maneuvers among the scruffy mountain grass and rocks. An Apache gunship then rattled their skins when it flew overhead at near a hundred miles an hour, twin turbo-fans roaring, four rotor blades blurring like a dragonfly's wings.

"Damn," whispered Ramon. "Almost scared the shit out of me."

"Army boys don't want us to have all the fun," she said. "We'll have to beat them to it. There, that outcrop." She pointed to a craggy uplift a hundred yards ahead. "That's where we'll look out."

"Sniper team moving to uplift north of gulch, over," Ramon reported.

"Roger," Bossman replied.

Tracers flew up into the air at the Apache gunship. The helo shrank over the mountains ahead, then banked hard left to escape the field of fire. Cooper counted the seconds until the sound of machine guns reached her ears.

"Three seconds," Cooper said. "They're about 900 meters away. C'mon."

Cooper and Ramon made it to the rock outcrop without encountering any insurgents. Cooper's heart pounded. Her lungs heaved at the thin mountain air. Ramon looked out with his binos.

She holstered her MP7 and pulled out the Barrett, setting it down on bipods. She used the carrying case as a cushion for her elbow against the rock, then dug her shoulder against the buttstock, letting her cheek slowly lower against the cheek well.

"Apache's circling back around, probably going to TADS."

"Let's see which of us gets the longest shot." She scanned the bluffs ahead, catching campfires in her thermals. She magnified her vision onto the targets, spotting several silhouettes scrambling to uncover equipment. The silhouettes of Kalashnikov rifles and RPK machine guns became clear and obvious.

"Positive enemy contact," she said.

Ramon reported in their location as well as the enemy's. Cooper searched for her first target, but just 300 meters down, on the road, she spotted four white silhouettes against the black earth of her thermals. Two men with RPG's set up on rocks overlooking the road. Their partners carried satchels with extra rockets.

"Bossman, Cooper, be advised, two RPG teams setting up an ambush on the road." She could already hear the vehicles echoing up the valley from behind and below.

"Take 'em out," he ordered. "We've got to clear some IED's."

Cooper reset herself on the big rifle. She aimed in on the first silhouette, then switched to daylight vision. She wanted to see the first man she killed. She wanted to see the kind of man who could beat his wife, his daughter, his sister for "shame," for "honor." The white silhouette vanished to reveal a bearded, bronze skinned man in fatigue jacket and dishdasha, a "man-dress" as grunts called them.

He set the RPG-7 on his shoulder and rose up slightly, right into her crosshairs. Cooper gently squeezed the trigger. The Barrett kicked like a mule, air pressure hitting her head like a smack in the face. The 661-grain round ripped through the man's chest. He flipped back with his legs raising into the air before they dropped limp to the ground.

His shocked partner jumped clear into the open. She adjusted on him, quick, not even thinking about the life she just ended. The round ripped out. Dust kicked into her face and neck. The .50-caliber round struck through the man's femur. She saw his mouth open into a scream, terror filling his eyes. The scope revealed almost every detail, but she only heard a faint echo of his cry much later than the movement of his mouth.

She wondered if that was how Malala looked when those who were supposed to care for her drug her flesh onto a burning skillet. She hoped the screaming man was Malala's husband, or a man just as heinous. Then wished it was Scotty. Or Lenny. She fired again, hitting him just below the neck. His body rolled over and stopped. The sudden limpness seemed unreal. Or fake. Like a bad movie dummy.

"Two down, Cooper," said Ramon. "Jesus, it just rips them apart."

He sounded far more stunned than she felt. Cooper became almost unnerved at her calmness, serene in her rage. She sent a round through the next gunner's head, then shot his partner flat against the ground.

"They're done," she said low.

A rapid one-two crump-crump report of detonations reached up from farther down the valley. "IED's cleared," Lenny reported.

She grunted inwardly, looking forward, wishing one had blown him to pieces. For a brief moment she contemplated letting some RPG gunners through to take out his Charger, but there were good men in there with him.

"Cooper, Ramon, push forward," Bossman ordered.

"Roger," they said.

Ramon quickly packed up his spotter scope. Cooper put up the Barrett's bipods and packed it into the carrying case. She readied her MP7 and headed on. Against the bluffs out ahead, 30mm cannon shells impacted from a circling Apache a kilometer away.

"Shit, been tracking them for months, now we got them in the open, flushed out," said Ramon between heaves of thin air.

"Thank you, Malala," Cooper huffed.

The Chargers and Humvees settled three hundred meters from the target area, pounding what they could see with their machine guns and grenade launchers, but more discovered IED's held up the only passable path for vehicles. Bossman led ten other SEALs in a push ahead on foot. Cooper and Ramon headed for a tall hill overlooking the gulch. They couldn't see any Taliban defending it.

They reached the top in five minutes, legs burning harder than they would have at sea level. Cooper groaned through the pain in her thighs and calves, fearing Malala's tormentors might not find themselves in her crosshairs. She set up the Barrett, Ramon on binos. SEAL snipers often didn't use spotters, they wanted every man a shooter with weapon in hand, but her Barret had his HK416 way outranged.

"Oh, shit," said Ramon. "Got a line of 'em. Almost looks like a trench. Dishka at ten o'clock, under camo net. Four hundred meters."

Cooper checked that area, finding the "Dishka," the DSHK Soviet-made heavy machine gun, looking straight down the gulch.

"We need to keep them clear of that gun," she said. "I got the current gunner in my sights." He looked old, gray beard, weathered face, old enough to be Malala's father. The one who betrayed his daughter's trust.

"Send it."

The massive bullet split through the gunner's head. Pink mist splattered with skull matter and black turban. The body fell so fast she couldn't even see where he landed. With four rounds left, Ramon set a spare magazine next to her elbow.

"Call the gun to the Apaches," she said. "Hellfire'll put it out for sure."

Ramon relayed his coordinates and then the distance and direction to the gun so the Apache could find it. As he did so, Cooper aimed in on a man tucked behind a crag of rock.

You can't hide from me, she thought, deeply amazed at her own predatory desire. She ended his life with a .50-caliber round through three inches of rock.

A Hellfire missile flew inbound. A flash and violent blast of black smoke ripped out from the machine gun position. The sound reached them seconds later.

The Taliban fighters abandoned their holes and trenches. They knew they couldn't hold, especially when Bossman's SEALs came into view, rushing up the hill. Two Chargers that maneuvered past the IED's fired the M240's on their backs in alternating bursts, "talking guns." The air crackled with snaps of flying bullets.

"Vaya con dios, amigos," said Ramon.

Cooper aimed in on a running fighter, then squeezed too prematurely. The round shattered the rock next to his knee.

"Shit!" She pulled out the empty mag, and loaded in the fresh one.

"Breathe easy, keep on them," said Ramon. "Lead up just a little, he's running straight. You got him. You are Zen, samurai with a gun."

Cooper let out a slow breath, letting the rifle rise slightly with the man moving ahead, then squeezed the trigger. It kicked and struck the man in the hip, right on the gluteus and he tumbled forward a bloody mess.

"Oh, mierda! En el culo! You're vicious, girl."

"Don't finish that one, Cooper," came Bossman. "We need a live one to interrogate."

"Roger," Cooper answered.

The two then continued on the ridge line, Barrett packed and personals out. They stayed high above the running fighters, keeping their advantage. The ridge gave them excellent overlook on the fleeing Taliban.

Cooper had three in her sights, damn near straight below at fifty meters. The two of them didn't have time to switch to the Barrett. Cooper aimed with the diminutive MP7. She clipped one more man in the shoulder.

Ramon killed one, shot straight through the back, and then her partner went pale. His first one of the day. The first in his career. His life. The first man he ever killed.

"Holy shit," he said. She lowered her weapon and looked at him.

"Don't think about it, Ramon. Keep focused." She grabbed his shoulder. "You're Zen."

Cooper aimed in at the others, catching one in the back of the neck with her weapon's nasty 4.6mm rounds. Then another in the kidney. Both fell dead. She let out a steamy exhale into the cold mountain air. She frantically scanned the rocky areas out ahead, a virtual maze of crags and boulders, the perfect escape route.

"Dammit!" she groaned.

"What?" asked Ramon, wiping his pale forehead of sweat.

"The rest escaped into there. Too many of them still alive."

He looked at her with his traumatized vision. "Are you okay?"

She rested back and looked at him. "I guess I needed to exorcise a demon of mine."

He nodded, breath uneasy. "They're not the ones you want. I know that, Cooper."

Cooper's lips flared in hate. "The ones I want, I can't touch. Unless they try it again."

"They won't," he said. "They can't. They know that."

Cooper looked back into the maze. The fighters had escaped into those rocks the way the other two hid behind their benefactors. No record left of what they had done, except what remained in her memory, boiling over every time she heard their jackal-like cackles.

With no more enemies they could see, they rejoined Bossman when he ordered to consolidate on the objective. Their sweat-drenched clothes began to freeze in the mountain winds. Cooper tried not to shiver, but her teeth clattered of their own accord. It wasn't even noon yet.

The team gathered in a 360, setting up their vehicles in a circle to cover every angle. Naval Human Exploitation Teams (HET) came up to interrogate the survivors once they had been treated by the medics. Cooper checked her weapons in the back of her assigned Charger, and warmed up. She removed her combat vest and opened up the front of her jumpsuit to let the warm air in beneath the soaked fabric, and dry out the sweat before it froze.

Ramon sat on the other side of her, quiet, staring out. She'd never seen his bronze skin so sickly.

"You okay?" Cooper asked.

He looked at her. "You make it look so easy, Cooper. You got what, eight, ten haji's? Shot an ass off one. I just...."

"Just think of all the people they won't be able to hurt now," she said. "You've seen what they do around here."

"Yeah. Guess you're right. Doesn't seem to make it any easier."

"If it was as easy as all that, we'd have zero survival rate as a species."

I've stopped them, she thought, *the way I'd want to stop those behind me.*

"Sometimes you just need the appropriate motivation."

Bossman strode over to Cooper's side of the vehicle, looking at her with his hands at his body armor's collar. A bit of Skoal rolled around under his lip. A large crump battered the air as another IED was destroyed.

"Five, huh?" he asked.

Cooper didn't say anything for a moment, just looked back at him with steel eyes. "Closer to ten."

He nodded. "Uh-kay." Then paused, eyes narrow, looking at the bared field of skin beneath her open suit. "The boys have always wondered something about you."

She cocked her head. "Which is?"

"How is it after BUD/S, and all that running, swimming, push-ups, and what not for the last coupla years do you still have them D-cups? Shouldn't you be flat-chested by now?"

Cooper lowered her sunglasses and said simply, "You should have seen them before."

"I did," Scotty said aloud from atop his Charger, cackling again. "Anchors away—"

"Hey, shut the fuck up!" Ramon shouted. "Last time I'm going to tell you!"

"Hey!" Scotty countered. "You're talking to an officer, Chief! You were warned before."

"Both of you shut your sucks," Bossman projected in a low growl. Cooper remained silent and stoic through the exchange, as she usually did, but this time reached over and silently put her hand on Ramon's shoulder to calm him. He let his hackles down at her request. She patted him on the chest with the side of her fist.

"Chamberman," he said to Scotty, "take your Charger to that overlook, I want plunging fire from there if they decide to come back through that gulch."

"Aye, aye, sir," Scotty said, kicked his foot on the plate beneath his turret and signaled his driver to move on. The vehicle rolled out over the rocks, away from Cooper.

She almost felt stunned, seeing Bossman shield her from him. Sometimes she wondered how much he knew of the incident. Being a commander in the Navy SEALs granted him a tremendous amount of authority and insight others of his rank in different fields would rarely touch.

The ground shook. EOD teams detonated more IED's found in the valley.

Bossman chuckled. "We'll be heading back to FOB Roberta in five mikes."

"What about the others? Are we heading after them at all?"

"Apaches, Cooper. Apaches."

She scowled at him. "We going to let them get all the kills?"

"Them fuckers really rubbed you the wrong way, didn't they?"

She didn't say anything, just looking at him with all the hate in her eyes. It was answer enough. He smiled on, this time, proudly, rather than tauntingly. For the first time, she thought the them he referred to weren't the Taliban.

"We're done here," he said.

"What about the village? Public relations?"

"Is that what they call mutual cunnilingus these days?" he asked.

Cooper's face went solid, adrenaline surging in her chest, fear crawling across her skin. Words, no matter what they were, seized in her throat.

"Don't worry, Coop. Secret's safe with me. What you worried about anyway? DADT's been dead almost a decade now."

"It's not about that."

He nodded, lips tight over the bulge of chaw. "I don't know any specifics, but you have a history with those two from Annapolis. Is it any reason to do with why you quit the Academy?"

Cooper looked at him tight-lipped. "I didn't *quit* the Academy."

Ramon leaned toward her, "Coop—"

"They raped me," she said through nearly clenched teeth.

Bossman went perfectly still, his eyes softer, but his face growing sterner. "Did they?" he started. "And they're still here?"

"Lenny's last name is Knox. It's very recognizable."

Bossman nodded. "Seventh fleet, ranking admiral."

"And the commandant at the time was best drinking buddies with him. They came up through the ranks together, old classmen. Lenny is practically Navy royalty, and Scotty his best, best ol' pal. I'm just the daughter of the manager of Big-o-Tires in San Clemente, who busted her ass the way most cadets did to even get in."

"Hey, Bossman!" yelled Sparky. "Navy Times is heading up the hill."

Cooper closed her eyes and sighed.

"Hm, looks like they want another story," said Bossman, then turned to Sparky. "Hey, tell them key-punching cock strokes to go down the village over yonder, look for a girl named Malala, she's got a story to tell."

"Wait," Cooper said, "she might—"

"She ain't going to say nothing," he said. "I think she has more to lose than you, but even more to gain when she rolls up that sleeve. That's public relations, Coop."

Cooper stepped out and yelled over to the radio man. "Sparky! Tell them to offer her a trip back to Kandahar if she cooperates."

"Roger," Sparky called back.

Good luck, Malala. And thank you.

Bossman spat a brown stream of tobacco against the rocky ground. It hit as another IED detonated in the valley. "Let's pack up these prisoners and get the fuck out of here."

Then he leaned toward her. "And at first opportunity, operations permitting, I'll get you out of this Team and to another. There's no reason you need to keep dealing with them."

"They'll follow, Boss," she whispered. "They always do."

"I'm the one signing the papers this time."

Cooper looked down and breathed a sigh of relief, holding the Barrett between her knees. Bossman moved off.

"What secret's he talking about?" asked Ramon.

Cooper shook her head and spoke softly to him. "I kissed that girl...Malala."

"What?" he asked, eyes wide.

Cooper turned and settled into the passenger's seat. "I'm bi-sexual, Ramon. I haven't told anyone this since Annapolis, not even my husband."

"Do you think he'd had have a problem with it?"

"No, it's not about him. It's about...them. I used to be different. I used to be very open about what and who I wanted, at any time. I used to worry when I was a teenager, but then Don't Ask, Don't Tell got repealed. I was so excited. I didn't have to hide it, but then those two happened."

"And your husband doesn't know?" Ramon asked.

"No," she said. "I met him after, never said anything about it. Never told him. He was the gentle soul I needed, to restore myself. I took to normalcy, one man, one woman, a child, a career. No more strutting, no more chasing girls, no flirty smiles to guys I want to pull my way. They made me feel like everything I did and lived for was wrong, like I'd brought it on myself."

"You know that's not true," Ramon blurted sternly. "No one's responsible for what happened to you except them. No one else, okay?"

She nodded. "I know. I feel like I have to protect myself."

"You have to protect yourself from them, not from yourself. But I guess that tears it, anyway. When we get back to the world, I'm taking you to a titty bar."

She looked over and smiled at him. "Actually, I'd rather be one of the dancers."

His eyes nearly popped out of his head, and she continued, "I'd love to be up there with those lights pulsating on me, all those eyes gazing, desiring me. I'd probably dance to some Slipknot, Before I Forget, strapped in black leather and a spiked collar."

Cooper noted the IED detonations had ceased, and another Charger pulled up to their defensive area. Lenny leapt out of the rear door, walked up to the front door and fist tapped his driver. Her eyes watched his every move, stalking, waiting for a move she knew wouldn't come.

"Path is clear, Boss," he shouted to Bossman.

Cooper talked back quietly to Ramon. "I used to be a Free Spirit. That's what my father called me. Likened me to a 'coupe,' fast and liberating, eager, always ready for adventure. He combined that with Gary Cooper, his favorite actor, and just started calling me Cooper. He said I had a very High Noon attitude."

Lenny looked at her, looking at him. Something was missing. The menace, the cackling jackal seemed vanished, unlike Scotty. She heard him ask Sparky something, but she couldn't hear. She only heard Sparky's reply, "Yeah, ten kills, confirmed."

Lenny's eyes turned to her again, brow turned upward, mouth slightly opened between his golden beard. Cooper didn't break her gaze beneath the black shade of her Oakleys, but he knew she looked right at him. Through him. Lenny got back into his Charger, tapped the driver from behind and gave him some instructions. The vehicle rolled off.

"A Free Spirit, Daddy," she said. "They took that from me. What am I now?"

"You have to ask?" Ramon asked, then reached over and tapped the sturdy barrel of the M82 Barret. "You're a woman of iron, waiting for high noon."

Cooper leaned back into her chair, rolled her head over to look at Ramon and smiled. She laughed, then her eyes winced at the bouncing light that began to shimmer off of everything around her. Several other SEALs looked about to see where it was coming from, but everyone eventually looked to the sky.

Cooper gazed upward, Ramon following. "What the hell?" he asked.

A massive streak of light exploded against the sky and trailed a great tail of white. It moved evenly over the curve of the blue.

"It's a comet!" Sparky said. "We're being hit."

"No," Cooper said. "It's moving too slow. If a comet was hitting the atmosphere it would be too fast to see."

"You sure about that Cooper?" asked Ramon.

"I studied thermodynamics at Annapolis, including study of celestial objects. A comet would hit at more than thirty kilometers per second."

"We lose another Space Shuttle?" asked Bossman.

"Way too big," Cooper said.

"Shuttle's been retired for years now," Ramon added. "That I do know. What about the ISS? It going down?"

"Still too big."

To everyone's amazement, the streak then changed direction, turning toward the far arch of the sky.

"Controlled flight," Cooper said. "Is it a ship?"

The crew of elite warriors stood about their vehicles and watched while the lance of fire traveled across the heavens, heading towards the horizon, eastward. The white and black smoke trail spread across half the sky, fanning against the breadth of the sun and dimming its light.

"Fray the strings. Throw the shapes, hold your breath. Listen...." Cooper quoted the song, calming the eerie fear she felt creeping in her gut. "I am a world before I am a man. Was a creature before I can stand. I will Remember Before I Forget."

At that point, it became brighter, and in seconds, disappeared behind the risen, broken horizon of the Hindu-kush. A flash darkened the sky, and over blackened mountains an image burned into Cooper's retina's for a split second. Wings of fire spread into the deep.

I: BORN

Cooper dropped onto her kneepads. One hand clutched at her belly. Blood poured over her black glove. The creature's pincers had stabbed through her back, exiting her gut.

She fell forward, bracing a hand against a deck made of crystalline, otherworldly material. A crimson pool turned black beneath her, awash in the dull blue-green glow of her surroundings. Cooper gasped and wept, the pain overwhelming. Fear crunched her like a ton of water.

"Fuck," she snarled through clenched teeth, sucking her next breath through locked ivory.

Spent casings littered the floor. The mutilated body of Ramon laid not far away. The smell of burnt powder filled the air. It pinched at her runny nose. A cold sweat glistened over her muscled physique, chilled by the cold air.

"Ramon," she whispered. "Can you...hear me, baby?"

She crawled to him. His own ribs jutted out of his chest, eyes cold. One hand still reached for her, and she managed to clasp her fingers onto it.

"Ramon, c'mon...come back...."

She wept to look at him, closing her eyes. Far too much pain in her emotions and body.

"Cooper!" a voice cried out from behind.

"Michael..." she whispered through the pain. His voice spurred her to action. Those things still prowled the ship. She reached for her assault rifle, laying near the hand that held her up.

"Baby," he said, much closer. His ebony hands fell on her exposed shoulders. The tails of his lab coat dipped into her blood. His long hair hung by her face, and she saw in her peripheral vision his personal talisman, a yin-yang with crossed feathers, hanging from his neck. "What happened?"

"One of those four-legged fuckers. It just hit and...."

"Sh-sh-sh," he sounded. "C'mon. Where's your first aid pouch?"

"Lower back. Help Ramon."

"He's gone, Cooper. I'm sorry. I know you two—"

"Shut up," she grunted. "Just...do what...."

Cooper barely had the strength to keep herself up as he pulled the medical gear out of a pouch at the small of her back. She grunted and he fixed the pressure dressing before wrapping every bit of bandage around her. At that moment she felt glad her ex-husband was a doctor.

Michael's loving hands touched her neck. "You're gonna be okay, Cooper."

Her black gloves prevented her from seeing the paleness in her skin. Michael lifted her into his arms. His touch felt like liquid heat against her cold flesh.

"Okay, come on."

The mere act of walking, even with Michael supporting her, sent pain shooting through her entire torso. Her spine felt like it had a vise squeezing on it from all ends.

"Keep with me, Cooper."

Michael picked up and carried her G36C carbine. It only had half a magazine left.

"I can use that better than you," she moaned.

"I don't think it's our best bet of getting out of here," he said.

Cooper snarled through the pain. "Figures...even now, you can't get over that hippy BS."

"It doesn't make me a hippy to consider other ways to get out of things besides shooting."

She chuckled. "So what's the...?"

Her vision faded. Cooper collapsed. Michael called her name, over and over, but it felt like it came from the other side of a thick, metal wall. Her memories drifted.

She felt the sands of San Clemente beach crunch between her toes. Her gaze drifted over the blue-green waves to her twelve-year-old son, Devon, wrestling with some seaweed.

The sun glistened on the burgundy paintjob of her father's '69 Charger. Its rumble filled her ears, flowing into the eyes of Commandant Kinkaid, looking on her bruised face while she laid in the hospital bed.

"You would admit to these two getting the drop on you? You'd admit to the humiliation?"

His voice wafted over her ears, as if she were numb. The terror she felt then felt not unlike what she felt now.

Sounds. Thoughts. Feelings. All drifted into darkness. Then came a sudden burst of warmth. The covers fell from their bodies. Moonlight gleamed against Michael's shoulders as he made love to her for the first time. Over a decade had passed, and she felt him now as she had felt him then.

A cleansing feeling, so far different than the painful, grunting thrust of Scotty. His hand clasped her neck, shoving her face against the ground, shower water nearly drowning her.

"Cooper!" Michael's voice roared into the confined space of her mind. "Cooper!"

A sharp pain struck her cheek, snapping her awake.

"Can you hear me?"

"Michael...."

"Hey, we're here. Stay with me."

"We're where?"

She looked around, trying to focus. Her vision didn't come like it used to. Nothing would sharpen up. Cooper blinked over and over, but it didn't help. The haze persisted.

"We'll take care of you."

"We? Who...?"

Through the haze a wholly inhuman thing appeared. A smooth, rounded head covered in purplish skin. Black, oil-slick eyes looked out.

"N-n-no," she pleaded. "Michael, get it away!"

She tried to move, but nothing happened. The world spun.

"Please...I have a son...."

"And a daughter." She felt his fingers string through her short hair.

"I can't go...."

"You won't. The eyphors will help you. They're our friends."

Cooper shook her head. The sensation was like falling off a cliff. "They brought the others here."

"It wasn't their fault. We'll save you. I need to put you in the cell. I love you, Cooper."

The woman didn't respond. Michael pushed her onto a different surface. It felt soft, gelatinous. The sensation grew over her skin. Cooper realized she was sinking into it. Her mind panicked, issuing out hurried commands to limbs that didn't respond.

Her eyes gazed out into the haze of existence. Black palls grew until they filled her vision. The cold, so bitter and harsh, grabbed her limbs. Emptiness. Oblivion. All pain and sensation disappeared.

The alien fluids filled her mouth and nose, covering over her eyes. Yet none of it mattered. Before she had sunk that far, Cooper died.

A massive shock wracked her body. Limbs warmed to the point of a burning sensation. Another shock. Jolting. Her hands shot out to the sides of something encaging her. Eyes opened to a milky haze, everything swirled and cascaded.

Another jolt, smacking her heart with heavy electrical force. She couldn't breathe, her nostrils and mouth took in liquid. Another jolt and she burst upward through the surface.

"Devon!" Cooper cried the name of her son with her first breath. Warm air touched moist skin. Light and darkness collided. She collapsed over some structure and into the ground. Bare flesh on brick bolted her mind awake in the tumble.

She finally stopped, laying on her back. Cooper looked up to a brick ceiling with dim white lights illuminating a dark space. Mind racing, nerves firing, she fought to calm herself.

"Where the fuck am I?" she cried out.

Rolls of paper still spilled out of printers. Cooling fans hummed. Various conduits snaked about the interior, like a large utility room.

As her breathing evened out and her mind calmed, she looked down to see herself naked, covered in some kind of film. In her tumbling she left a trail of the gooey stuff, emanating from where she had awoken. She gazed upon a swirling assortment of cables and conduits grouped around a white, tub-shaped vat.

She couldn't recognize any of the technology. Automated surgical tools hung from mechanical arms in the ceiling. Steam wafted out of cooling vents. Hoses, cables, and wires stretched from the vat to the ceiling and walls. Cooper got up, reached back into the vat and picked up some of the fluid, thick as it slipped off her fingers. It smelled organic, like a kind of synthetic olive oil, much thicker than water.

It jostled her memory. "Eyphors?" she said. The vital fluid that filled their ship. She'd been lowered into it when....

Cooper looked down and ran her slimed hands over her belly. No sign of her wound. No pain. It felt thrilling just as much as it unnerved her.

"Hello?" she cried. No one replied. "Ramon?" Her voice shook with his name.

A glass case, similar to a gun locker, gleamed under the dim light. She looked into her naked reflection. Her body and skin gleamed in a perfect healthy light, as bright in her porcelain radiance as she had ever been. She felt her face, her shoulders, down over her breasts and belly, to her thighs. Everything the same, if not better than she remembered.

The object inside shined like black chrome. It beckoned to her. She looked past her reflection. It resembled a sleeve of some kind, two tapering cylinders connected at a joint like an arm.

"Where am I?"

A sharp noise compelled her around. A metal hatch swung open across the room. Light from outside illuminated the silhouette as it walked through. A harsh, wheezing breath cut into the after silence. Cooper controlled her breathing, terror surging, arms crossed over her breasts.

"Who's there?" she demanded.

The wheezing figure closed the door with a sharp clang. Footfalls slowly approached. A dark-skinned man hobbled towards her, long hair and beard turning white. Eyes filled with fear looked out from his wrinkled face. His hand clasped his stomach. Blood pooled through his fingers and stained a green jumpsuit.

"Cooper?" he said. His eyes settled on her and teared up. A pitiful gasp escaped the labored breaths. "Cooper, my darling."

Cooper's eyes narrowed, now taking her turn to gasp. She recognized him now despite the weathered face. A necklace with a yin-yang symbol and crossed feathers hung from his neck. Dark, worn eyes looked out from his ebony face. His beard now looked rough, graying, along with his long hair.

"Michael?"

"Thank all that is holy," he said softly, then hobbled sideways into the wall. Cooper ran over to him as he slid to the floor.

"Michael, what's happening?" She moved his hand away from the wound and looked. A gunshot. Powder burns. Close range.

"Cooper, listen." He grunted and grit his teeth. "There's no time. Nothing's...going to be the way you remember."

"I need to get a doctor."

"No!" His eyes went wide, teeth shining as he clamped them together. "There is no doctor to help me...No doctor I'd want to help me. Now listen."

His breaths became shallow and rapid. His free hand grabbed her arm. "Go over to that glass. Break it."

Cooper looked around for a second, then picked up a chair next to a read out. When she hurled it, the chair flew with such force, she did a double-take as glass cascaded to the ground.

"Now grab th-the gauntlet. Put it on."

"What is it?"

He nearly growled. "Just do it."

Cooper picked it up, wary of her bare feet around the glass. She shook the crystalline shards off the oily black material, then looked at it. Her fingers felt electrically charged to it. She chuckled at the pleasant feeling.

"Please, put it on, Cooper. Hurry."

She nodded, then slipped the gauntlet up her arm. It fit all the way up, adjusting like cloth. The pleasant feeling went all through her arm, then clamped down with a force of pain she'd never felt in her life. She screamed and fell to her knees.

"I'm sorry," Michael whispered against her howls.

The gauntlet liquefied into a rotating spiral, cutting through her skin and digging into her bone. Tears rushed down her cheeks as she grit her teeth. Then it settled. She watched in both amazement and horror when the cuts closed up. Skin fused back together like nothing had happened. Not a drop of blood had fallen.

She shook like a leaf, chilled. "Why didn't you tell me what would happen, Michael?"

"Because, you might not have done it."

"Fuck you! Tell me what's going on!"

He shook his head and reached for her. Despite her anger, Cooper moved toward him. Her pain paled in comparison to seeing him there, dying. She watched him just as he had watched her. It felt like moments ago.

"Locker...over there...." Michael gestured to the far wall. "Boots...suit."

Cooper went where he said, opened the locker to find a green jumpsuit similar to his, plus a pair of boots. The suit had a red patch marked GNP, with yellow ones beneath that said "Preserve at all costs, KD3605."

She dressed, put on the boots, properly sized. When she went to zip up the suit, she ripped the fastener clean off. Eyes narrowed, she held it up and shook her head, then tossed it.

"You'll be genetic priority...." Michael said, swallowing hard. "Don't... don't lose that suit...."

Cooper returned to him. Took up his hand. He looked up to her, the suit open down the middle to below her belly button thanks to the broken zipper.

"I seem to have trouble with, um...." she began.

"You'll be stronger than you think," he struggled to say. "Whatever you do, blend in." He grunted, suppressing a cough. "Don't ask more questions th-th-then you have to. Get to Synchro Point."

"Synchro Point?"

He blinked, slowly. For a second, she thought his eyes might not open. "Find the rest of th-the project. It's there. Get to Red Eagle. H-h-hawkeye will find you. She always finds things."

"You saved me. What about Ramon?"

He furrowed his brow, confused and impatient. "I don't know who that is. Listen—"

"My partner, Michael," she interrupted. "He was there when you found me."

"I don't remember."

"How could you not? Or is it you don't want to remember because you refuse to believe you weren't the only one I loved."

He shook his head, teeth almost grit. "That's all over, Cooper. I'm over."

"No, I can help you. Tell me where to get help. Where are we?"

"I am finished...." he gasped, grabbing the back of her neck and drawing her closer. "There is a second gauntlet."

She shook her head. "No. Don't tell me...." she trailed off.

"They will help you, Cooper. They will help you to fix things. But just like the first one, once you put it on, you'll never lose it." He chuckled, but then his face turned sad.

"Cooper," he whispered.

"Yes?" She drew in closer, his hand sliding to her cheek, his fingers dark against her porcelain skin.

"I'm so sorry."

She touched his cheek. He felt so cold. "Shh. It's okay."

"No, I j-just want you to know, that I-I-I never wanted to take the kids from you. The j-j-judge...."

"It's okay, Baby. I know." A tear fell.

"B-but you don't know how long I've wanted to say this...You were perfect for this. You have to believe me." He pressed his teeth together against the pain. "They missed you, they r-really did, darling."

"What happened to them?" she whimpered. "Michael, where are our children?"

He shook his head. "Everything happened so fast. No one knew where they came from. I don't know...." Hate rose from his dying breaths, an agression she'd never experienced in him. "They burnt down the world, Cooper. They set it on fire."

"Who, Michael?"

He kept fighting, but she saw him losing, fading. "Tell me who, Baby." She gently stroked his sunken cheek. "Tell me where Devon and Alyssa are."

He looked into her eyes, his dark brown irises as passionate as she remembered, but with a sting of anger she had never heard from his gentle spirit. "A phoenix is born from ashes. Rise, Cooper...help us rise, again."

His lips went still, eyes gazing at her through a window of eternity. His jaw didn't move. Eyelids relaxed and his head leaned heavy on her hand. Skin went ashen. In his last breath, she heard one word escape the grasp of death.

"Run."

Cooper barreled through the door into the bright light of the day. The rays sheered into her eyes. Tears still rushed from them. She looked out into an empty lot next to a large concrete building. Graffiti stained the walls. Her trained instincts set her on autopilot despite the emotional whirlwind. The smell of rain mixed with the faint scent of cordite and smoke.

Her boots smacked pools of water. She did as Michael told her to. Run. She ran like she never had in her entire life with their names blazing through every footstep.

Devon. Alyssa. Where are you? Where am I?

The sound of pistol shots bounced around the industrial urban surrounds. A whine of jet engines mixed with the metallic grind of trains. Cooper barely took track of how fast she ran, but knew without a doubt she hadn't run so fast her entire life. She cornered with one push of her foot then drove into a dead sprint, running between a rundown train and a graffiti-covered brick façade.

Up ahead, armed figures ran by. She skidded to a stop and pushed herself up against the wall. No sooner had she finished the move, the figures were already past. She ran on, and came to an opening where they gathered.

White armor and camouflage jumpsuits, blotched urban combat patterns. Patches on their arms simply read MD. Gas masks concealed their faces, helmets their heads.

Most carried pistols, a few with sub machine guns, another with an RPG. They waited with weapons drawn.

"What the fuck we gonna do with forty-fives here?" one of them asked, voice tainted by the voicemitter. "We might as well be spit-ballin' against those things!"

"Reinforcements are en route from Synchro Point," the apparent commander stated. "So just sit tight until they get here. We gotta evacuate the citizens."

"Well, aren't you a fucking hero!"

What kind of whiny troops are these?

Feeling a little less threatened by them, she came up to the end of the train car and meekly sounded, "Uh, could you tell me the way to Synchro Point?"

They all turned in unison, startled and jittery. "What? Get to the goddamn metro rail. Didn't you get the evac—?"

Before he could finish, the far brick wall enclosing the rail yard erupted in a flurry of red dust. Out from the cloud ran a monstrous machine over ten feet tall, streamlined and fast on two legs. Clawed arms struck out.

"Eyphor!" one man shouted.

Cooper ducked behind the bulk of the train while scythe-like claws swung back and forth, cutting the men to shreds. She heard their child-like screams mix with useless pistol shots.

The RPG gunner didn't even fire, cut in two. Cooper gasped when a head flopped down in front of her, gasmask and helmet intact. When all the men lay dead, the blood-spattered machine stopped and stood there, looking at her.

Cooper eyed the dark thing. *An Eyphor*, she thought. *Killing people. Dammit, Michael why did you trust them?*

It stood there, apparently looking at her as she pressed her back against the train car. A deep sound broke free around it, hitting her ears like a voice.

"Get to Synchro Point," it said.

Cooper slowly stepped away from the train car, feeling strange that this inhuman thing said the same words that her now dead ex-husband had.

How did it just speak to me? she thought. *Only Michael figured out how to speak with them.*

Before she could reply, the flare of a rocket smashed into the machine's flank. It collapsed into the ground, sprawling around like a dog that had just been shot in the hip. As it stilled, the words came out again.

"Get to Synchro Point."

A thick, clear liquid gushed out, smelling like that layer she woke up in. Smelled like that stasis fluid.

Vital fluid, she thought. *They live in that stuff.*

She thought of going to it. Opening up the compartment to see the little creature within. Five years working at the facility, she'd rarely seen them. Only in glimpses, even in their ship itself. And never had she heard them. But she remembered Michael's words, and the eyphor's as well.

Get to Synchro Point.

Cooper sprinted past and headed in the direction the men had come from. A jet roared overhead. The shadow passed, but she didn't get a glimpse of the plane.

JD3603

Cooper came onto a street and struggled to stop before running into a large, armored vehicle. Six wheels braked, filling the air with white smoke and the stench of burnt rubber.

Cooper slid to a halt and fumbled onto her back. She looked through the white haze at a dark, gray-blue hull. Battle scars marred its matte surface, along with orange markings.

Bootfalls ran out from the back of the vehicle, two of the MD men with Kriss submachine guns. The first grabbed her collar and yanked her up.

"GNP!" his modified voice said, the letters on her suit.

The second man led her into the back of the armored vehicle. Unsure of their intentions, she kept on the defensive. The other MD men hadn't tried to kill her, but then neither did the eyphor that killed them.

They left the back doors open as they moved forward. The engine had a sound she'd never heard before. It whined in an electronic way, whistling like a supercharger and thrumming.

An MD man pulled off his helmet and gas mask and threw them on an empty piece of bench. He looked back at Cooper as she lay on the floor, backed up against the opposite side.

"Lookit this, young Watchman," he said, his face pitted, ugly, and old. "Goddamn perfect GNP. She's a tall one too, with excellent form. Hard to come by any day. What are you, six foot, honey?"

The words set off a fire inside her, talking as if she were a piece of meat. He cackled and leaned back against the hull wall. So familiar, but even uglier. The other "Watchman" kept his gaze out the back.

All around, Cooper saw through a series of wide windows. But she remembered the solid hull outside, without a seam let alone a window. She pulled herself up onto the bench, watching the event unfold.

"Letting 'em jiggle free there, honey?" the ugly one asked with eyes on her chest. Cooper adjusted the sides to cover herself more, not giving this one anything.

"Zipper broke."

The area outside looked like a mix between small town America and various villages she'd seen in third world countries across the globe. They passed a burning car or building every few seconds. Sounds of gunfire echoed over the humming of the armored car's engine. Tracers crossed the sky. She shook her head, thinking her children could be somewhere in this, hoping she hadn't lost them.

"Lookit this, though, sport," the ugly, unmasked Watchman said. "Gotta protect this one, and not just cause I like big tits. Protecting GNP can get you big rewards."

He looked at her like he eyed a meal. The same look Scotty had. Dark eyes empty, all hunger and hate. He approached, tongued his lips.

"She's GNP," the other Watchman began, "you can't have any fun with her." His voice carried an air of sarcasm.

"I don't need to wet my wick just to have fun. So what's up, JD?" he asked, a gloved finger rubbing down her cheek.

"Don't touch me," she warned.

"Oh," he said, his look both playful and threatening. "You mean you're not used to it by now?"

"Am I supposed to be used to old pervs drooling at my sight?"

His hand snapped around her throat, forcing her back against the hull. "You're damn lucky we got to get all prime material out of here. Secondary Protocol's been announced."

He relaxed his grip and fingers brushed down the center of her exposed chest as he retreated. A flush of rage boiled through her, but she resisted the urge to plant her fist in his skull.

Try it one more time, she thought. *I'm not going through that again.*

Both sides of this conflict seemed interested in keeping her alive, for whatever reason. Cooper refused to believe Michael was with these men. She couldn't handle that. Not so soon after seeing him die.

Behave as best I can, she thought. *Without letting them do what they want. But I'll break Pig-Face's neck if he tries something. I have to. I can't let it happen again.*

Pig-Face leaned back and cocked his Kriss SMG, laughing and howling. "Look at 'em go!"

With a quick glance, Cooper saw other green clad people running on the sidewalks. Pig-Face kept howling.

"Secondary Protocol!" he shouted, then raised his sub machine gun and fired into the running crowd. "No GNP tag, no luck!"

A sick, burning sensation simmered through Cooper's body. A familiar yet shocking ¬thump-thump-thump popped off in sequence. Heavy brass casings bounced off the roof and slid past the open back door, clacking into the streets, .50-caliber rounds.

Reality hit like a thunderclap, chills running up her spine as the ear splitting cracks of gunfire rattled her limbs. The sight of those bodies falling, twisting, and contorting under murderous impacts sent only one thought into her mind. Her children could be anywhere. Even there, among those people.

The thought barely formed before she struck down on the man's submachine gun, pressing it against Pig-Face's waist. Cooper yelled as she shoved him into the bulkhead, and tore his weapon away. Immediately she went to the other man, who barely had enough time to register what happened.

She caught him right as he dropped an empty magazine from his Kriss. She aimed in and moved back into the APC to open space between her and him.

"Put the weapon on the deck!" she shrieked. "Do it!"

The Watchman braced his arm on the bench and hunkered down to drop his weapon. At that moment the driver slammed on the brakes, and both Pig-Face and the other Watchman flew forward at her. She lost balance. The second Watchman pinned his body against her arm, then pressed her submachine gun to the deck.

Pig-Face's fist wailed once over her face, and then he screamed in pain. "God fucking dammit!"

Cooper barely felt a thing.

"What?" asked the other Watchman.

"Like hitting a fucking brick." He pulled out a .45 caliber pistol and pointed it straight at her. Cooper's body froze, and then shook, jaw tight.

"You dumb fucking bitch," Pig-Face spat. "You lucky you didn't shoot. I'd have every authorization to blow your fucking head off. That's as far as a red tag will take you. Try your luck again. Please." He pulled the hammer back.

Cooper let go of the weapon, and the other man recovered it.

Pig-Face's other gloved hand darted underneath her open suit and clasped one breast so hard she nearly yelped. "Move an inch, not even these will save you."

She froze against her reeling anger. Skin nearly sizzled with rage. But she couldn't move with that barrel gaping at her face. After a couple eternal seconds he let go and retreated. One after the other, they reloaded their weapons, making sure they had a loaded gun trained on her at all times. The vehicle continued on at their signal. The firing commenced again.

No, she cried in her mind. *No. Don't let them be anywhere near here. Don't let them be. Please. Let them be safe.*

Heavy slugs tore into the people and buildings. Puffs flew when the bullets gouged brick and concrete. Out of the dust, a young man appeared, running as fast as he could. Desperate, he waved his arms to plead. A single slug hit him dead center in the chest and knocked him to the ground. Cooper closed her eyes, grounding her teeth together in all her fury.

They will pay. I swear it. I swear. I swear. They will pay. Whoever made them will pay, whoever pays them will pay!

The armored car slowed. The engine died down. She heard other voices, many of them, and hundreds of footsteps. The metal clacking of trains and sounds of a rail station echoed all around.

"We're at the metro," came the driver. "Off load any passengers."

Cooper didn't wait. She bolted for the open back. The old man body blocked her first. His hand fell onto her waist. She froze again to prevent from killing him.

"As you can see, life is so short," he breathed on her cheek. "I'll be sure to look you up at Synchro when I get done here, JD. You owe me one now."

She slipped past and her boots hit the asphalt. The car slid away. More jet noises filled the air, followed by the hard throbs of another sound. Cooper saw strange, incandescent lances of light shoot into the heavily overcast sky. Pitch black beams surrounded by brilliant blue light. She'd never seen a weapons discharge like that before.

An unfamiliar gunship roared overhead. Dark, sleek. Brimming with armaments. Co-axial rotors blurred above it with a winged tail balancing out the back. It moved faster and more controlled than even the Apaches she'd seen most of her adult life.

Cooper arrived at an overpass. She looked down into a tram yard. Hundreds of people filed into fewer than a dozen cars. Gas-masked Watchmen administered the on-load. Cooper ran down from the overpass to the station, getting into line.

Everyone around her looked frightened and anxious. She couldn't blame them. The distant crumps of large explosions shook the ground. Wind rustled her short, neck-length hair. It seemed longer than before, when she kept it scruffy but short. It looked like a couple months extra growth, but much more time had to have passed for Michael to become so old, and for all this to happen.

Where are my kids? she kept asking in her mind, then felt another, deeper chill as she noticed there were no children to be seen anywhere. No couples. No families. The youngest person might have been in their late twenties.

"Howlers," the man in front of her said, pointing to the sky. Cooper looked. Against the gray clouds, she picked out several black marks. A swarm formed.

A harsh sound grew as they approached, becoming louder and louder. The small, robotic things screamed overhead. Cooper grabbed her ears. "Howlers" seemed like a good name for them.

"What the hell?" she asked.

Another call went throughout the crowds, two words she'd just learned. "Secondary Protocol! Secondary Protocol's been activated!"

People screamed and Cooper felt panic surge through the orderly lines, turning the formation into a mob. The crowds disintegrated into a mass surging at the trains.

"You're a GNP!" one man hissed, eyes wild. "Give me that tag!"

Cooper looked down at the red "GNP" badge on her chest.

"Give it to me!"

He reached for it. She batted his hand away. "What are you babbling about?"

Others gathered around, knowing they were too far back to get into the train.

"GNP. It's mine!"

A man leapt at her. Cooper lashed out with her left fist and cracked him against the cheek. Another rammed her from behind, sending her to the deck. They piled on and clawed at her suit, trying to pull it off of her. Cooper did all she could to protect it.

She pushed upward on one leg. The entire mass blew off of her, men and women. She didn't know how she did that with one push.

Adrenaline surged through her body, much faster and fiercer than she ever experienced. Her head became so light she felt ready to fly off. Everything moved in slow motion.

"Woah."

"Hey, come here!" a voice said, muffled by a gas mask voicemitter. She turned to see a couple Watchmen marching towards her, fighting to get to her with shock sticks and drawn pistols.

"C'mon!" he cried out and knocked another person over the skull. Cooper charged forward. She flew past the Watchmen and into the car, a crowded, hot mass of people.

Watchmen used shock sticks and pistols to clear the doors. In a minute, the train started moving. Trees and buildings passed by the window. Flashes of explosions lit up the overcast sky.

"The bombardment's begun!"

Coming in the opposite direction the train rolled, a swarm of aircraft filled her view. More of those Howlers. Hordes of them. Squadrons of bigger, low flying craft came within a hundred feet of the train. More gunships led the way.

Slower behemoths made of a spiny, gray-black material flew low to the tree tops. They resembled giant, flying flatworms.

Not eyphors, she thought. *No way. But...working with the Watchmen? Maybe?*

So many pieces. Cooper tried to put the puzzle together, but the disparate elements all fumbled into a giant pile at the base of her mind. Still, she marveled at the display of power, like nothing she'd seen of any army before.

"Oh, no," a woman said. "The bio-carriers. They're gonna turn all the survivors into puppets. We'll never go back now."

"So what?" another man said. "Not like you owned anything there that's not on your back."

"No troop carriers. They're not interested in retaking the city."

"The Planetary Army is gonna get hammered!"

"Try not to sound too happy about that."

"PA's probably already gone. They got what they wanted and bolted."

"What the hell would they want here? The war's down south."

Cooper looked away from the window and leaned back against the wall. She tried to relax, but as her mind slowed, she thought more and more about her children, Devon and Alyssa.

How long has it been? How long was I out? I hope they survived. Let them be alive, please.

A solitary tear fell and she covered her mouth. She tried to find a corner she could bury her face in, but instead had to fight the emotional onslaught.

Memories flashed, seeing her children in their old home. She could hear Devon's cry of joy when he slipped passed her with a football. Frantically, out of desperation, she searched people's faces. Her fingers tingled with the touch of Alyssa's dark hair, the one time she attempted to braid it.

Where is this? she thought. *Where are they?*

II: THE ANT FARM

"Looks like another scorcher out here over Salt Lake City, this Tuesday, June 22nd. Going to be a high of 102 degrees, low of eighty around midnight tonight, possible rain showers from a system moving in from the north. Alien auroras might make an appearance, since it's rumored they come around in the heat. I don't know, I've seen them in January in pouring snow, but what the hell does anyone know? I don't think we've known anything since a three mile long spaceship crashed into the city. It's anyone's guess."-92.9 KKXM, The Oldies But Goodies

Salt Lake YMCA, Salt Lake City, County of Salt Lake, near Salt Lake, 0830, 06/22/2024

Cooper and her son Devon dove into the water at the deep end, then pushed into the lanes. Twelve year old Devon started strong, but Cooper could only sandbag so much. She fought a chuckle when she suddenly soared ahead ten feet, then slowed.

Devon's dark brown skin was easy to spot in the water, his complexion much more like his father's. The genes for her pale porcelain skin didn't even seem to have registered. She switched to a slower sidestroke to avoid the appearance of enabling him.

When he reached the other side, she was only a few inches behind. Cooper stood, her six foot height rising high out of the water. Devon planted his feet, panting as he looked at her.

"Don't let me win!" he blurted, water gleaming on his dark braids and cornrows.

Cooper snickered and covered her mouth. The water had pressed her short brown hair against her scalp.

"Don't laugh."

"Sorry," she admonished, hands up. "That was bad sportsmanship. You're so competitive, I shouldn't have to go so easy on you. You'll win eventually."

"Eventually? I can take you now!"

Cooper lowered her gaze at him, hands on her hips. He'd learn to talk smack at a young age. Cooper found it oddly adorable. "Okay, I'll tell you what. We'll go again. I'll swim outright, as fast as I can. But, to be fair, I'll go under the surface the entire lap, back and forth. I won't come up for a breath."

Devon's eyes conveyed his disbelief. "What? That's impossible."

"Oh?" she patted his cheek. "So much to learn."

"You didn't stay under that long at the beach that one day."

"You were on my back. I didn't want to drown you."

"Okay, prove it."

Cooper turned her back against the edge of the pool, stretched, and Devon got ready.

"Say when." She took in a deep breath from her nostrils that didn't seem to end. The trepidation already showed in his eyes.

"N...." he started, but then halted, doubt creeping into his eyes. "Now!"

Cooper went beneath the waves while he cut through the surface. She still went slower than she could, but this way if he tied her, it would build up his confidence. Holding her breath beneath the entire time would at least make it look like her handicap had been fair.

She kept an eye on him from beneath. Without goggles he was a little blurry, but his dark silhouette was easy to make out. She smiled and a few bubbles escaped between her teeth. He was putting out a maximum effort, but keeping control of his strokes, not splashing the water like some drowning dog as children his age were prone to do.

They reached back to the other side and she surged back up again. She put hands on her hips as he watched, still holding her breath. He shook his head.

"Okay, breathe now," he said.

She crossed her arms. After a lifetime of freediving and Navy SEAL training, three minutes was nothing. She hadn't even turned blue yet, just a little red.

"Come on, let it out! Breathe!"

"She's good at holding her breath, y'know," came the voice of his little sister, Alyssa. She laid belly down on the bleachers, drawing with pencils. Devon glared at her, and Cooper put her finger under his chin to bring his gaze back her subtle smiling and tight, unbreathing lips.

"Okay, you've made your point! Take a breath!"

Cooper saw genuine concern build up in his eyes, and she blew out an audible huff, and sucked in another through her nostrils to reassure him.

"All right?" she asked.

"How did you do that?"

"Years of practice. Here," she sat up at the side of the pool and patted her hand on the tile for him to join her. "Practice breathing slow and deep." She put her hands on her stomach. "It's about learning to trap more oxygen in your body than a normal person. Watch."

She straightened her back and took in a deep breath through her nostrils, holding it for a few seconds as if she were doing it for the first time, then letting it go through her mouth.

"Train your lungs. It takes a long time, but if you stick with it, you can swim with greater freedom than anyone else."

"Where'd you learn this?"

"Freediving photographers around where I grew up. They'd go underwater to take pictures for nature magazines and such. SCUBA bubbles can scare away certain things in the water, so they'd freedive to get their pictures. Hammerhead sharks, for example, scatter from the bubbles, but I always liked swimming with the dolphins whenever they showed up."

"Dolphins?" he asked with a smile.

"Yeah, some of the ultimate freedivers. They're amazing. Come on, let's practice. Straighten your back. Hands on your stomach, or hips, and keep your eyes open, otherwise you'll just be putting yourself to sleep."

He did everything as she said. For a couple minutes they took in deep breaths, islands of calm as more people came into the pool with beach balls, floaties, and foam boogie boards. Children screamed and shrieked, but they kept up their concentration.

"Now, go for a couple laps," Cooper told him. "If you feel some convulsions, ignore the first couple, but come up if they're too much. I'll keep the lanes clear. Go ahead."

He nodded and rushed into the water again. She watched for a bit, until other forms caught her eye. Not too far away, a young woman with a very dark complexion, almost as dark as her ex-husband's, stood in the waist deep water. Long dark hair, well curled, elegant, hung about her shoulders and down a smooth back exposed by her rather insubstantial gold and black bikini.

Cooper gulped, but then looked away and took in a calming breath. Then she glanced back. The girl turned as she played with some of the children, like some kind of event coordinator. No parents, but a lot of kids. The ebony beauty saw Cooper's eyes looking over her curves, then a chill shot up Cooper's spine and her cheeks went red.

Cooper looked away. *Oh, fuck, she saw me staring,* she thought. *I'm rusty as hell, that's embarassing.*

She didn't dare look back, but then she felt the water disturbed next to her legs. She looked to see the woman approach, droplets of water falling down chocolate colored skin that gleamed without blemish. The whites of her eyes and the shine of her smile looked so bright.

"Hi," she said, then narrowed her eyes. "You're Jordan DeBlanc, aren't you? US Navy SEAL's?"

Cooper cocked her head, then quickly checked on her children. Devon swimming, Alyssa drawing. "Oh, uh, yeah. That's been a while, like six years."

"Really? Thought they'd fast track you to Admiral or something. I didn't have the career you had obviously, but you were on the *Constellation* back in '17, right?"

"Oh, yeah. Yemen. Oh, wait, I'm not supposed to say that."

They both laughed together. The woman braced her arms on the side of the pool and sat up next to her. Cooper's eyes were treated to the water flowing down the woman's thighs. She started wishing she'd worn something more provocative than the simple black one-piece she had on. At least it was thonged.

"I'm Amanda, formerly Seaman First Class Peterson. I was only in two years before I got my BCD," Bad Conduct Discharge, "but I remember hearing about you everywhere."

"Oh, yeah," Cooper rolled her eyes. "There wasn't a week I didn't see my face on the Navy Times. First female SEAL graduates BUD/S, first female SEAL gets her duty station, today she had corn beef hash for breakfast. At least when I went operational in Afghanistan they had to stop all that shit for OpSec. Silent professional counts for jack when political firsts are involved, I guess."

"Guess that was pretty annoying, being a military celebrity. That makes us quite an odd pair to sit next to each other. The ultimate woman warrior, attended Annapolis, first female SEAL. They probably would've given you a carrier as a retirement gift."

She cocked her head. "If you don't mind my asking, how'd you get your Bad Chicken Dinner?"

"Oh, working part time on weekends."

Cooper shrugged. It seemed odd, working part time at a civilian job wasn't unheard of for active duty military. "Where at?"

She bit her lower lip. "Déjà vu, San Diego."

Cooper's eyes widened, and excitement sent her heart racing. She checked the location of her kids again. Devon had just tapped the side of the pool and turned back for

another lap. Alyssa hadn't moved a muscle except her drawing hand.

"You were a stripper?"

"No, I was a waitress. But it's still an 'establishment of ill repute,'" she made air quotes. "An ethics violation, according to the regs."

Cooper looked away for a moment, the words nearly making her wet hair stand on end. Ethics violations.

"Yeah, there're so many things I could say to that useless shit."

The woman was apparently taken aback by her venom. "That's not something I expected from someone like you. You seemed like, like—"

"The ultimate embodiment of military élan, an uncompromising warrior and individual of exceptional physical courage and moral fiber?"

Amanda cocked an eyebrow.

"Admiral McWest, commander of SOCOM at the time. I played the part for the opportunities I was given. But," her gaze drifted up and down over Amanda's beautiful body, before stopping to look deep into her soft eyes. "I always wanted more than what that narrow, self-righteous path would allow me."

Amanda smiled slightly. "Don't Ask, Don't Tell was repealed over ten years ago. Coulda been a playa just like the boys."

"Who says I'm not?" Cooper nearly moaned, and read the eager reception on Amanda's face. It made her tingle deep down. "But I had...complications."

"Family?" Amanda asked.

Cooper immediately felt thankful the other woman had thought of a different angle, and not the predators that had stayed in her midst.

"Yeah, well, the Navy still takes marriage seriously." She shrugged. "Call me Cooper."

"Nice to meet you." Amanda offered her hand forward, Cooper took it, looked into Amanda's eyes and slowly lifted her hand to her lips.

"All of that's not to say, however," Cooper began, "that I haven't since come back into my own."

She gave Amanda's hand a slow kiss, her body so warm, then just gazed into her eyes.

Devon halted up against the edge of the pool, splashing water over the edge. Cooper's attention broke back to him. "I got to use the bathroom."

"Hit it," Cooper said and he dragged himself out halfway before she grabbed him up and he managed to make it the rest of the way. She could feel his muscles turned to jell-o.

"Your son?" asked Amanda.

Cooper looked back beaming with pride and nodded. "Yes, he is. He likes to take after me. I worry about that sometimes, Afghanistan was...."

"Amazing how everyone's forgot about that place ever since the crash. I've got a terrific view of the ship from where I live. I could show it to you, especially at sunset."

"I'd like that," Cooper said. "I work there, actually. I went private, Rangewood Security, Rapid Reaction Force. And, uh, my ex-husband, works at the facility full time. I don't know if you read about him in Navy Times, but he's the world's top biologist. Got his second PHD when he was nineteen."

"Wow! Why'd you get divorced? Is he socially awkward? I heard those prodigy types can be that way."

"No. I got divorced for the same reason I left the Navy. I felt trapped. I wanted out. I wanted more. And...." Cooper considered the next line, maybe too fast, but decided hell with it. "He didn't approve of my second job."

Amanda cocked an eyebrow.

"I also work at Deja Vu." Cooper smirked. "I don't serve drinks, though."

"Bouncer?" Amanda asked with a mischievous gaze, and Cooper laughed. "Which one? I'd like to drop in."

Cooper shook her head. "Let's skip the cover charge. Your place sounds good enough. I'll give you the VIP treatment."

Amanda gulped then. "Okay, then. Seven tonight, good?"

"Good for me."

Amanda backed away a bit, looking over her charges to see one boy slam a beach ball into another's face.

"Oh! Reggie! Stop that!" she turned to Cooper. "Sorry, I'll be back. I've got to settle them down before there's a riot."

Cooper laughed and watched her move off, barking orders to the unwieldy group of kids she had to watch over. She used the opportunity with her and Devon gone to go over to Alyssa. She dripped as she walked, and stopped over her daughter's space.

"No! Wait, go away!" Alyssa screamed in panic when some of the water dripped onto her pages. Cooper barely caught sight of what she was doodling.

"Oh, don't worry, it's just a little water," said Cooper.

"What?" the little girl protested. "No, you're ruining them."

"Okay!" Cooper backed away, hands up. "I'm sorry."

Alyssa looked at her with enraged brown eyes. Her skin was a much lighter brown, golden color than her father or brother. Cooper's genes seemed to have more effect.

"Why can't you do anything right?"

"All right, that's enough," Cooper nearly snapped. "You don't talk to me that way, I'm your mother."

She noticed her daughter's hair getting a little ragged as well. "I'm going to have to fix your hair up when we get home too."

"No," Alyssa said. "You don't know how to do it. I want to wait to go back to Daddy."

"Daddy's working hard, honey. He won't be able to come get you for a couple days."

"Nooo. It hurts when you do it."

Why did I even bother coming over here, Cooper thought forlornly. *She hates me.*

She turned away, unable to find the right words to say. Devon approached from the locker room and she smiled at his arrival. She couldn't understand how her relationship with him was so warm, and her daughter could barely stand her sight.

Devon smiled, but then he looked up past her, still a good thirty feet away. Fear filled his eyes. She knew the look.

"Mom!" he screamed. "Look out!"

She barely turned in time to see a bright wave of light wash over her head. Her skin tingled and lungs nearly seized up.

"Mom!" Devon screamed again and ran toward her.

The aurora of light passed on and rose into the air. Devon wrapped his arms around her waist. Children screamed and panicked.

"The auroras," Cooper whispered. "Calm down, honey. They've never harmed anyone."

Aside from panic stricken morons wrecking cars, crashing planes, and stampeding over each other.

She wasn't going to take any chance, and refused to admit the protective rush to either of them. She'd never seen them this far from the ship. The alien crash site sat fifty miles away. In her training at the facility, she had seen them dance high in the air near the tops of buildings and antennae. This close to the ground wasn't unheard of, but that made it no less a surprise.

Amanda gathered up her kids as well as she could, and got them into the locker room.

"Rain check?" Amanda asked running by.

"Sure," Cooper replied quickly.

In that quick distraction, Cooper returned her attention to note only Devon stood by her.

"Where'd Alyssa go?" Devon asked.

With a quick, honed searched, Cooper found her girl standing twenty feet away near the edge of the pool, gazing upward at the pirouetting lights flashing in tornadic swirls above. Her tiny hands reached for them.

"Alyssa!" Cooper shouted. "Come here!"

"So pretty!" Alyssa giggled. She looked up at the banners of light, shimmering in gold and white. She stood straight up, hands out, smiling.

"No, Alyssa come here."

The dilemma tore at her. She stood near Devon, and couldn't leave him, but her daughter drifted further away, enraptured by the light. The conflict froze her legs in place.

"Alyssa!" Devon shouted. "Come on, leave it!"

With a mighty effort, Cooper moved away from Devon to get her.

"Stay back, Devon," she bade him, and he nodded with all the fear in his eyes.

Cooper approached Alyssa, slowly. She wanted to tell Devon to run, but he didn't know where to go. She didn't know where to tell him to go. Maybe home, but he had no way to get there. He couldn't drive. And with each step, Alyssa grew in her vision. Closer. Closer.

She reached for her girl, hypnotized upward, and then light dove straight toward her.

"No!" she shouted.

Cooper gasped in further surprise when the lights darted away from her daughter, only to envelope herself, her entire body. Every muscle fiber tickled with delight, but fear filled her chest.

She turned and spun with them, trying to find where they were going next.

"What are they doing, Mom?" Devon shouted in terror.

"I don't know."

Alyssa laughed in pure joy. "They're dancing with you, Mom!"

A blinding flash erupted within her eyes. Everything went black, and then out of the darkness an inferno burst forth into her mind. Great wings of fire unfurled to reveal a screaming eagle's head rushing her way, feathers made of flame. Its maw filled her vision,

shrieking into the depths, before her vision returned.

In one swipe the lights moved from Cooper to Alyssa, swooshing over her with such intensity her curly hair rustled. Wind twirled through the enclosed space. The auroras tingled on her outstretched fingers, and the child's eyes radiated out into the air. Cooper had never seen anything so beautiful.

Fear and awe struck her limbs still, but when the lights finally flew past her daughter and vanished through the walls, Cooper rushed in and picked up her girl. She looked into her eyes to see only pure happiness and life.

"They danced with you, Mom. Did you see? You were beautiful, and they loved you."

Cooper could barely breathe, just so relieved her daughter and son were okay. She pulled Alyssa tight to her, rushed her back to Devon and grabbed her son's hand. Cooper pulled them both into her.

"Are you okay, Mom?" asked Devon.

"I think so...." she trailed off. Her cell phone rang. She gasped at the sound coming from her bag at the bleachers. She put Alyssa down and pulled it out. "Hello?"

"Cooper?" came the hated voice. One she couldn't escape, especially in these days. Scotty Chambers. "That you?"

"Yes...this is Cooper." They had followed her from Annapolis to the SEALs, and then to Rangewood. Somehow, he had become her team leader.

"We've got a situation at the ship. Wheel's up in thirty."

"But, we're not on QRF right now. It's Team Five's—"

"Cooper, all team's are activated. For all intents and purposes, we're all on Quick Reaction Force. Get in as soon as you can."

Cooper hung up the phone, breathed an anxious sigh, and turned to her kids, grabbed the bag and handed it to Devon.

"No time to explain guys. I need to drop you off with nana and go to work. Okay? There's no time to—"

"But, Mom the auroras!" Alyssa pleaded. "You need to go to them."

Cooper shook her head. "Don't argue, Alyssa, not now. Grab your stuff."

"This is much more important."

"Alyssa!" Cooper shouted and clasped her little shoulders. "Enough of your day-dreaming. This is serious. There are no unicorns and faeries like your little pictures, so get with it. Even pretty things can be dangerous, now let's go."

Cooper grabbed Alyssa's sketchbook with a wet hand, soaking into the pages. Pencils went flying when she picked it up and tucked it under Alyssa's arm.

"Hand!" Cooper commanded and Alyssa put hers in her mother's, though she teared up. "Let's go."

Cooper ran to the exit, Alyssa in her grasp, Devon at her heels.

The train rolled into a large urban center an hour after it had taken off. It passed through some industrial areas filled with large, rusted factories and mills. Some signs still hung, though often broken and crooked, but Cooper recognized the American styling and system.

Must be somewhere in the States, she thought. *I hope.*

Fences topped with barbed wire blocked out other parts of the train yard. An advanced train design sat on a rail line higher up on an embankment. Angular, dark, and menacing, she'd never seen a machine like that. It sat on its own line, separated from the others by security gates and Watchmen. It hardly matched the dilapidated surroundings.

In a few seconds it went out of sight. The train came to a stop and people filed out. Cooper waited and observed at a window. Watchmen directed the people to processing centers at the end of winding corridors of chain link fences. At a far corner, she looked at another type of guard, but then nearly buckled over when she realized her vision zoomed in on him like a pair of binoculars.

She gasped and put her hands over her face, trying to realign her senses. When she stood back up, Cooper looked again.

What's going on with me? she thought.

But, after a moment of discomfort, she used the zoom and checked out the other guard. Sandy-colored armor covered him from head to toe. A large bug-eyed helmet concealed his entire head. As the crowds cleared, Cooper moved on. She tried to stay with the mob. Then chaos broke out. People shouted and ducked for cover. Cooper double-backed against the head car.

"No! I don't want to be sterilized! Don't let them do it!"

A sweaty man ran back in the opposite direction.

"Counter-evolutionary!" some in the mass shouted.

The armored guard lifted his arm at the man, palm open. A ripple of noise and burst of heat incinerated the running man's head and left shoulder. What was left of him fell into a heap. Cooper froze.

One Watchmen started grabbing people for the clean-up, while the rest kept the people pressed into the processing center. She looked for several seconds at the smoldering corpse, thinking about his words. *He didn't want to be sterilized?*

As she walked towards one of the processing areas, a large monitor near the ceiling flicked to life.

"All new citizens, welcome to Synchro Point." The words came out in crisp English. A clean shaven, mid-aged Asian man appeared on the screen, his head filling it from nearly edge to edge.

"As you may have heard, Synchro Point is the base of operations for the human arm of Nexus. I am Professor Robert Liang."

Liang? Cooper remembered. *Olympus's President? He's definitely older. Just like Michael. What's he got to do with this?*

"During your stay, you may hear me referred to merely as Overseer. Well, that is my duty, to oversee the operations of our very important work here. That work of course includes protecting you, mostly from yourself."

Very important work?

"At Synchro Point we take this work more seriously than at any other place. This city is the grand experiment in humanity's accelerated evolution, the cauldron from which a new race will rise. All qualified GNP's will be closely guarded. If you are an unqualified male and have not received your sterilization packet, you will receive it before exiting processing. And you may ask, why must I be contained in this way?"

Cooper looked down from the screen. The vision of the screaming man's smoking, smeared remains still locked in her vision. Human sterilization.

"Uncontrolled breeding has been the bane of mankind since the beginning. By not properly mixing the gene pool in proper quantities, using controlled selection of traits, we have squandered our potential again and again. The protections of civilized enclosures permit the promulgation of undesirable genetics. The blind breed the blind. Behaviorial disorders pass from one generation to the next. The abused abuse their own successors in the way they had been taught, with no interruption in the cycle."

He spewed this shit back in Olympus, Cooper remembered. *Back then it was only theory. For fuck's sake who put this maniac in charge?*

"Societies rise and collapse. we grow in fits and starts, always back-sliding whenever a great society stops adapting. We cannot allow this to happen anymore, we cannot afford it with the world as it is now. Nexus has shown us a way out of the endless chain of calamity, and we must all make sacrifices if we are to achieve the greatness we are capable of attaining."

Michael, were you in on this? The line kept moving forward. *What happened at Salt Lake?*

"I know how it is, you feel drawn to one another. The human is a social animal and enjoys contact with others, but you must understand that the natural urges no longer have a place in the world we are trying to build. Sexual selection is based on long obsolete instincts, selecting traits that may have been useful on the savannah, but counterproductive in technological civilization. Selection is now artificial, based on genetic algorithms I have devised to create that which Nexus needs."

Nexus. Keep hearing this. What is it? All I knew about were eyphors.

The line continued forward. Cooper had no choice but to listen in the narrow confines of the chain-link fence. The volume was such no one couldn't hear. Lest they were deaf, but then Cooper figured the deaf might already be weeded out.

"The threat we face is one of oblivion, and we cannot afford to let selfish, biological impulses ruin us. A direction has been laid out before us and I have been chosen to lead you through the difficult times we have ahead. But the benefits to our future cannot be denied, and all measures are in place to make sure that we reach those goals. Sterilization is key to preventing the propagation of unwanted genes. The rebels that plague us—"

"Hey!" The voice dropped Cooper's attention back down. A Watchman looked up at her from behind a large black console curving around him. "JD3605, you are marked as GNP. Have you brought any contaminated or relic material from City Omega-Three-One-Seven, or did you contact any in the attack?"

"Uh, no." I hope that's the right answer.

"Your GNP designation is not in our system. Where were you scanned at?"

"Um," Cooper took in a breath, forced herself not to hesitate. "Up in City Omega...." the numbers escaped her.

"What facility?" the Watchman demanded, voice shorter. "C'mon, do you rate that badge or did you just titty fuck a watch commander for it? And zip up, you're not getting it any easier showing off the sugar."

Cooper huffed and touched the bottom of the zipper line. "It broke. I...uh—"

"She strip it off a dead one?" asked another Watchman.

"The number wouldn't match up then. Fuck, your dense, man."

Another Watchman pushed through the slowly milling crowds and barked, "Send that one to me!"

His mask seemed to enhance his voice to a terrifying degree, but Cooper thought that might have been in her mind.

"She doesn't get into the city without my clearance," the Watchman at the console retorted.

"Watch Commander's orders," the new one said, "he'll inspect her himself."

Cooper caught a few chuckles muffled by gas masks.

"He usually does," said the man at the console. Then waved her off. "Ask the commander to save some of her for the rest of us."

Cooper took in a deep breath, muscles lighting on fire, set to alert. The Watchman approached her.

"Come with me."

"I'll die first."

He grabbed her arm. She pulled back to fight and he pulled an electrified baton from his belt. It sparked from a forked tongue.

"It won't be as bad as all that, just cooperate."

Cooper's breaths turned short, shallow, rapid. *They all say the same things.*

"Let's go!"

Cooper warily obeyed. She followed him.

"I'm GNP," Cooper said. "You can't kill me."

I've learned that much at least. I don't even know what it stands for.

"Stay quiet," the Watchman said, much quieter. "And stay even. I know your number."

She furrowed her brow. The other said he didn't have her number in the system. Yet *he* did? They entered a hallway of steel doors. From behind the metal, she heard muffled cries and some yelling voices. A chill went up her spine.

The Watchman led her into the room at the end of the hall, a wide open area with a series of strange computer consoles on the other end. A little metal mesa sat in the middle. Some instrument arms hung over it from the ceiling.

"Take off your clothes, and hurry up," he demanded.

Cooper fixed her gaze on him, waiting for him to make a move. She slowly moved her hands the edges of her broken zipper. She couldn't read anything into him. His helmet and gas mask covered everything.

"I said hurry up. We've got over five thousand citizens to process today."

Cooper pulled the fabric from her shoulders, let the suit drop, shrugged out of the sleeves. The Watchman stood absolutely still. The jumpsuit clumped above her boots. She couldn't read his expression, but knew the sight of her bared body struck a blow. A raspy breath escaped the voicemitter.

"Boots too?" she asked, almost coyly. She had a power over him. He was no threat. Nothing like the others.

"Yes," he said. "Uh, go ahead."

She bent over to take them off. When she rose back up, his gas mask and helmet were off. He ran a gloved hand through scruffy dark hair and shook his head. Cooper beheld a gaunt and handsome man with deep eyes and dark, brooding sincerity. His eyes looked upon her softly.

"Who are you?" she asked.

He croaked when he tried to speak, then cleared his throat. "No time for that... please, step up to the platform."

"You said you know my number."

"JD3605. JD, for Jordan DeBlanc. I've been waiting for that number to appear from up north. Now, c'mon, there's no time. I have to get you scanned for GNP. Don't worry, you'll pass."

"What's GNP?"

"Genetic Priority. Now, c'mon, get on the platform."

As her bare feet touched the cold panel, the door opened. In walked one of the large, armored guards. She froze, fighting the urge to escape. To fight. But he didn't make a move.

Had he heard us?

Now up close, he looked even more tremendous. She saw things that weren't quite human about him. His legs bent too high at the thigh for human knees, and then angled back until another joint sent them forward again. Armored, pneumatic hooves dropped with strong thuds. A thumb closed dead center with the middle of three fingers. Armor encased every part of him, blotched beige and dark green. But not metal, almost alive, with fine hairs and cilia shimmering over the surface.

"Don't mind the guardian," said the Watchman. "Now just hold still on that platform and it'll be over quick. In the process it'll scan for any contaminants."

Contaminants? Oh, shit! That gauntlet!

Before she could do or say anything, the various instruments on their mechanical arms lowered around her. Others from below. She stood still, pads touching her, needles poking, and lasers scanning in a whirlwind of light up and down from head to toe.

"Why do these damn things have to take so long?" the Watchman groaned.

The guardian spoke, voice deep but with a rough, hissing quality. "You primates have no patience. Despite the good that will come of it, you simply cannot wait."

"We're not the ones trying to accelerate evolution." The Watchman huffed and looked at Cooper. "Especially when it looks like there's nothing to evolve."

The guardian's hoofed feet sent out faint vibrations. Jet nozzles gaped over his back.

"You get too attached to the chemical drives," the guardian said. "In the end, biology is what drags you down and keeps you an animal."

The creature stood before her in two strides, scowling with those multitude of black eyes. A cold claw touched her chin, lifted her head back.

"Free yourself of this flesh and there is more power and freedom than you can imagine. This freedom is not a matter of rights, or the ability to choose, it is the achievement of pure will. Will free of desire, free of your body's chemistry, free of emotion or drive. Your reproductive systems are obsolete in the new order. In achieving such a state, even a slave cannot be touched. Not in Nexus. Embrace the metal destiny."

The guardian turned on its hooves toward the door, slipping its bulk through and shutting it behind.

"Damn guardians," the Watchman said. Cooper stepped off the platform and recovered her clothes. "Always sermonizing."

He turned back to the console and typed some things in while she got dressed.

"I appreciate what you said."

"You're welcome," he replied. "Name's Jamison, by the way."

A printer spilled out some papers. "I've taken the liberty of expediting your processing. This is your housing assignment, food card, and access key. I've printed out a standard map, but it's not really needed. You can't go through any checkpoint that's not on your assigned living route, so you're pretty well channeled to it anyway."

He put them into a duffel bag that he grabbed from a pile. When he handed it over, they looked into each other's nearly matching brown eyes. She couldn't help a girlish bite of her eager lip.

"Thank you," she whispered. "If you hadn't shown up...."

"I barely got the news in time. Things aren't exactly going as planned."

Cooper looked around, wondering all of sudden why no one knew. "Isn't there surveillance in this room?"

"I've taken care of it."

"That's saying something."

He nodded once. "I'm good."

You are, she thought, though she wasn't even sure what that meant. It felt like the thing to think.

"What do I do now?" she asked.

"Follow your route to your assigned living space. Try to keep out of trouble, stay quiet, and wait. We have others that will help you. Then Hawkeye will get you out. In the meantime I'll try to get you a replacement issue sent to your quarters. GNP patches are hardcoded into the fabric, I can't just give you a new suit."

"Can't just hand out badges?"

"Too easy to replicate. A uniform requires more material and separate manufacturing. Believe me, I miss the days they just used badges."

Cooper nodded, looked him up and down, wondering what was beneath his own uniform. "It must be difficult to wear a uniform that isn't worth the thread it's made of."

"Yeah," he said softly, then handed over the last of her papers with a slight smile. "Hopefully, it won't last forever."

Jamison moved in closer to her, whispered. "I can't tell you how long we've all waited to see you. How long we've waited for this day."

"I'm not even sure what this day is," Cooper said. "I don't know what any of this means. I've been...asleep."

"We'll fill you in when we can."

Or you could, she thought, almost laughed at the pun in her mind.

"But for now I need to get you moving. We've already spent too much time here, they'll get suspicious. My anti-surveillance measures won't last forever."

Jamison led her back out into the main metro area once he replaced his gas mask and helmet. She nodded her good-byes to him. He stayed stoic and silent, now as anonymous as the others. Nothing else could be done.

Cooper followed other refugee citizens from City Omega 317. The metro station looked like something late twentieth century, but unkempt and rotten. Papers and trash flittered about the corners. A large rat followed his nose about twenty feet away.

She walked down the front steps into the streets. Synchro Point looked like it was once a normal city, with concrete sidewalks and old-fashioned brick façades like some

mid-Western city. Brown leaves littered the ground, trees and bush either hibernating or dead. The air stunk with fumes. It reminded her of an oil refinery, probably a reason for the Watchmen's constant wearing of gas masks, aside from the obvious psychological effect.

Watchmen stood on every corner and patrolled the sidewalks. Armored cars acted as their workhorses, and now she could see the turret up top, sporting a new type heavy machine gun she didn't recognize. The armor sported dark and light gray camouflage schemes, others were white, but they all shared stark, orange markings. She didn't recognize any of the machines.

Above it all, a tremendous white spire reached into the sky. In the gray light of the clouds it gleamed a shady blue. It too had orange markings, stripes and various shapes themselves larger than the largest buildings ever made by man. The vast structure made her light-headed just to look at it, filling her with awe and dread.

Its sheer scale failed to properly register in her mind. Her psyche felt compelled to resist believing what she saw truly existed. A structure stretching into eternity, a streak into the sky. She couldn't see the end, fading ever upward, more like a surrealist painting than anything that stood like a building, yet it was there.

At the base, a few well-sized skyscrapers reached upward, though dwarfed by the great spire. One of the tallest buildings looked like a maroon, old-style cash-register. She recognized it, then it dawned on her through the terror.

The Wells Fargo building. Is this...Denver?

Cooper approached the first checkpoint. Heavy machine guns bristled out of a fifteen foot tall, stark white barricade that stretched across the street from one building to the next. She got in line with the others.

Keep in line, she thought. *Don't stand out. Be a good drone.*

On her approach, a scanner above the door flashed a light to her GNP badge. A portion of the barricade opened up and she walked through.

No fuss, no muss, she thought with an inward sigh.

Buses moved by, rusty things packed with citizens. Other citizens operated stench-riddled dump trucks, but no personal vehicles.

Cooper reached a T-intersection, with checkpoint barricades bristling with machine guns at either end. She checked her map to see which way she needed to go, but then a face flashed before her eyes. A man passed by and she couldn't help but see his likeness.

"Devon?" she barely whispered. He walked away in the opposite direction she needed to go.

Cooper slowly followed. *How many years have passed? Could he be...?* His dark brown skin reminded her of his complexion, closer to Michael's than hers.

She quickened up her desperate steps, reaching out to catch him just ten feet from the barricade.

"Hey," she grabbed his shoulder. "What's your name?"

He turned to face her, eyes furrowed. "Name? JK9081."

"No, I mean your first name."

He twisted out of her grip, and the fabric slipped from her fingers. "Look, are you crazy? We aren't allowed to use those anymore."

"Do you remember me? Look at my face."

"What the fuck is going on here?" shouted an approaching Watchman.

The man started running away towards his opening and the Watchman blocked her with his baton.

"No, wait, Devon! Is your name Devon? Do you remem—?" The crack of the Watchman's shock stick silenced her.

"Get back!" He jabbed it into her gut. The blow barely registered, and then he pulled his pistol. "I said get back!"

Cooper slowly backed up, watching as the barricade access closed. Three machine guns had trained on her. Their barrels gawked her way.

"Do you have any business past this point?"

"No, I—"

"Then get to where you're supposed to be. Now!"

"All right," she said, then turned. As she approached her assigned path, she tried to keep the groundswell down. "Please...where are they? Someone tell me."

Cooper passed three more checkpoints before coming up to a rundown apartment complex. Looking for the right number, she entered the middle commons area. A rusty old merry go-round sat in the center, surrounded by other worn playthings.

No children, she noticed with a chill. *What happened to mine?*

At the far end, four Watchmen held down an entrance to one of the buildings. Cooper kept her distance, moving over to a swing set. From there she stood and watched.

"It's only a matter of time before they come for you," came a soft voice. She turned to see a young woman with black, scraggly hair sit into one of the swings. "Especially you. You don't have long to wait."

"Why?" Cooper demanded. "Why me? And why soon?"

The woman cackled, a hideous, disturbed sound, then looked Cooper's way. Cooper noticed the scars on her face, like three knife cuts. "The Watchmen like their women. They like 'em fresh, and that's what you look like." She rubbed a hand over her scarred face. "They like 'em pretty."

"My God," Cooper whispered. "They did that...?"

The woman had a GNP designation on her suit as well. Cooper couldn't understand how they could get away with it.

"How could they do that to you? Aren't you...uh, priority?"

She snickered. "Messing up the skin doesn't mess up the genes. They have to get creative in torturing us when we get out of line."

She stood and approached Cooper, stopping inches from her.

"Have they got their hands on you?"

The woman gently reached at Cooper's chin, her touch electrifying enough that Cooper didn't resist. Fingertips glided along the open zipper line of Cooper's broken suit.

"They'll probably try to get creative with you, until they disappear you."

"Disappear me?"

She pointed to the great white monolith rising to the sky. "They'll take you there, and no one will ever see you again."

Cooper looked over her shoulder at the Spire, menacing in its bright white luminance.

"Beauty is a curse," said the girl, before her hands slipped under the fabric and cupped Cooper's breasts.

Cooper's eyes widened and she looked back to see hazel eyes just inches from hers.

"We shouldn't waste it while it lasts," she whispered against Cooper's lips while her fingers kneaded pliable flesh. "Let me have you first, JD, please...."

Cooper froze, fearful if the Watchman saw them. She pushed forward, set her hand on the wall behind the woman to brace herself and cover what she was doing beneath Cooper's jumpsuit.

"Your skin's like nothing I've ever felt," the woman continued.

Cooper tried to speak, but still felt the electric shock seizing her throat. If she hadn't been interrupted with Amanda, a moment that was just this morning for her, they would've been doing untold acts on each other. The touch of soft feminine fingers on her body again, the look of those pouty lips and icy hazel eyes, overpowered her will.

Then guilt tainted her desire. The father of her children died just hours ago. Ramon, not long before that, but in a different time and place. She still felt their hands. Strong. Manly. Powerful chests and arms to hold her, a contrast to the silken touch of this young woman here. What happened to Malala? Or Amanda? Were they still alive?

Only the scars broke her inner revelry, marring the woman's lovely, innocent young face. Scars, brought upon her like the poor Afghan girl. Cooper shook her head, anger overcoming her. It silenced her guilt. She closed her eyes and felt simply the other woman's kneading touch.

"Why do they get such a free reign?" Cooper asked. "Why aren't they sterilized like the others?"

"Watchmen are undesirables. The Nexus doesn't want their genes, but Liang said to let them have their incentives. 'Sides, so long as they only fuck other undesirables and don't break the real merchandise, then collect the GNP's when called for, the Nexus gets what it wants."

"What does the Nexus want? Who are they? Why are they doing this? What have they done with the children?"

The woman looked at her, slightly suspicious. "You ask a lot of questions."

The sound of broken glass forced Cooper's attention to the other building. Window shards fell from the third floor. Shouted voices chased gunshots and screams.

Cooper took a knee next to a small brick wall, pulled her jumpsuit back over her chest. Swarms of Watchmen filed out of the building. They held men with hands tied behind their backs and black bags over their heads. She noticed the GNP badges on their chests. Armored cars rolled up and Watchmen tossed the prisoners inside.

A Watchman broke off from the group and approached the two women. "Is there a problem here?"

Cooper looked at him, fumbling for the words to say, letting out only faint croaks.

"Shut up," he said and pushed her aside, then approached the girl. He pulled out a knife. Cooper went defensive, watching for any sudden move.

"Now, Kelly, we've gone over this before," he said, touching the side of the blade to her nose. She shook and turned her head away. "Don't be snooping where you don't belong. You keep behaving, I'll be easier on you when I take you down to the guardhouse. All the other boys will too. Don't you like it when they're easier on you?"

Cooper's hands tucked into fists.

"*Let us kill him!*" said a voice. Cooper looked around for who said it, like a whisper

on the wind. "*Settle this anger, we can kill him!*"

Of all the alien things she'd heard today, that by far sounded the strangest. Before she could figure it out, the Watchman moved away from the whimpering Kelly. He followed his comrades into the armored cars and they drove off.

Cooper knelt next to Kelly and placed her hand on her shoulder. "Are you all right?"

Kelly's whimpers turned to grunts, and her scarred face contorted into anger. She slapped Cooper's hand away and rushed to the door.

"Don't touch me!" she snapped. "Find your own trouble."

Kelly disappeared behind the entrance, her footsteps storming up a flight of stairs. Cooper sighed and sat back against the wall, closing her eyes.

Where the fuck am I? What's happened? She opened her eyes and stood up. In a few minutes she found her building and went to the fourth floor. The old wooden planks creaked. The stench of rotten pine tickled her nostrils, along with that piss/shit smell of poorly kept bathrooms. Paint chips littered the ground.

When she finally got to her unit, she went through a doorless entrance, though brass hinges still hung on the frame. She walked into the tiny kitchen. A man sat at a round table with his head down on his arms. Empty water bottles stood on the table top. A shaggy old rug laid in the middle, sending up its rotting stench.

"No door," he mumbled, then raised his head and looked over his shoulder at her. "There's no door. Used to be but Watchmen had the wrong room once, and they kicked it in, and they didn't replace the door. It's made of wood you know."

"Uh." Cooper nodded. "Yeah, I know."

"No, you see," he stood up out of his chair and walked passed her to the frame. "The door was made of wood. Like those trees in the park, though, I don't know if they used trees in the park to make the door. Well, if there are still trees there, they must not have used them. Yeah, that's probably right. That's right isn't it?"

Cooper pressed her lips together and nodded. "Mm-hm."

"If you find some wood that fits on the frame, we have the door. But," he strode across the kitchen, "we have windows. And they work."

"Uh, what's your name?" *Do I really want to ask that?*

"Name?" he cocked his head. His brown eyes seemed empty. "Name, you ask? I don't have a name. Well, yes, of course I do have a name. We're all assigned one aren't we? But, what is the point of those names if we do not use them. I mean, the Watchmen come around they call me 'citizen.' A guardian comes around he calls me 'citizen.'"

He approached and stood just inches from her. "You see, they call me citizen. 'Hey, you, citizen come here!' or 'Quit dry-humping that light pole, citizen!'" He laughed at the last one. "They don't really say that, but you get it. They call me citizen, they call you citizen, they call everybody 'citizen!'"

His voice came down to a whisper. "So, I guess that means, we are all 'citizen.' We are not many, but one, and our name is Citizen. It's who we are."

He sat back down and grabbed his forehead. "Too much thought. Too much thought."

Wary and tired, she searched the unit. An open door connected them to an adjoining unit where she saw a woman sleeping on a couch. Next to the kitchen with the madman was the bathroom with a single toilet, sink, and shower. No door. No shower curtains.

She groaned. "Are you telling me that I have to shower where you can see?"

The man snapped his head toward her. "You need not worry, citizen. I have achieved a near null state in my sex drive. I am the most advanced mentality in this building. Your bared form causes no rise in me, because my mind is nearing freedom from all biological imperatives. My guardian keeper says that something may be done with me soon, and I will serve Nexus."

Cooper cocked her head and faux smiled. "That's so good to know."

"Or, you can understand that the sex drive is counter to accelerated evolution, because it controls people's minds. With the sex drive, they do things that are counterproductive, all to fulfill obligations of an obsolete reproductive system."

Obsolete? she thought. *I gave birth to two. I think mine still works.*

He bolted up straight. "Evolution is based on mutations. Mutations that prove adaptive and productive are passed on because those who don't have the mutations die, and the dead cannot breed. Well, what happens when you must deal with nuclear weapons, or travel in hostile environments? Technology puts us in places we can't live, in space, in the oceans. We can go there but the bodies will not survive, genes cannot adapt fast enough. Technology outpaces mutation and therefore technology must be the cause of mutation, and that is what Nexus is!"

III: TWINS

06/22/2024, 8:30 AM. "*Welcome back to Fox and Friends. This, just in: strange goings-on at the Salt Lake Facility. The Rangewood Rapid Reaction Force, or Triple-R as it's known to Salt Lake employees, has been activated and is rushing its people into the facility. Olympus International officials are reporting 'no comment' on all fronts. Several others are saying that Olympus has been issued a government gag order, and that the US government is ordering the company to stay silent to media.*"

Rangewood Triple-R, On Approach to Salt Lake Facility, 1230, 06/22/2024

The MV-22 tilt-rotor approached Salt Lake City at five hundred feet, all power on and nearing three hundred miles an hour. Cooper sat among twenty other people, all readying their weapons and gear. She did a final check on her G36C carbine, then tucked the cover flaps of her ammo pouches behind the magazines.

A black, skintight piece of nomex and memory molecule matrix shaped like a one piece bathing suit gripped her torso. Gloves of the same material came up over her biceps while stockings of it went thigh high. She found it better suited than normal fatigues to the semi-aquatic environment of the spaceship. The aliens lived in a kind of gelatinous "vital fluid."

Panels of chrome material held nano-mechanisms that could extract oxygen from the vital fluid, and provide the scuba hose and mouthpiece about the shoulders with air. She also didn't mind how she looked in it, despite protests to practicality.

Yellow, UV visors darkened her brown eyes, and she hid her emotional distress behind a solid expression, as well as the exotic sensations running through her limbs and torso. Something about those lights, interacting with her synapses maybe, set her nervous system on fire. It flared up and down, but she felt near the cusp of ecstasy. She kept seeing Amanda's skin glisten with water, and ached for someone's touch.

She took in deep breaths to keep herself calm. It didn't help that most of the male specimens she traveled with had their strong, muscled arms mostly exposed, their faces gaunt, bodies shaped, trim, and virile. Only seeing the those two could dampen the flame in her limbs. Scotty Chambers and Lenny Knox. Rangewood had recruited them into the same team as her. Even out of the SEAL Teams, she couldn't escape them.

The entire operation boggled her mind. She joined Rangewood because it would get her closer to Michael, and in turn, closer to her children living fifty miles away from the crash site. Michael was one of the few who had actual contact with the aliens inside the vessel, and he had said many times they were largely non-aggressive to humans.

Olympus International had kept the alien ship locked up tighter than Area 51. She'd sent Michael a text message through her smartphone, but still hadn't gotten a response thirty minutes later. Trying to stifle her worry, she fixed her equipment, readjusting her pack, ammo pouches, breathing hoses. Yet her muscles still tensed and ached to make love to someone. Hell, she'd hook up with her ex-husband at this point.

"You all right, Cooper?" asked Ramon, her partner, who'd also managed to stick with her.

"Yeah," she replied.

"You seem kind of wired."

She shrugged. He nudged her arm with his elbow. It sent electricity through her bones. "I'm sure your beau's all right."

She smirked, nearly chuckling. "My beau, huh?" She hadn't referred to Michael as her "beau" in almost two years, but he remembered it.

Ramon had comforted her through the divorce. She'd put on an act of sadness at the time, since she couldn't have been happier when she was set free from those vows. It had been merely another façade, illusion, lie she pulled up around herself like a curtain. An attempt at normalcy to erase what had been done by the two at the front of the Osprey.

"Yeah," Ramon said. "You hadn't found anyone else since."

If you only knew, she thought.

"Sides, I'm sure it's just a brown out."

Lenny Knox snorted back toward them. "Y'know, I wouldn't be too bothered by a power outage if weren't for the fucking three-mile long thing from space right next it."

"Should've spent more time in the thing during drills, Lenny," Cooper responded in a firm voice to make herself clear on everyone's intercom. Laughs and chuckles filled up the cabin. Lenny had earned a reputation for avoiding training ops deep inside the ship, preferring to stay on its perimeter. Cooper only wanted to get even deeper into the ship than they would let her.

Coward.

"Shut your sucks and listen up," boomed Team 2's commander, Scotty Chambers.

She saw his ebony face at the end of the bench, the whites of his eyes bright against his skin, like the gaze of a demon in the dark. She continued to avoid him as much as she could, but never requested transfer to another team. She needed to keep him in sight, even more so than Lenny. He'd only become more menacing since Afghanistan.

"I just got an update. We have comms with a few of our security officers down there. Our bird's diverting to his reported area near the Number Eleven Gate."

"What did he say?" asked Cooper.

Scotty shook his head. "We didn't get that. Advisory sent the intel in, they said he was going out to investigate a disturbance, but they don't have a description. Then he went silent."

The Osprey banked to the right. Cooper looked out the window. Three other Ospreys came into view, veering away to the original landing zone. Beyond them, the smooth, elongated shape of the vessel appeared. Nuclear cooling towers barely rose to its base. It always filled her with a sense of awe and dread. Gray-black storm clouds approached from beyond.

Lenny made his way back toward her and Ramon. Her eyes observed him from his first movement. Like a hawk on its prey, she never took her eyes off of them. Lenny only looked more afraid, softened in recent months. When passing in the halls, he tended to widen his path around her. He avoided looking at her in the tight gear she preferred.

Ramon and Cooper both watched him approach, before he sat across from her, lifted his intercom mic to above his visor. Cooper did the same, slowly.

"Hey, Coop," he said shakily, barely audible over the Osprey's noise.

"What do you want, Lenny?" she asked flat out.

His blue eyes looked out to the black ship beyond. "We got a real incident here."

"Scared, boy?" Ramon taunted. Cooper put her hand on his wrist. The feel of his warmth under her hand released a sudden ignition she grunted to control.

"Yeah, we do," Cooper said, sweat breaking out on her brow, dripping out from beneath her visor. "Not your first time, Lenny, why so pale?"

Lenny matched her gaze. "First time going live in an alien ship. Threat unknown. You don't call react for a brown out. Something's down there."

"There's lots of somethings down there," Cooper said. "Eyphors, people, guard dogs, even rats. Probably ants too, somewhere."

"Look," he began, leaned forward, spoke quietly. "I know what we done, it wasn't right. Didn't seem wrong at the...I mean, Scotty seemed to make it make sense, some how."

Cooper nearly shook. "Broken heads like you two can justify anything."

"He didn't know how else to take you down a peg. You were too wild, too smart, outpacing him even as a lower classman. You practically invited it."

Cooper set her fingers around the charging handle of her rifle, leaned forward like a cobra coiling up for a strike. "Careful, Lenny."

"Hey, hey," he said, put up a hand. "I ain't trying to be like that. I felt bad. Still do."

Cooper couldn't believe it. She still felt his breath on her neck. Heard his words in her ear.

"So good, so good. You look so good," he had panted on her. The words still rankled her neck, where he had kissed again and again. Each spot lit like a Zippo flame.

"Go condition one," Scotty ordered throughout the cabin.

Cooper racked her G36C carbine, putting a round in the chamber. Weapon on safe. Her thumb readied to flip it off at the wrong word. She wrapped one gloved hand around her pack strap.

"Two minutes," Scotty alerted.

"I got a family now," Lenny said, almost pleading. "I got a wife."

Ramon shook his head. "Sure, she doesn't know what a piece of shit you are."

Lenny reached into his glove and pulled out a picture. "I even got a daughter now. You heard, I'm sure."

He held up the small photo to her. She beheld such a sweet face. Tiny and fair skinned, black hair, and hazel eyes.

"She's over a year old now," Lenny said. "Her name's Kelly. Kelly Knox. I never understood until I had a daughter. C'mon, Coop. Cut me some slack here."

Her gaze went from the girl back to him. She only felt the fuze ignite in her gut. "I won't accept your death bed apology, Lenny. You're scared. You want forgiveness because you got a girl now? Fuck you. And if I ever meet your daughter, I'll let her know just what kind of man her father is, and I hope your shame breaks you. One way or the other, I'll have the justice your daddy denied me. Now go back to your guard dog."

Lenny looked down and away from her. He silently put the picture back under his glove and returned to the front of the Osprey, back to Scotty's side.

Cooper looked at Ramon, who held up a fist. She smirked and knuckle-tapped him. He wore another version of the nanofiber armor, looking like he was in a wet suit underneath his combat gear, with the sleeves cut out. Her eyes briefly followed the vein running down his bicep.

Her mind filled with memories ofBUD/S, being surrounded by such well shaped, athletic men. Their wet bodies dripped in the sunlight, everywhere she looked, wearing nothing but those little brown shorts.

She nearly grunted and visibly shook her head. *Holy shit, snap the fuck out of it you raging fiend!*

"Cooper are you okay?" asked Ramon.

"What? Yeah, fine. Good to go."

"You're sweating and, well, you're radiant."

"The fuck you talking about?"

"One minute!" Scotty yelled.

He talked quick. "Hey, you trust me. I'm your partner. Have you had sex recently?"

Her eyes widened. "I wish. What has that got to do with anything?

"Your hormones are all over the place. I can tell by looking at you. If you're pregnant, you need to stay on the Osprey."

She closed her eyes and swallowed. Her throat seemed so tight. "No, I'm good. I'm not pregnant."

"You sure?"

"I'd know if I was pregnant, Ramon. I have experience in these things."

He nodded, smiled. "All right." He patted her on the shoulder. His thumb lingered there long enough to send a fire racing through her shoulders into her neck and breasts. A hot flash of pleasure forced her to whimper and shake.

Ramon looked at her again, incredulous. The Osprey slowed, rotors tilting into the vertical. Dust flew about the craft. Cooper's heart raced, readying for the ramp to go down. It always sent the adrenaline rushing, not helping her current state.

She had seconds to look around, see her surroundings. A chain-link fence to port. Guard house on starboard. They landed behind the gate. A parking lot packed with cars filled out the space in front of the Osprey. The ramp lowered. She unhooked her safety belt.

Ramon looked her dead in the eye as the seconds disappeared.

"Stay on board, Cooper. I'll explain to Scot—"

"Go!" came the command.

One after the other, they grabbed their assault packs, slung them over one shoulder, and kept their weapon in firing hands. Cooper headed out and heard nothing else from Ramon. She came to her sector and took a knee. As the Osprey lifted off, the seventeen man and one woman team got to their search.

Cooper quickly got her light pack on both shoulders, then checked the guardhouse first. She entered the console. Computer on, account locked. Phone off the hook. Half-eaten sandwich on the desk.

"Clear here," she reported.

"Any sign of the guard?" asked Scotty.

"No tenemos nada aqui," replied Ramon.

"English, Ramon, god dammit," spat Lenny.

"Search the parking lot," Scotty commanded next.

Cooper took the number three place as they headed towards the cars in front of an office building. The structure stood beneath one of the tremendous vehicle access ports of the alien vessel. The Freedom Tower could have fit inside the opening, used for the entry and exiting of whatever machines the vessel carried. Distant thunder rolled gently over them.

The intense desert sun beat down on her tight black fabric. The nano-fiber reacted and cooled her body. She kept sweating like crazy, though. The movements of her legs sent her loins raging.

What's happening to me? she thought. *This isn't like hormones during pregnancy. What did that aurora do to me?*

A sharp clanging sound, like something beating on the cars, hit her ears. She and Ramon readied their weapons. Cooper waved him forward, keeping him covered.

"Hey, I got something," Ramon said.

Lenny and Scotty moved up. Cooper spotted a man in black uniform pants and white shirt, wearing a security guard's belt. She made out the black and yellow Rangewood patch on his sleeve. He stood, back to the team, beating into the hood of a dark Cavalier.

Something's wrong with him, she thought. Steady on her approach, she noticed a shiny, black patch of some kind on his upper back. It looked like it had ripped through his shirt.

"Hey, Chambers," she alerted.

"I see it," Scotty replied. "Cooper, Ramon, provide cover. Lenny, you with me, dawg."

"On it, Boss."

The four formed a forward wedge in front of their other twelve team mates.

Cooper kept a steady stance, putting her 3.5x sight on the guard. The black thing on his back shined.

Looks like some kind of...leech?

"Hey, man, you all right?" asked Lenny.

The security guard turned around, wobbly. One shoulder dipped lower than the other. Varicose veins crawled up his neck and cheeks, eyes blood shot. Cooper's own eyes widened when she spotted his hands, fingers far longer than they should have been, extending into...claws?

"Look out!" she warned.

The guard hobbled at the team lead, covering the short distance and slashing at Scotty.

"Shit!" he yelped and leapt back. Cooper tried to come in for a shot, but Lenny got in the way, brandishing his shotgun.

"Freeze! Get on the ground!" Lenny Knox followed corporate policy to warn first, unaware or unbelieving of the situation.

"Shoot him, Lenny!" Cooper shouted.

She saw only blood spray. Claws slashed through his body armor, cut into flesh beneath. He fell back, hit the asphalt with a thud. Blood gurgled from his throat. Cooper nearly screamed. In all her career she fought the urge with every rush of fear.

Then the barriers went up. The emotional firewalls she had built in the Academy-,BUD/S, Afghanistan, went on full power and she aimed in. Her finger squeezed out an even, controlled burst.

"On him!" Ramon shouted, circling to her left.

The...whatever it was, didn't go down, even as half her magazine filled its torso. Ramon plastered it with three buckshot hits from his AA12 auto shotgun. A spray of yellow-white gunk ripped out of the wounds. The creature finally dropped, spasming on the ground until all movement stopped.

"Hay dios mio!" Ramon hissed. "Es del infierno. Le chinga!"

The rest of the team came up behind them. Scotty Chambers looked over the body. Four strips had been torn across his armor. Lenny hadn't been so lucky. The claws dug deep. He moaned through a mouth full of blood, dripping down his cheeks.

"Help...." he whimpered.

Cooper could only think of how she must have looked, body broken and beaten on the shower room floor. The taste of her blood mixed with spilled shampoo when the water flowed over her mouth. She'd spat it, and so Lenny spat blood.

"Coop," Ramon said, waving his fingers forward to the guard's body.

She focused. Cooper inched closer, aimed in on the black thing. It looked like some kind of crab-shaped creature the size of a dinner plate. A putrid, gaseous stench filled her nostrils.

Some kind of pulse ran through the thing and nearly made her jump. It reared up, exposing a pinkish-red underbelly and sharp mandibles. Cooper fired everything she had left in her magazine. The creature exploded into a white spray.

A hot substance splattered against Cooper's boot and thigh. The sensation, like hot cheese, sent Cooper scrambling back.

"Oh, God, what is that! Get it off! Get if off!"

She grabbed the substance. Her glove came up covered in whitish mucus, bare fingertips felt it, a slimy puss. She shook like she never had.

"Cooper!" Ramon shouted. He tried to help wipe it away. "Doesn't look like anything bad. You all right?"

"Oh, God what do I have?"

He touched her cheeks and looked closely into her eyes through the visor. "C'mon, girl. You're Zen. You with me?"

Cooper's senses came back gradually, but she nodded.

"Advisor, advisor," Scotty said, his voice raspy but calm. "We need an immediate evac now. Send the birds back, get us out of here."

That fired a shot of clarity through Cooper's system. She walked up to him. "No, Scotty. Something's going down here."

"Yeah, no shit!" he exploded back. Sweat soaked his dark face. "No shit something's going down."

"It wasn't supposed to be like this," Lenny managed to gargle while the medic tended him. He groaned when they lifted him onto his side to get the bandages around his torso.

She shook her head. "We've got a job to do. The people—"

Scotty turned and stepped to her, dark eyes empty, the right one twitching, mouth

stuck in a dead frown. The predator's look. She remembered it so well she froze.

"The people in there are already dead," he growled.

"Wasn't supposed...to be like this. Scotty. Chamberman!" Lenny yowled in pain. "Not what he said...."

"Not what who said?" Cooper asked directly to Scotty.

"Just trust me," Scotty Chambers replied. "Leave. Now."

"And you're not?" Ramon asked.

"I've got a job to do. You don't."

Her face went solid and stern. "Scotty, the father of my children is in there. And we need to get everyone out."

"We need to assess the threat," Ramon added. "Find out what's going on."

Scotty narrowed his gaze. Frown turning to a slight smile. "Never give in do you?"

Cooper knew what he meant. Referring back to her grunts of defiance, her insults, every moment she tried to escape their grip.

"Until I see their bodies," Cooper retorted, "I'm not giving up on them."

"You don't get it. Even if they're alive, they're dead."

"Everyone's dead," Lenny nearly screamed. "Unless they made the bargain. Right, Scotty? That's what he said. But look at me, dawg. I'm...I'm...."

The medevac Osprey rolled in and brought up a pall of dust, drowning out the relative quiet of the facility. He looked around to his people, some looking to him. Others looked toward Cooper.

"All right," he said bemusedly. "Let's be heroes. Everything else is in place."

"Spill it," Ramon said. "What the fuck is Lenny babbling about?"

"Cool your heels, Speedy. We go on that ship, you'll find out quicker than it takes me to explain."

Scotty put his gaze back on Cooper, gave her body a look up and down, bit his lip while he sneered. "Lead the way, Coop."

Cooper walked passed him and talked directly to the rest of the team. "Rogers, Aimes, get Lenny on the helo. Everyone else, on me. Let's go."

They readied their weapons. Cooper ran on to their first objective, Ramon and the others behind.

Long after night fell, Cooper still laid awake. Outside her window, the massive Spire stood in the night. City lights illuminated its enormous base. A map on the wall showed it sitting at the center of a complex of checkpoints and barricades, like the goal of some circular maze.

Helicopters flew about. From below, the occasional thrum of an armored car cut through the night.

The gauntlet moved around in her arm, pulsating and reforming. Her muscles tensed. She saw them bump around under her skin. She tried to steady it with her other hand.

"*We cannot wait forever*," the voice repeated, another reason she couldn't sleep. It had been saying the same thing all night. She moved over to the window sill, looking outside with the binocular vision she learned to control.

"*We cannot wait forever.*"

She chuckled with a harsh breath. The song wound around in her head until her lips sung it out in a whispered voice. "More human than hu-man, more human than hu-man."

Michael loved White Zombie. One of the last things they agreed on. The song kept throbbing in her head. "I am the astro-creep, a demolition style hell American freak, yee-aaah, I am the crawling dead, A phantom in a box, shadow in your head saaay...."

"Phoenix," came a whisper in the dark. "Phoenix."

She looked at the door adjoining both rooms. A dark figure approached out of the shadow, a beefy black citizen with graying hairs in his beard and scalp.

"Move quietly, Phoenix. Don't let that *citizen* hear us."

Cooper looked down at Citizen Mutant, as she'd come to call him, while he slept on his mattress, then crept her way to the opening.

"Call me Shadowman."

She came to within a foot of him. "Okay, I'm the real Slim Shady. What do you want?"

"I am not at liberty to give you answers. But Hawkeye is coming. I'm here to tell you to lay low, and to help you out till Hawkeye gets here."

Shadowman reached into his jacket and pulled out a piece of cloth wrapped around something a foot long. "You will need this."

He moved the cloth away, revealing the black form of another gauntlet. Cooper's eyes widened.

"Oh, no sorry. Already got one."

"You'll need both for what lies ahead."

Cooper grit her teeth. "The first one hurt enough, and it's still acting strange."

"What was once strange will become normal, Phoenix."

"My name is Cooper. Jordan 'Cooper' DeBlanc."

He shook his head. "We all have names, and when used carelessly they prove our weakness. We're all down on their books. If they ever connected one name with another, it spells death. We speak of you as Phoenix, never to say he or she, and never your real name. Shadowman, Hawkeye, Red Eagle, Walleye, Dead Meat, Prometheus, and Phoenix."

"I feel sorry for Dead Meat."

Shadowman pushed the gauntlet forward. Cooper took it.

"If they come for you before Hawkeye, which is possible, I will find you as quick as I can. But I want you to know, live or die, it will be an honor to be beside you."

Cooper recognized that language, the one of soldiers. "Tomorrow then?"

He nodded. "Work detail, North Canal Zone. Try not to act too...strong."

He disappeared into the dark room beyond. Cooper decided to take that shower, but first used a pair of scissors to cut her hair back down to size. She learned to cut her own hair in the Navy. She set the gauntlet down on the edge of the bathtub next to the wall. Hot water cascaded over her, feeling wondrous. Her nerves felt restored, even as she looked at the black thing on the sink.

She turned off the water. Night winds from the window cooled her down. She picked up the gauntlet and walked over to the mirror, feeling more relaxed than before. She looked at the slick black material, then slipped it on, waiting for the....

"Dammit!" she hissed. It split into strands which rotated and cut into her skin. Again, no bloodspray. She grit her teeth. The strands dug in, fusing with bone and muscle, reshaping and forming it to where it wanted.

"*Yes....*"

I'm really getting sick of you too!

"More...give us more...."

Go to hell!

Cooper closed her eyes and waited. Finally, it finished, and she expected to see it gone just like the other one. Instead, she looked into the mirror and found a woman with golden irises. She almost yelped and covered her mouth, finding both gauntlets armoring her arms in a slick, black material.

Silvery claws stuck out from her fingers, each an inch long. Curved crests formed swept back wings on her upper arms. She could feel it all, the claws extending and retracting at her command.

Then, pure ecstasy filled her torso. She sucked in a breath and fought from moaning. Something moved within her. Hatches opened on her upper back. Slippery, segmented tendrils flowed out slowly. Curved blades clicked out of every segment.

More blades extended from the heads of the tendrils. They circled around her. Cutting edges hovered over wet skin. Cooper felt their every movement, exquisite. Her legs trembled, pressed together. Eventually she couldn't hold, obeying her desire to drop to her knees, so much more intense then after the aurora had touched her in what still felt like yesterday.

Every part of her felt ready to explode. Muscles expanded and contracted, pulsating with rapturous energy. One of the bladed tendrils circled behind her head and stopped face to face. She felt some kind of friendly consciousness coming from them. She licked her lips and smiled at it, giggling.

The tendrils clicked back into her. Cooper reared back. She ran her clawed fingers up her thighs and torso. Small, red cuts formed and vanished, healing instantly. She stretched back and dipped her hands between her legs, trying to ease some of the sensation, but only intensified it throughout her body.

"Oh, dammit," she whispered when she realized what she needed to do.

She moved her fingers ever faster. Smooth, even circles. The other hand moved low to caress her lips. The claws cut, but skin healed up. Rapid pricks of pain followed by euphoria when the hurt vanished. She desperately tried to keep quiet, nearly biting her tongue off when her thighs shuddered and she dripped on the floor.

The tingling relief rushed to the very edges of her limbs, and Cooper regained her footing on shaky legs. She looked into the mirror, cupped her milky white breasts in black resin hands and silver talons.

"Yes...we are becoming...."

Becoming what?

She reached up to her mouth, and stuck out her tongue to find a golden stud there. She touched it with one claw. Her tongue felt the light sting when the tip cut flesh, but she didn't recoil.

"Huh," she said. "Interesting."

No, she countered in her thoughts. *Not interesting. It's freakish. What did Michael do to me?*

"He gave you power."

Power?

"To control."

To fight?

"To win."

To win.

"To find your children."

To...find...my children.

"Yes...."

The black gauntlets retreated back into her skin. Eyes went from gold to brown. Her mind calmed and everything seemed strangely harmonious. She wobbly strode over to her bed and passed out. There she laid until the first sunrays crept in through the window and Robert Liang's voice clattered in her ears.

"Good morning, citizens."

She awoke to his face on a flat screen monitor on the rotten, paint-chipped wall. "We have much to say this morning, some good, some bad."

Cooper moved to get up, but in a sudden dizzy spell she spilled, stark naked, off her bed and crashed on the wood floor. She gasped and pulled the covers over her. Mutant sat at the table, eating, almost unaware of her.

"First off, a congratulations to one of Nexus's newest neo-skin commanders, DD1066. He's been in many of our reports, but his achievements and that of his heroic soldiers have earned him the name Kul-man, bestowed upon him by the guardians, a hero of the Mass Departure."

Mass Departure? Cooper thought.

The report displayed a headshot of a man with bluish, grayed out skin, yellow eyes and a terrible scar down his face that deformed his upper lip. She focused on him, disbelieving of the image.

What the hell is he? Or it?

Cooper grabbed her clothes and dressed

"The bad news I have to report, is that some people have been abusing certain privileges. The covenant of marriage is an out of date practice, no longer having any place in its economic or reproductive contexts in our society."

The sentence drew her attention completely to the monitor.

"I have allowed some couples to declare their marriages, though there is no legal context for them doing so. Instead, I recognize that human beings feel drawn to each other. Considering the use of selective sterilization, I saw little to worry about when it came to reproduction. However, some 'couples' are beginning to ask for certain rights, for certain measures to be taken to ease times apart."

Yeah, no shit, pal.

"But we must all keep our eye on the Endstate." The last word flashed in white letters as he continued. "To remain a competitive species in a vast, multi-dimensional universe, we must follow the edicts of accelerated evolution given us by Nexus."

Cooper blew out a breath. "What the fuck is Liang on about?"

"Overseer," said Mutant. "He is called Overseer."

Cooper turned to the man, scarfing down ration packs like they were candy. At that moment, she realized she wasn't hungry, and didn't remember the last time she ate.

"Overseer will open the way," he said. "We shall all be perfect in the image of Nexus, and we shall have him to thank. One day he will call for me, and it will be my time."

Psycho. Oh, wait, who am I to talk? I'm hearing voices and talking back.

"Marriage is obsolete," said Mutant. "If it is obsolete, it has no purpose. Skin is skin. Wood is wood. Purpose serves for a purpose. If there be no purpose, it should not exist. And so it is for work that we find purpose."

He suddenly stood ramrod straight and Cooper backed away. Mutant turned to the door and shouted into the corridor. "Complex Seven-Zero-C form work detail on street and await transportation."

Mutant walked out at a brisk pace. Others followed in ones and twos. They didn't respond in any kind of disciplined fashion. Cooper put on her boots and peeked out the door. Shadowman arrived quickly and took her back into her own apartment.

"All right," he said. "This is just a regular work detail, nothing too complicated. Bus'll be here any minute. We play it cool, like it's an everyday thing."

"Do you have any answers as to what happened here?" she asked. "This is Denver isn't it?"

"We don't have time for much, but it had to do with the ship, okay? Now, we gotta get down there before—"

"Salt Lake?"

Heavy bootsteps arrived at the end of the hallway. "No, the bus will wait for you. Get your fucking shit and hit the street!"

A Watchman strode forward, bootsteps hitting the rotten wood floor, running his shockstick against the wall. He stopped at Cooper's room.

"What is this? You trying to get some nookie? Move out!"

Cooper and Shady bolted for the hallway, having to squeeze through. They ran for the stairs.

"Jesus, woman, when I tell you to go, we need to go!" he chided.

"Well, I'm sorry but this hasn't been a typical fucking week, all right?"

They hit street level and joined the rest. Four buses arrived, Greyhound logos scratched and worn off. A dozen Watchmen corralled the citizens along the sidewalk.

"Why would they assume we'd be trying to have sex?" Cooper whispered. "Aren't they sterilizing people?"

"Don't stop people from trying."

"Where are the children then? I had a son and daughter. I need to find them."

"They'd be grown by now, now shut it," Shadowman hissed.

I'm going to snap his neck he tells me to shut up one more time, she thought.

"*Death is our calling*," the voice said. Cooper shook her head, fighting the urge to jump up and slice at something. "*We're not killing. We are not fulfilled*."

Cooper's teeth ground together. Strange things rolled around inside her. A voice in her head. Tamperings with her body. And now everything and everyone wanted her to keep quiet when she felt like screaming.

The Watchmen channeled the citizens onto the buses. They used their shocksticks like cattle prods.

If they hit me in the ass with one of those—

"*We kill them*."

Cooper rolled her eyes. *You can shut up, too*.

She and Shadowman sat near the middle of the bus. Right across the alley sat the girl named Kelly. Cooper sat there for a minute, then looked at her. Despite the knife scars, she was still a very pretty girl with soft features. Her dark hair created a lovely contrast with her pale skin.

"What are you looking at?" Kelly growled.

"Sorry." Cooper turned away and shook her head.

Citizen Mutant took the wheel of the bus, apparently a place of privilege. Two Watchmen stood up front, with two behind. The diesel engine growled poorly down the road. A Watchman from behind walked up. His knuckle brushed Cooper's shoulder. The sensation turned her numb.

"Look at you. You made it," the Watchman said. Cooper looked up as the man removed his gas mask.

"Pig-face," Cooper quipped. "You made it too. Well—"

The old, ugly man lifted his shockstick at her face. "Hey, I might like to play around a bit, but I don't take lip like that. You still got to pay for your misbehavior."

He turned to Kelly. "Right, KK? Hey, KK2856." Kelly's gaze shot back up at him. "Remember when you gave me that lip?"

Pig-Face cackled and looked back to Cooper. "Took her to the back of the bus and got a quickie between stops."

Cooper could barely maintain the flame burning inside her.

"Course she just couldn't take it. Reported me to the Watch Commander. Must have sucked his dick or something. Had me demoted and sent to that shithole up north. But, uh, my man Stokes took care of that. Ain't that right?" He called to one of the men up front.

One of the Watchmen pulled a knife from his belt. "Damn straight did. Pulled a train on her for it too. Just about the whole guardhouse."

Pig-Face laughed again. Kelly looked straight ahead, lips quivering. Cooper couldn't stand that look on her face. The pain in her eyes. She couldn't bear it. She wanted to hold and comfort her, to shield her from these predators.

Give me a chance at 'em, she thought.

"*For once we agree on something*."

The bus arrived at the work area. A concrete canal filled with mud and junk. The stench riled in Cooper's nostrils. Then she recognized a particular tinge to it, a solid repugnance like fungi grown in a dirty shower sponge.

The creatures. Salt Lake.

Gathering at the edge of the canal, mangled, mutated bodies floundered in the muddy banks. People passed around clumps of meat hooks.

"Hurry up with the tools," a Watchman shouted. "If you ain't got one, you're using your hands."

Several other Watchmen were already on site when they arrived. Cooper examined their weapons. Kriss submachine guns. AA12 auto-shotguns. Shells littered the ground, and the smell of cordite mixed in the air.

"Fish out those bodies and get them to the incinerator."

Cooper and Shadowman readied to go down until a group of Watchmen stopped them. One held Kelly's arm. She had an empty and distant gaze in her eyes directed at the ground.

Oh, no. Give me a fucking break.

"Let's go, JD," said Pig-Face. "We ain't got all day."

"Genetic Priority," Cooper countered. "You can't touch me."

"That depends on how creative we can get. C'mon!"

Cooper looked at Kelly again, still and expressionless. Shadowman stepped forward but a shockstick waved in his face stopped him cold. Cooper braced her hand against him.

"It'll be okay," she said.

"That's what I like to hear. She's game!"

"C'mon," Pig-Face grabbed her arm. She twisted away.

"I know what's going down," she snapped. "I can walk myself."

He glared at her for a minute, but then smiled. "Okay, then."

How the hell am I going to get us out of this? she thought.

They left the group and walked about a block away, into a canal duct. Her mind raced for ways to get them out. Cooper entered a dimly lit area. Concrete surrounded her. The two women stood with the men blocking the way out.

"Well, what you waiting for, Kelly?" asked the masked Watchman named Stokes. "You know the drill. Strip her down."

Kelly didn't say anything, just slowly approached and touched the edges of the jumpsuit's open zipper.

No, Cooper thought. *Not like this. This can't be how it happens for her.*

"I'm sorry...." Kelly whispered.

"Don't be."

Cooper sucked in a breath as Kelly pulled pulled the fabric from Cooper's shoulders. The touch of Kelly's fingers sent lightning through her skin.

"Oh, man," said Pig-Face. "Look at that."

Cooper's tight waist blossomed into buxom hips and buttocks. Deep inside, she felt it boiling. Power. Energy.

"Oh, look at that ass, man. Panties are perfect."

"Yeah, can't cover nothing."

"It's strange," Cooper said softly, staring into nothing. "When I came here, there was a Watchman who was pretty nice to me."

"Fucking pussies everywhere," Pig-Face spat, hand down at his crotch. "Think I got time for that shit? After seven billion dead, human race is dying dumb-ass, but I'm gettin' mine."

Seven billion? Cooper thought. *Are we on the brink? Are assholes like this all that's left?*

Kelly hunkered down to remove Cooper's boots and pull the fabric of the jumpsuit away, leaving her in tank top and underwear. Kelly's fingers slipped under the waist straps of her black panties, and started to pull down when Cooper grabbed Kelly's wrists.

"No," Cooper said. "I can't take you like this."

Kelly shook her head. "We have to. Please, they'll hurt us."

She gently touched Kelly's scarred cheek. "I want you, but I can't."

"You were game a few minutes ago," Pig-Face spat.

"I won't let this happen to me or you again," Cooper promised her.

"Fuck it," said Pig-Face. "Stokes, give me that knife."

His partner handed over the blade. He approached Cooper with bootfalls that sounded like thunder. Kelly backed away, moving like a frightened puppy. Cooper had never seen such terror on anyone's face. Not even Malala's.

Pig-Face put the blade next to Cooper's cheek. "I ain't putting up with your shit, JD. You don't need your face to pass on your Priority genes. Get kissy or I get cuttin'."

Cooper gazed into him. Through him. He had all the hunger of Scotty Chambers, all the malice, but none of the ferocity. Nor the skill. She knew he had no power over her.

"You're probably the most pathetic piece of shit I've ever met. At least the goddamn Taliban had an ethos."

He looked confused for a second at her words. "Taliban? How the fuck you know about them? You weren't even born then."

"Maybe I'm not as young as I look."

"Fuck it," he said, then grabbed Kelly's arm and tossed her to his cohort. "Start stripping that bitch."

Kelly gasped, a gloved hand around her throat, the other unzipping and pulling at her suit.

"Leave her alone," Cooper demaned, when Pig-Face body blocked her, but she barely moved.

Pig-Face grunted and touched the cutting edge to her cheek. It stung as it moved down to her chin, but then the pain vanished. He opened his mouth for his next threat, but went silent when he realized the cut had already disappeared.

"What the fuck?" He cut again across her other cheek, and Cooper simply glared into his eyes as if to drill holes in him.

"*He's beginning to realize*," said the voice.

"You, hold her!"

Another Watchman got behind Cooper and pulled her arms into her back. She didn't resist. Didn't even feel theatened.

"I'll never be afraid of you," Cooper said.

The terror she saw in Kelly's eyes slowly became apparent in his. Desperate, he lowered the knife and drove it into Cooper's gut. The blade cut through the top layer of soft skin, but stopped barely half an inch beneath. He tried to push the blade in, but Cooper pressed against him, abdominal muscles reacting, turning to steel. Gauntlets formed, and her eyes became gold.

The grapples shot out of her back and wrapped around the Watchman holding her, one bladed head gouging through an eye socket.

In an instant, lust turned to shock. Cooper shoved Pig-Face back to his companions. Before the first gun came free. Bolts of pleasure flared through her body from coursing energy.

Cooper rushed to Stokes and jammed her knee into his gut. The grapples stuck blades into the two men at his side. With him hunched over, she dropped a hammer blow to his back and flattened him out.

She back-kicked into Pig-Face's stomach and sent him to the ground. He barely braced himself. A grapple struck into another man's face, plowing head blades through his gas mask's eye socket.

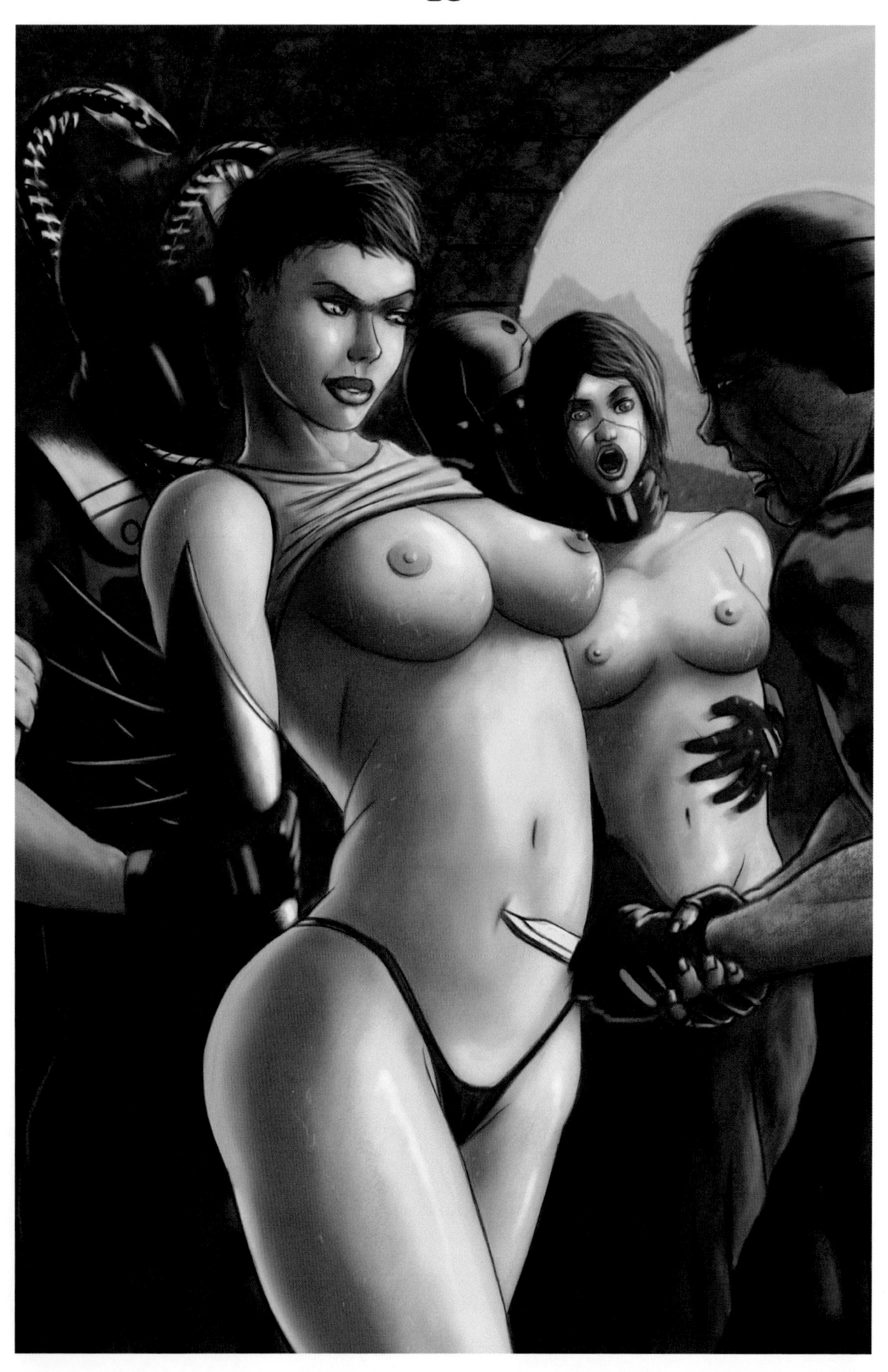

The other grapple had its slicing grip around the last Watchman's throat. With a twist, it sawed off his head. The helmet separated and tumbled one way while the head bounced another. Cooper looked at herself then, standing there in the light.

The grapples arched at her sides, as if looking for approval. Blood and gore dripped from their bladed rails.

Oh, I want more.

"*We must find more.*"

Pig-Face shuffled and grunted on the ground. Cooper smiled. Her body shivered in delight. Terror reigned in his eyes with a delicious glint of pain.

"*Yes!*"

"More human than human," she sang barely above a whisper. "More human than human. More human than human."

Cooper lifted him to his knees. His lips quivered. Cooper looked at him, savored the moment, then drilled a fist into his face. Bone cracked beneath her knuckles and skin tore from his cranium. She pulled her fist out. Blood and other bits stained her resin skin.

Cooper looked over to Kelly. She breathed deep and quick, hazel eyes glistening against the shadows behind her. She looked afraid, but not terrified. A cautious confidence dominated her complexion.

"You killed them all. How did you do that?"

Cooper chuckled. "Rather easily."

"Are you her?" Kelly asked. "Are you...the Phoenix?"

Cooper strode towards her. "I don't know what I am. Not anymore."

She touched Kelly's lovely, scarred face with her unbloodied, armored hand. She could feel the girl's skin, as if the resin shared her nerves.

"But I won't let them hurt you. Never again."

Kelly closed her eyes and leaned her cheek into Cooper's touch, holding the other woman's hand there. Cooper gazed at Kelly's full, pink lips. She moved in closer, the heat bouncing between them.

"They'll never hurt you again. I swear to you, Kelly." She moved in and kissed her on the lips. Kelly responded, pressing her lips back, opening her mouth. Life surged through Cooper's limbs. Her grapples reached lower and out, as if to shield their embrace.

Kelly moaned and wrapped her arms around Cooper's tall body, feeling her back and buttocks. Their first kiss deepened with their embrace. Kelly licked and pecked down Cooper's neck, drifting to her breasts. Cooper held her there, cheeks mashed onto her soft mounds.

"I...I can't believe this," she said.

"I don't know what to believe anymore," Cooper replied. "Just let me hold you."

"You can hold me, Phoenix. Hold me anytime you need to."

Another set of footsteps approached. Cooper and Kelly looked at a panting Shadowman barreling into the tunnel. He stopped in his tracks before he nearly tripped over a dead body. "Holy shit!"

Then he looked at Cooper and froze. "Woah." He went silent, staring at Cooper's glistening physique held in Kelly's arms. After a second, he covered his eyes. "Oh, damn. Uh...."

"It's all right," Kelly said and backed away from Cooper, but holding onto her arm.

"It's not what I was expecting either."

He looked around at the bodies. "All right, we got to hide these. Help me pull them further into the tunnel."

As he grabbed the nearest body, Cooper stepped forward and planted her bare foot on it.

"First, some answers," she said.

"Hey, are you crazy or something?" he protested.

"*Yes.*" The voice made Cooper pause.

"While we've got a second, I want answers."

"We ain't got a second, all right!"

"Hey, I'm the one standing here tits out. If I've got a second, so do you."

"Look, the Nexus has been running the show for fifteen years, all right? They were chasing that ship that crashed here. It belonged to the—"

"Eyphors," Cooper interjected. "My husband was communicating with them."

"Who?"

"Michael DeBlanc, my hus—" She stopped herself, and looked back at Kelly's hazel eyes. "Ex-husband."

Kelly nearly laughed, and Cooper smiled at her.

"Listen, those eyphors had the key to taking the whole thing down. The whole Nexus. But something happened in the crash. Then they came up with a plan, called Phoenix, and you're it. You're the key to destroying this whole damn thing."

"How?"

"That's above my pay-grade. Now, can we do this?"

"What is Metro Defense?"

"They used to be the army for Nexus here on Earth. But then Liang split them into the Forces, an army of supersoldiers Liang designed with the Nexus. They're part of the ultimate plan, the EndState."

"Which is?"

He shrugged. "The plan to be part of Nexus. It'll wipe out anything it can't use. But to do that, we'll have to surrender ourselves, become machines. Nexus sees the flesh as too soft. I learned that much just listening to those fucking broadcasts all day."

"The Metal Destiny," Cooper said.

He nodded. "Yeah. Some bad shit."

"And the children? I had a daughter named Alyssa, a son named Devon."

"Liang directs all reproduction in Nexus territory, which is pretty much the entire world. Priority citizens are selected, processed at the Spires."

"Spires?" Cooper asked. "Plural?"

"We think there could be as many as twenty across the globe. From there they're taken to a place called the Depot. You won't find any children here. But, like I said, yours wouldn't be children anymore. It's been fifteen years since the incident started."

Cooper let out a breath. "But, seven billion dead. That's what he said. That's almost the entire human race."

Shadowman stood there, silently nodding with a shrug. She felt better that she had some answers, but they only raised new concerns. She looked over at Kelly, who gathered up her clothes and offered them to her. Cooper smiled and took them, giving her a quick kiss.

Kelly pointed at her gauntlets. "Those'll be hard to hide, though."

"Oh," Cooper looked at them, then gave it a little thought. They shrunk and melted into her skin. The gentle sensation made her sigh, then they vanished from sight. Her eyes became normal. Much of the blood had been absorbed into her skin, processed, dissolved.

Kelly laughed out a bit of her nervousness and amazement. "I can't believe it. Sometimes I thought you were just a myth. A false promise."

"I don't know what I am. But I'm definitely not false." She stroked Kelly's cheek with a knuckle, and rubbed her shoulder. "And we'll get out of here together."

"I'm with you, JD."

"Cooper, actually."

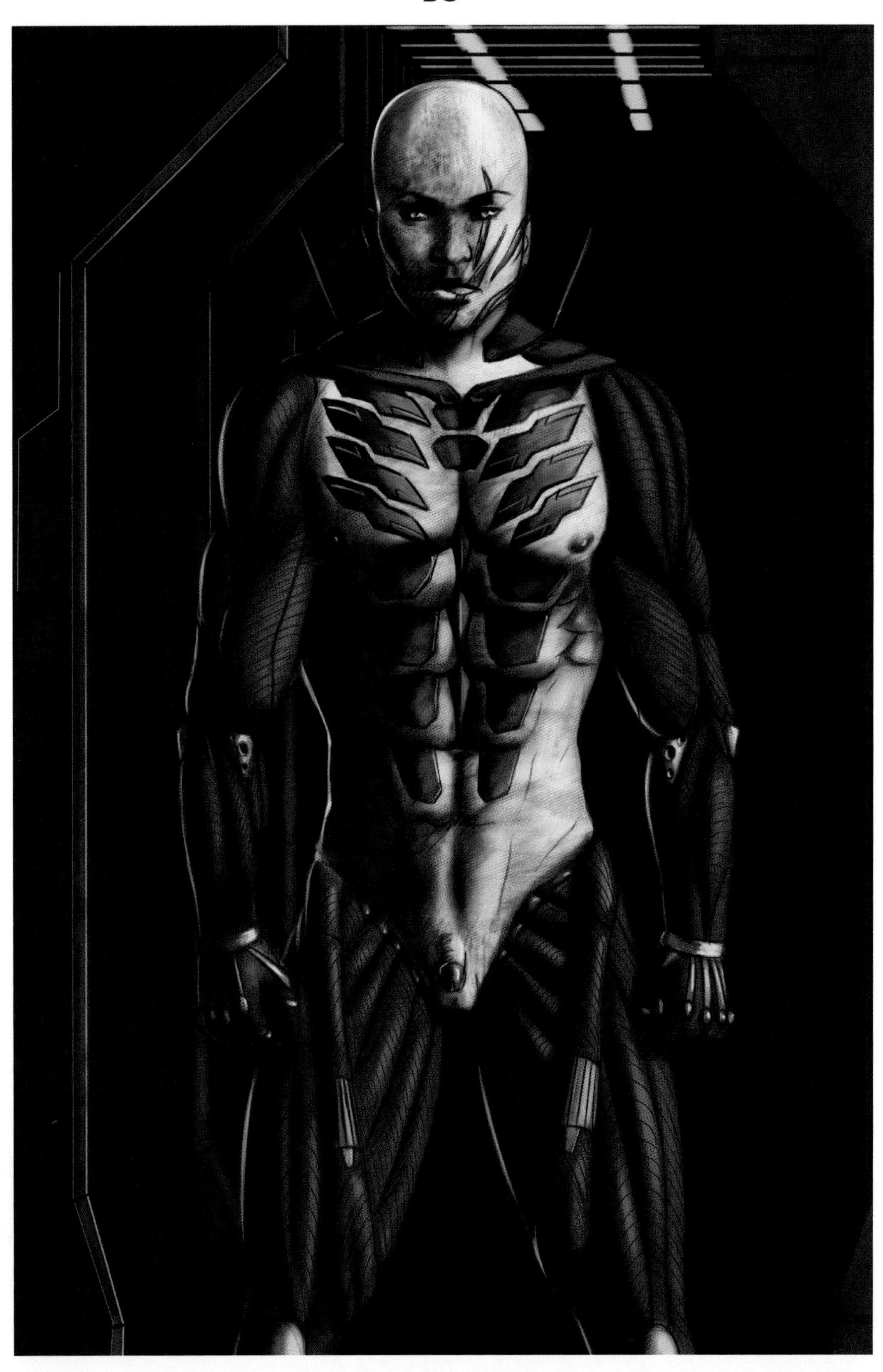

IV: RUN LIKE HELL

The clouds rolled beneath Robert Liang's boots. He'd never gotten used to that, but enjoyed the godly feeling nonetheless. High altitude mists sped between the columns that formed the corners of his complex atop the Spire.

Nexus material technology allowed them to create solid, armored surfaces that translated the light through them, allowing enclosed structures to see outside. Even a tank could see anything around it. As clouds moved along, he looked at the city beneath.

The mass sprawled to the mountains on one side and to the new North American Sea coast on the other. Interdimensional travel required tremendous amounts of energy just to move small things. The immediate transdimensional shift of an entire Nexus army caused a catastrophic shock wave that shifted whole continents.

With the epicenter of the Forces' arrival somewhere in Missouri, the east coast of the United States had become an archipelago, with sea waters filling the great cavity all the way to here, where Denver used to be. The once gradual rise of the continent toward the Front Range now resulted in a mile deep drop off to the sea below.

Now Synchro Point, a city of fifteen million, sprawled on the back of what was once Colorado's capital. The Spire, center of his administration, saw over most of it. Observation and listening posts within the great white tower looked out into the mountains and to the coasts.

Its frame formed a containment bracket that could prevent further calamity, a portal to the rest of Nexus. A dozen chambers, each the size of the Empire State Building, could bring in reinforcements from all throughout the domains. Twenty other Spires had risen in other parts of the globe, but his reigned supreme.

Colonel Kul-man walked down the steps to the viewport. Even though Liang had designed the neo-skins, the culmination of fifteen years of work, the sight still thrilled him like the first time he witnessed this success.

High tension, nano-muscle tissue replaced his arms and legs. It required no coverings, so the red-orange sinews looked like limbs with no skin. His torso remained bared. Angled segments of metal and polymers reinforced his skin and endodermal armor. Wetwire filaments wound just under his skin.

The neo-skins wore no boots, their foot structures bare. Kul-man's skin bore a pasty, browned out color. Scars crossing his face had since deformed his upper lip. Fields of burn marks littered his physique. Yellow, mechanical eyes stared out above gaunt cheek bones.

"Colonel Kul-man," said Liang, a genuine smile spreading across his face. "It's good to see you."

"Overseer," Kul-man began with a nod. "I came to say, well, I appreciate your gifts."

Liang detected a bit of forced platitude in that statement. He fished around, stepping forward and putting his hand on Kul-man's shoulder. The metal fiber nano-muscles had a texture of wires wrapped around each other.

"Was the girl to your liking?" he asked. "You've definitely earned it. Your exploits on the Mass Departure are the talk of the guardians. They are quite proud."

Kul-man hesitated in his response. He looked down and away for a moment. "She was rather young."

Liang shrugged. "She's at prime breeding age. Besides, isn't that a relative term for you?"

"And she was helmed." Kul-man used the term for wearing a mind and memory altering headset called a helm. Nexus used it to alter behavior in soldiers, to tweak them, as well as teach muscle memory drills.

Liang let a breath simmer out. He turned and walked away with hands clasped behind his back. "You're too chivalrous, Colonel. Not quite something that's beneficial to Nexus's aims on this planet."

Liang turned back to the stoic soldier who stood still as a statue. "They are not delicate little flowers nor precious, unique snowflakes, Kul-man. If I give you a woman to breed, you will breed her. It's not just for sexual satisfaction. It must have a purpose. If not, we can let the Depot be all there is. Accept your reward."

Kul-man continued his dead, yellow-eyed stare. "There's something me and the other soldiers have wondered, Professor Liang. The space-time bending that occurs with trans-dimensional travel over great distances means that while only fifteen years have passed for you, it's been over forty for us. After such a time, to come back and see the state of affairs here, we cannot but voice our disappointment. Our service on the Mass Departure has earned us a degree of independent thought from by the guardians."

"So General Ahri-man has told me. Mankind has not been very compliant in accepting Nexus's will. But it's not as bad as it seems. Many good specimens will be joining the ranks very soon."

"Out of what's left," Kul-man retorted. "Our mission is to save humanity's future. But we return to see most of our species gone."

"The human population had existed for too long outside the bounds of natural selection, causing the propagation of unfit genetics. The current course of events has reduced that blight to the prime core of what we need."

Liang walked back to the nude cybernetic soldier, speaking with his slow steps.

"Everything in Nexus must have a purpose. Our emotional states had a purpose before, but not now. Laughter could help us overcome fear. Pride allowed us to excel. Love helped preserve our breeding partners and affection spurned us to protect our progeny. Reason and logic allow us to see these things, so we do not need our passions to override us into action. So, quell your fears of impending doom. We are not past the point of no return."

He stopped before the soldier. "You know all this. Don't throw away all you have accomplished. Realize that after thousands of years of uncontrolled expansion and reckless compassion, much of the human species was worthless material. Separating it out has been a painful, but utterly necessary process. The woman designated EL1101 may have been your first sexual experience in a very long time, but don't get distracted by your emotional attachments to her. She has no memory of who you are, and the embryo has been extracted. And that is the future of our kind, that is how we will refurbish our tattered banner."

The professor backed away and looked out in the sky again. "Mankind is such a unique animal, that's something the guardians were convinced of from the start. Reproduction is such a powerful drive, the most powerful in all of nature. Controlling it is a task that requires constant vigilance. We cannot let it slip out of control. We must be unique in the universe to earn Nexus's admiration and attention."

Kul-man nodded. "The other worlds are quite...alien."

"You would know. You've seen far more than I. I am quite envious."

Liang turned back to his observations, looking out over all that he controlled.

The work detail bussed out to a damaged rail junction. The rail sat sandwiched atop a grass covered rise, between a brick façade below street level and a chain link fence. The ground had given way beneath.

Guess this Nexus never learned how to keep things in shape. Might have something to do with the local admin, probably.

The rails appeared newer than anything in the city. One of the black trains sat atop it, angled side panels shut.

"The train cannot fulfill its purpose," Mutant chimed. "We will amend this."

"Thank you, Mr. Speaker," Cooper said.

"He's so good," Kelly whispered into her ear. "Almost impossible to believe he has an IQ of a hundred-and-fifty plus."

"Really?"

"Yeah, apparently quite the brain for math and spatial relationships, I hear. That's what they want him for, but life here has made him more than a little crazy."

Watchmen took up position around the work site. Everyone depended on muscle to get it all done. Cooper and Kelly tried to look busy, and fought the simple urge to hold hands. They had to hide their feelings while the work detail continued on its routine. Watchmen kept their eyes on every little aberration.

One thing they couldn't fight was the occasional gaze into each other's eyes. Kelly seemed reborn ever since discovering who and what Cooper was, even though neither of them truly knew what it meant. Cooper wanted to explore just what she had started with this woman, but couldn't until the Watchmen were gone.

During the work, a metal bar dropped from one of the train cars. Air rushed out and sent people scrambling. Cooper walked ahead into the gap. Panels opened, lifting like DeLorian doors.

Figures appeared inside, incomplete. Human torsos breathed and writhed in the grip of some kind of apparatus. No legs. No arms. Heads concealed in harnesses. But they sweated and moved as if living, fed by the machines. All male.

Cooper's jaw quivered and then all the disgust and terror begged for release. Hands rushed to cover her mouth, but her eyes couldn't close. Chests rose and fell. They shifted and pulsed in agony.

Watchmen rushed up the embankment until Mutant shouted out.

"And so evolution comes!" He waved his hand to the torsos.

Cooper didn't notice that the Watchmen stopped at his approach.

"We cannot mutate fast enough. Mutation takes too long, and so to go where we are not evolved to go, technology must be the cause of evolution. This is closer to perfection."

Kelly rushed to Cooper and braced her shoulders. "You okay?" she whispered, then gasped. She embraced Cooper then.

"Strive for perfection and you will go to the Depot. Skin is skin. Flesh is flesh. All tools in the battle of evolution. Be prime material or...." he looked at the Watchmen around them, "...be stuck in obsolescence and await extinction."

Shadowman and others took care of the dead Watchmen. It would buy them time, but nothing more. The MD usually assumed murder if their men went missing for more than 24 hours. Cooper found it kind of funny they would wait that long. It meant Watchmen often vanished.

She couldn't get over the rotten stench of the apartment complex. As she lay in bed, Cooper's thoughts kept drifting to what happened at the canal, how easily she killed six armed men.

What am I? she thought.

"*We are the answer.*"

We are Legion!

"*Fool's tales.*"

Take a joke why don't you?

Cooper feigned sleep for about an hour while Mutant snored away. Sleep never came. Eventually, she flung off the covers and stood over at the window in white tank top and black underwear. The putrid air filtered in on the breeze.

"Hey," came a whisper in the dark.

Cooper looked to see Kelly come from the next room. "Uh, hey."

They met in the dark, and hugged before entering a deep kiss. Kelly felt over Cooper's back, hands finding skin smoother than anything she ever imagined possible, so soft and lively.

"I really want to know what you're made of," Kelly whispered. "You're like no other person I've ever felt."

Cooper giggled quietly into the dark. "You probably know more than I do. Feel more. Feel everything."

Cooper pulled off her tank top, and Kelly's fingers pulled down at Cooper's panties, letting them drop to her ankles. Kelly then pulled the zipper down on her own jumpsuit, and it fell from her shoulders with a shrug.

Cooper's heart pounded like a jackhammer. She felt another woman's body on her own in what seemed for the first time. So long. No cloth between them. Just skin. Terrible things had happened, but Cooper wasn't going to waste the opportunity to rewrite the rules. If any good could come of this, she would make it. She lifted Kelly into her arms, the other woman wrapping her legs around Cooper's waist. She carried her over in the dull light to the shower and turned on the water.

Both women explored each other in the water's flow. The world shrunk to the size of their little corner. Nothing else mattered. Only the feel of their warmth passing between wet skin. Fingers lit each other on fire.

Kelly clasped and suckled on Cooper's magnificent breasts like a starving baby. She went down her belly with lips and tongue. Kiss. Lick. Back up to suckle on supple nipples. Fingers delved deep between Cooper's thighs, feeling up to warm stickiness that clamped onto her penetrating fingers.

Cooper could only lean back against the tiles, surrendering her body. They rubbed their chests together, breasts feeling over each other's. Pliable flesh smoothed against pliable flesh, too soft for purchase while water cascaded down between the tight gaps.

"Oh," Cooper moaned out, almost too loud, "fuck I love women so much."

Kelly laughed and wrapped her lips on Cooper's. Tongues danced in a wide open twirl beneath the stream of the shower. It wetted their kiss even further. Cooper wrapped her arms around the girl's torso while Kelly clamped her fingers hard and wide on Cooper's ass. There they held each other tight.

"Kelly...." Cooper whispered against the water's noise, then kissed her shoulders and neck. "Where do we go from here?"

"We get the fuck out of here," Kelly replied. "We might have to use the railroad."

Cooper held Kelly so tight to her, hand through dark, soaked hair. Their breasts nuzzled together, legs intertwined. They lowered to the bottom of the shower, held each other, and kissed. Kelly's hazel eyes looked into Cooper's browns.

"Can you make the other eyes come around?" Kelly asked.

Without even thinking about it, before she could answer, Cooper's eyes turned gold and Kelly smiled with amazement. "That's incredible."

She felt at Cooper's belly, where Pig-Face had tried to stab her. She pushed and felt Cooper's muscles stiffen and harden.

"Don't tell me I'm made of memory molecules," Cooper said, then chuckled.

"What are those?"

"It's an experimental armor type back when I was with Rangewood, guarding the ship. Molecules realign and turn to hardened materials when under some kind of stress, like when a bullet hits."

Kelly braved to put her hands around Cooper's neck. She gently rubbed her thumb against her trachea.

"What are you doing?" Cooper asked.

"You still breathe, I was just wondering if...." she closed her grip around Cooper's throat. The skin atop was still soft to her touch, but everything beneath gradually hardened in response to her increasing grip.

"You want to try choking me, then?" Cooper asked.

"I've...been trying." Kelly squeezed as hard she could, then shook with nervous laughter. "It's like trying to choke a steel pipe."

Kelly's fingers then ran down Cooper's face. "And your skin heals instantly. The knife...it just...."

Cooper reached up and touched the long scar down Kelly's left cheek, following it from under her eye down to her chin.

"You're so beautiful, Kelly," said Cooper. "There's nothing they could do to you to change that. I'll get you out of here, somehow."

"Nothing they could do to me?" Kelly nearly sneered. "Nothing they could do worse."

"I've pieced together parts of it, from your scars and what they said." Cooper paused. "I'm sorry, we don't have to talk about—"

"I'm GNP," Kelly replied. "So, no vaginal penetration allowed. They went the other way. I couldn't walk for a week after they dumped me back in the cell. They cut my face before they started."

Cooper nearly shook with the anger. It made her light-headed, to see red while she sat on the shower floor. The flowing water brought back those memories. An odd sensation. Lenny's words echoed in her mind against the din of falling water.

"I hear you like anal," he'd said.

"Hit it, man!" Scotty challenged him, wide smile shining from his dark face.

She closed her eyes to shut it out.

"I know something of what they did to you," Cooper said. "Just...not like that."

"You?" Kelly said incredulously, eyebrow cocked. "You can't be serious."

"It was a long time ago. I wasn't like I am now. I was more like you."

Kelly shook her head. "I can't believe it. You're the Phoenix."

"I wasn't always, Kelly. I don't even know what being the Phoenix means."

"*You wouldn't.*"

Cooper's eyelids twitched at the voice's sudden quip. She had to close her eyes till they stopped. Kelly leaned in and kissed her again. So long and deep. They held each other, whispering to each other as the water turned off.

"Can you tell me anything of what I was supposed to do?" Cooper asked.

"Kill Nexus thugs, kick them off the planet, something like that," Kelly said, cheek on Cooper's shoulder. "I guess you'll be pretty busy, cause there's a lot of them. How don't you know?"

Cooper shook her head, rubbing Kelly's back. "Kelly, I've actually been asleep for fifteen years."

"Asleep?"

"The last year I remember was Twenty-Twenty-Four. I was part of a rapid reaction security team stationed near the eyphor's crashed ship in Salt Lake City. Something injured me there, four legs, pincers the size of sabers."

Kelly shook in Cooper's arms, she could feel the other woman tense in fear. "Mantids. They spread across the world from the gateway. I heard some say they killed a hundred million people before the world surrendered. They'd...they'd barrel into people's homes, harpoon them, cut them to bits."

"It's what they did to me. My ex-husband found me and put me in some kind of stasis with the eyphors' help. I woke up two days ago."

"Explains why you don't know much." Kelly shivered again, this time from cold it seemed. The warm water chilled. Cooper felt it on Kelly's naked, wet skin.

Cooper closed her eyes and concentrated. She felt the energy running through the sinews of her muscles. It radiated from her skin, warming against Kelly's touch. It radiated from somewhere in her core.

"Are you doing that?"

Cooper laughed. "Yes.

Kelly sighed and relaxed. She stopped shivering, holding on tighter. "What was it like from before? I wasn't even two when it happened."

"Well, people dominated the world. We were all over the place. We had almost no knowledge about different worlds, other planets. The greatest threats we faced were each other."

Cooper pulled back from their hug, and looked into Kelly's hazel eyes. "I was a member of the Navy, a military force that was supposed to defend the country that used to be here. I was part of an experiment to see how well a woman could be one of the Navy's top warriors, a SEAL."

Kelly smirked. "Sounds like the experiment is ongoing."

Cooper huffed. "Two men who were supposed to be my brothers in arms attacked me in the Academy. They feared and hated me, so they raped me. Tried to break me."

"You couldn't have gotten back at them? It was like it is here?"

Cooper shrugged. "In some ways. One was the son of a powerful admiral, the admiral who was a career long friend of the commandant. They swept it under the rug, made me stay quiet. But it didn't end there. Those sonsofbitches managed to follow me to every hellhole the Navy sent me to."

She sighed. "What's worse, they trapped me inside myself. I was so different before. I felt this untapped reserve of intense desire within me that I couldn't answer. I was afraid to, felt like it would attract a repeat of their attack. There were days I felt like screaming, trapped in a cage. They sent me off to war and I killed...several men. Some of the cruelest kind, like Pig-Face and Stokes."

"Those Tala-, Tali-, what did you say?"

"Taliban. I killed many men like Lenny and Scotty, but never them."

"Those were their names?"

Cooper nodded. "Scotty Chambers and Lenny Knox."

Kelly began to nod but then stopped. Her body froze. Neck tightened. Cooper noticed it as if warning lights flashed in Kelly's eyes.

"Something wrong?" she asked.

"No," Kelly said. She loosened up, rolled her shoulders, then smiled. Her eyes betrayed her though. Cooper didn't press the matter, but wondered if Kelly recognized those names.

Kelly eased her lover, running fingers through Cooper's damp, short hair.

"I have to leave," Kelly said. "Patrols'll be inspecting the complexes in a few minutes. There's something I have to give you first."

"You have to give me something?"

"Shadowman gave it to me, said it was for you. He wanted me to give it to you since he had to take care of the mess. And...I guess he thought it would be better for me to do so, since he, well, saw us."

Kelly left the shower and reached into the breast pocket of her jumpsuit, then pulled out an object that gleamed so tiny in her vision. Cooper's throat knotted when she saw it and walked up to her lover. The heart-shaped locket hung from a delicate gold chain.

"Is that...?"

"I didn't want to open it. I didn't know what it did."

Cooper bit her lip as Kelly lowered it into her hand. When Cooper opened the locket, bright, holographic images of her family appeared. She gasped at their likeness.

"It was only flat little pictures before." She shook her head then when she realized just what they were. The angles, the way the figures moved. "These...these are my memories."

Kelly nodded. "Memory extraction technology is pretty common nowadays, for both sides."

Cooper shook her head, not sure what to think, but feeling a little mad. Her memories. Who else had them? Why'd they take them.

"Why did they do this? Who else has seen it?"

"Everyone who carried it had strict orders not to open the locket," Kelly tried to reassure, seeing Cooper's obvious frustration. "It's taken a long time to get here, through some dangerous places. They wouldn't take the risk if they thought it wasn't vital."

"Who's this 'they' you're talking about?"

"The Planetary Army. They were formed shortly after Nexus arrived from the last remaining governments and armies. They have kind of an underground mail system going on so we can get stuff from Pikes Peak."

"Pikes Peak? That's Colorado isn't it? So this city *is* Denver."

Kelly shrugged. "I don't know what that is."

"Don't worry. What's at Pikes Peak?"

"The head of the PA. It's where the eyphors drilled out their hive."

Cooper felt thunderstruck. Colorado was next door to Utah, to Salt Lake City. Those creatures she fought. They spent the morning pulling their carcasses out.

"But there it is," said Kelly.

"Here," Cooper held it up by the chains. "Put this on me, Kelly. I'd like you to do the honors."

Kelly took up the locket, then reached up around Cooper's broad shoulders to clip it in place. Kelly collected up her clothes and backed away to the entrance of the adjoining room.

"I'll find you in the morning," Kelly said. "Good night, my Phoënix."

Cooper smiled and waved good-bye. She recovered her tank top and black underwear then dressed before she got back into bed. She pulled the covers up and made them thick around her head, created a little tent, and then opened up the locket. At first she felt joyous, even as the knot welled up in her throat. Her own memories lit the air before her. Devon's smile shined in the little space.

After a moment, she couldn't take it anymore. She curled her hands around the locket and shut it, sobbing under the rough wool.

Walleye couldn't get the image of the woman out of his head. JD3605. The Phoenix. When the word came down, he scarcely believed it. Something of it had to be true. No reason the PA and eyphors would've risked sending a suicidal strike north of Synchro Point. No reason, unless it was true.

She's here, he thought while pulling his Watchman flight suit off and sticking it back in his locker.

"So glad to get off that street detail," said Rodman, his co-pilot, fresh out of the shower. "Strange how you don't see all that filth even from a hundred feet up."

"Hard to see details at three hundred kph," Jamison, Walleye, said low.

"I know, right? Except for the ta-ta's. Once they shower at least, y'know?"

He slapped stoic Walleye on the shoulder. "Hey, buck up, man. Something got you down?"

Walleye shrugged. "Seven billion dead people."

Rodman pff'd. "Waste products. Don't sweat it."

Walleye's co-pilot dressed up in a spare flight suit, packed his duffel bag and headed

away.

"See you at the barracks, bro," he called after him.

Walleye said nothing, merely took off his undergarments, grabbed a towel and bar of soap, then headed for the showers. This late at night, he found himself thankfully alone. He set the soap on the ledge, turned the water on. It hit his scalp like a shockwave.

Cascades flowed down a well trained physique, trim and cut. The wet hair clung to a strong neck atop broad shoulders. He let out a breath, turned and leaned his back on the wall. The falling water felt like a cleanser, removing the disgust of what he witnessed every day, renewing with the hope.

He thought of her. Remembering the image of her naked body standing atop the scanning device. She hadn't been coy about it. Baring herself only gave her an emboldened gaze.

The Phoenix, a truly unique woman, he thought.

The torrent flowed down the ridges of his chest and abdomen, droplet curving over the shape of muscles. Highlights speckled at the peaks of manly ripples. All while he imagined her moving and shaking. The slightest step sent ripples up her fit body, breasts swaying with momentum.

He grew at her thought. Such a wondrous feeling that tingled the nerves throughout him. The hot current traveled down the shaft to drip and caressed the rounded curve. He blew out a breath.

JD3605, he thought. *The number I've waited so long to see.*

He opened his eyes and looked out into the steam. "Now what?"

"Phoenix!" a desperate voice shouted. Cooper bolted upright with a surge of adrenaline. Dawn light filtered into her room. "Phoenix!"

Deep footfalls hammered the wooden floors. A male citizen with blood running from his forehead stopped at her door.

"Phoenix, they know. Run!"

A clamorous blast hit Cooper's ears the same instant the man's chest ruptured in a bloody mess. His body dropped to reveal a masked Watchman who then leveled the shotgun at her. Cooper jumped from her bed and kicked the weapon from his hands. It discharged and shattered the thin-screen monitor and kitchen window. Her back-fist sent the Watchman spinning to the ground.

"Subversive!" Mutant shouted. "She's subversive! Counter-evolutionary!"

Cooper charged him, clamping down on his neck and pressing him against the cupboards.

"Mutant, it's time to rethink your priorities."

Cooper dropped him, then thought, *I've got to get Kelly.*

More Watchmen approached. She ran into the hallway, wearing only her tank top and black panties, glimpsing a column of Watchmen entering the floor. The first shotgun muzzle gaped ten feet from her.

Buckshot plowed into her belly and pushed her to the ground. Cooper scrambled away in a panic, stopping against the corner. She looked down to see the hot pellets roll off from beneath her tank top. Not a scratch. When she looked at her hand, the gauntlets had formed.

The Watchman stood frightened by the sight of gauntlets from nowhere and gleaming yellow eyes. Cooper pushed off the ground into a sprint. She flew past the doors like nothing she ever knew.

Shots rang out and she bolted upstairs. Her toes barely touched the concrete. She darted out of the stairwell into the top level of the building. Static, disoriented voices caused her another moment's hesitation.

"Subject is running. Too fast, cannot pursue."

"Subject possesses inhuman ability. Suspect unauthorized accelerated evolution. Mark target as counter-evolutionary, 10-59, requesting maximum force authorization."

"Unidentified enemy capabilites. Mark as unexplained phenomen, unexphen."

"Requesting guardian support at my twenty, over."

The Watchmen, she thought. *I'm hearing the Watchmen, their radios.*

"Phoenix." She jumped at the voice, twisting to see Shadowman barreling toward her from down the hallway. "We've been flushed out. They know about everybody."

Cooper picked up more radio chatter. Bootsteps approached from the stairs.

"They're coming," she said.

"Follow me."

They came to a roof stairway and linked up with two citizens brandishing pump-action shotguns.

"Here," one of them said, handing her a drop holster with .45-caliber pistol. "MD issue."

Cooper slung the drop harness to her bare thigh.

"We'll hold them as long as we can," said Shadowman.

"Wait, where's Kelly?"

"Don't know, we tried to find her."

"I'm not leaving without her. Or you."

"Kelly's fine," he said. "She knows the streets. But you gotta go. Now!"

Cooper's limbs suddenly felt made of stone. "I can't believe you're willing to die for me like this. Why? Why me?"

"There's nothing else in this world like you," Shadowman replied. "They say you're the only one who can end this. I can't know that for certain, but I'd rather die for that chance, than live like this another day. Now get the fuck out of here! Find your kids."

She couldn't say anything. One of the citizens fired his shotgun around the corner. Pistol shots and MD shotguns responded.

"Go on!" Shadowman shouted. "Get the fuck out!"

Cooper bolted for the roof, breaking through the door. A swarm of birds went skyward, drawing her eyes up to a massive, descending tilt-rotor with Watchmen aiming out the doors.

"Oh, shit!" She sprinted off. A flurry of shots flew around her.

The forty foot distance to the edge of the roof closed in eight strides. Cooper leapt and cleared the alleyway to the other roof.

"Where the fuck did she go?"

"She was there a second ago."

"Central Control, we need those guardians, over."

Cooper kept running. She body-slammed into the roof exit and the door surren-

dered. She glided down the stairs, panting.

"*Do not hesitate again*," said the voice.

Or, what? You'll sound spooky again?

"*We must not die*."

Thanks.

Citizens screamed and dodged out of her way.

"She's a subversive!"

"Counter-evolutionary!"

All around her, she heard vehicles moving on the street. The radio traffic of the MD kept running through her head.

And I now have radio intercept capability in my brain. Oh, this is genius.

"*You make a joke of us!*"

Shut up.

She kept moving, quietly. A masked Watchman stood in an entryway, raising his hand. "Don't move—"

Cooper snapped up his wrist and tossed him to the ground. She pulled the pistol from her drop holster and leveled it at his head. He put his hand up again.

"No stop!" He ripped the gas mask from his face, helmet falling back. "I'm the one who helped you."

He met her gaze, fright filling his dark eyes, framed by curly black hair. Stubble grew on his gaunt cheeks and chiseled jaw line.

"I was the one at processing two days ago. Jamison, remember? Please...I told you there were ways to get out."

Cooper relaxed a little. Lowering the pistol.

"Guess things still aren't going to plan," she asked. "Why are you with these squads?"

"I'm not, I came ahead of them. I tried to make it earlier. They found out just an hour ago. Those guardians can piece together anything, no matter how small the clues. Now, look, Hawkeye is looking for you, but you move too fast for any of us. I was lucky. Once you lose the Watchmen, stay low and hang tight. Hawkeye'll get to you."

Cooper nodded. "Doesn't sound like the best plan. I've got people I'm looking for." The Watchmen radio chatter came as close as the floor below. "Who are you, anyway? I doubt Jamison's your real name."

"Call me Walleye." He stood up, his handsome face much closer, virile and intense, as tall as her. "I'll see if I can't plant some information and lead them the wrong way. In the meantime, the only way out appears to be from window to window.

"Okay." She shook her head. "This is so insane."

"I know, but it's the world I grew up in. The Nexus is all I know, and I hate it. If you truly have the power to end it, I'll do everything I can to help. My actual job here is flying gunships. I don't know how, but if we can get you on one, I can fly us out. But for now, shake these guys. I'll go lead them off."

Cooper tapped him on the shoulder and ran to the stairs. She went up one flight, hearing Watchmen coming from both above and below. A single window at the end of the hallway presented her only escape, a patio on the building beyond.

This is crazy.

"*We can do it*."

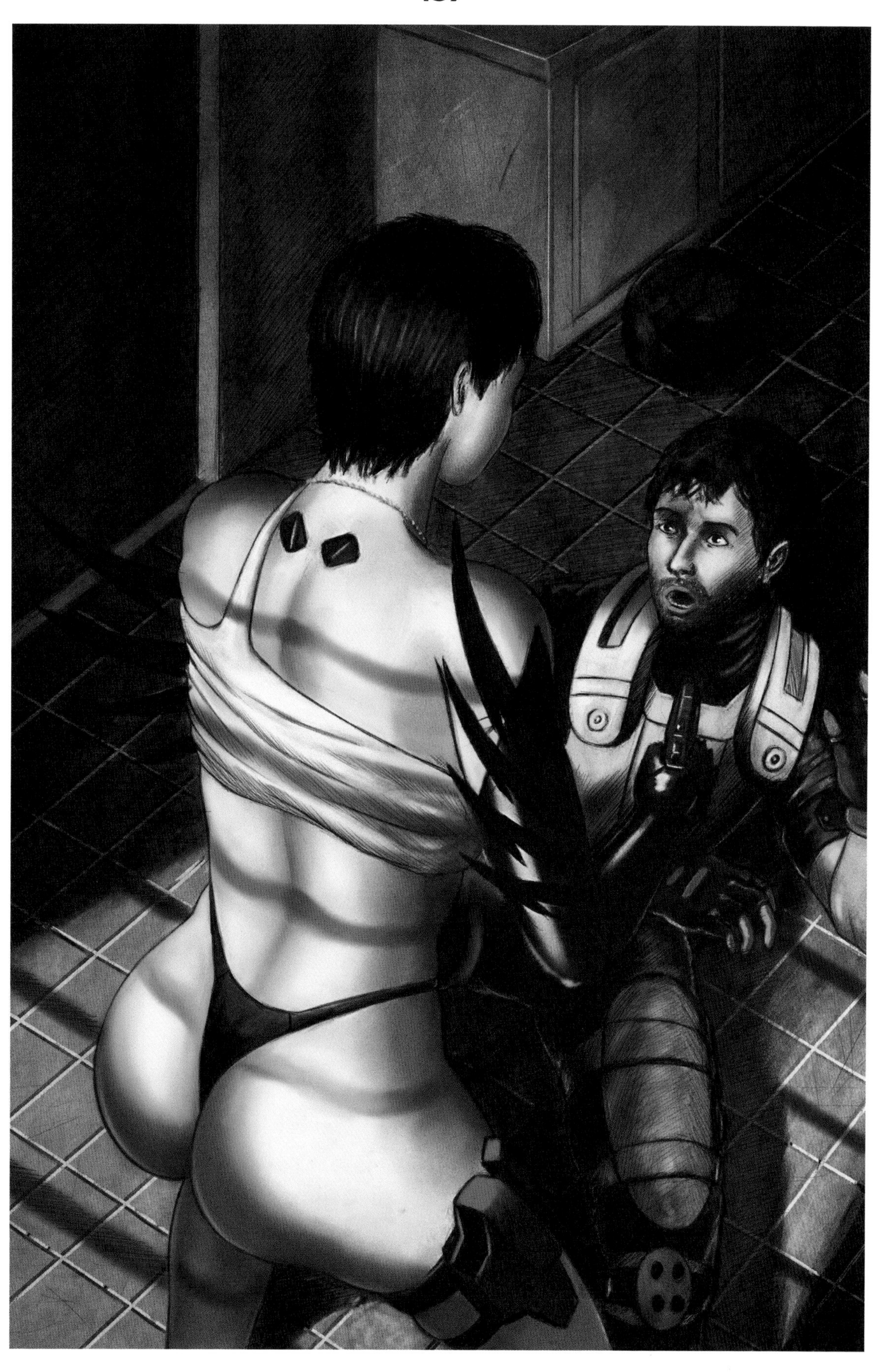

Let me guess, I just need to 'believe.'

"*No, you just need to do it! Do it!*"

The first Watchman kicked through the stairwell entrance. Cooper sprinted towards the window and plowed through the glass. She scissor kicked through the dropping shards like a long jumper. She sailed onto the far patio. The falling glass attracted MD gunfire. Cooper ran into the hallways and looked for another way out. She made another long jump into a far window.

Residents screamed and bolted for their lives. Cooper reached the next opening to the outside, looking out to just a red brick façade.

"Shit!"

"*Jump!*"

"Oh, no way."

"*Do it!*"

Cooper stepped up onto the railing. A little woozy. No matter. No time. She had bypassed the cordon, but the MD would come around in a matter of minutes. Going by the stairs would be too slow.

She sucked in a deep breath and took the plunge. The ground came up in a hurry, but then slowed. The space between her and the ground vibrated with an unseen force, slowing her drop. The concrete bowed into a crater beneath her, cracking. Her feet planted into it and her fall stopped.

"What the hell was that?"

"*Gravity,*" the voice answered. "*Now move!*"

The whine of alien turbines came around the curve. The massive guardian set down and pointed an open palm toward her.

Cooper ran. Flames flashed out of the guardian's palm. White tracers followed her trail. Cooper ducked into an alley to see it was only a dead end five feet deep. The guardian piled on. Across the street, a stairway descended into an underground access. Armored cars approached.

She pulled out the .45 in her drop holster, checked ammo. When the firing stopped, Cooper turned past the smoking and mangled corner and aimed in. The guardian stopped firing with one arm, and swung the other toward her.

Cooper fired in that precious second, then took off to the door across the street. A shell darted out of the spray and glanced off the armor. Heat splashed her face. She leapt down from the top of the stairs and knocked the door off its hinges, then charged into the unknown beneath.

V: HAWKEYE

06/22/2024, 1300: "*Good morning, welcome back to the Josh Kimmel program. We've got a lot to talk about today, like why in the hell our government, the one we elected, the one we want to get a job done, the one that's supposed to report to us, is all hush-hush about people dying around an alien spaceship that crashed into our country. It's days like this you wonder, why can't they ever land in Russia or Albania or something? We can expect this kind of behavior from their governments.*"

Salt Lake Facility, 1320, 06/22/2024

The elevator opened into the hallway. Cooper and Ramon held their weapons at the ready. Corridor lights flickered. Blood lined the corners. Echoes of gunshots in other parts of the facility racketed against the walls. They approached one of Michael's labs.

A body laying against the wall sent her heart racing, but she kept focus. Turning on her carbine's attached Maglite, she saw it wasn't her ex-husband.

"Is that dead?" asked Ramon.

Cooper hunkered down, trying to ignore the sensation of the tightening fabric on her hypersensitive loins, and looked through her sight. The bloody body had varicose veins, discolored skin, and whited-over eyes.

"Looks like it," she said. "Infected too."

A sliver of oily black behind the shoulder showed it had one of the creatures on its back. It jittered, and both mercenaries fired into the body. Human blood and yellow-white sputum splattered onto the ground and walls.

What diseases did that thing have? she thought, the notion haunting her all day. *Turned randy as hell by an alien made of light, and then infected by a slime monster. Just a fucking awesome day.*

They reached the entry airlock. Their emergency access cards let them in. One door closed behind and another opened before them. The two kept weapons ready and everything went silent on the inside.

Double panel glass blocked off several sections. Behind them, creatures and bodies lay on the tables. Red stained the sterile area, two men in bio-hazard suits worked around the specimens.

"Cooper!" a voice called out. She moved to see Michael running towards her. Her heart raced.

Her weapon hung loosely from her hand as Michael wrapped her in his embrace. She felt his scruffy beard against her cheek. She was way too sensitive to be so close, but couldn't pull away.

"Michael...." she nearly whimpered.

"Oh, Cooper," he whispered. "I'm so glad you're here."

"I had to come rescue my damsel in distress."

He chuckled. The sound made her smile. She hadn't felt this passionate about him in years.

What was that thing that touched me?

Michael looked her over. "Y'know, I heard rumors about the outfit you wore. But, this is quite interesting in person."

Cooper looked down at the one-piece shaped leotard that shined like black leather spandex.

"Real S&M vibe it's got going," he added.

"This material is memory molecule armor. It's thin as cotton, but hardens under direct impact. I've got more coverage with this than my tactical vest back in the day."

"Whatever you got to tell yourself."

She cocked an eyebrow. "Are you complaining?"

He shook his head. "You look fantastic, and ready to kill, at the same time. One woman in a million could pull that off."

"Ready to get out of here?" she asked.

Michael paused, the joviality escaping his eyes. "I think this problem's too big to walk away from."

Cooper furrowed her brow, trying not to show the fear that rose up at his words. "Uh, what do you mean?"

"Have you studied the infestation projection schematic rates?"

Cooper blinked and shook her head. "Uh, no, I've been too busy lifting weights and pounding pussy."

"Come here." He took up her free, gloved hand and guided her over to a series of displays detailing the examinations of creatures.

"We started finding them around the facility about two weeks ago," Michael said. "We thought they were harmless, just eating rats."

A single creature lay dead on a lab table, its body the size of a dinner plate. Four stalked legs stretched from it, with a tail out the back, two pincers up front, and the head in between.

"Why weren't we briefed on this?" asked Cooper. "Did you think it a good idea to keep this secret from your security personnel?"

"There weren't that many, we had them contained. Or so we thought. We dissected a few and found a number of what we thought were neurotoxins, but completely incompatible with human DNA. Harmless, we thought."

"And...then they started attacking?"

He nodded. She shook her head, looking away into the contained lab area.

"You should've been told," Michael admitted, eyes low.

"Yeah, well, we know about them now. What else do you know?"

"The ones we've dissected in the last few hours, the toxins and hormones in them are completely compatible with human DNA. Two weeks, Cooper. We can't figure out how the hell they did it. But if we don't contain this, we'll have an epidemic on our hands."

Cooper looked at all the grotesque things on display. A sense of disbelieving dread nearly stunned her to silence.

"This can't be happening. Where'd they come from? The ship?"

"No, the eyphors had nothing to do with this." Michael rubbed her bare shoulder and smiled, dark fingers on her light skin. She fought from shaking, wishing everyone would stop touching her.

"I think their enemies have followed them here."

Cooper gulped and broke from his loving grip. "Their enemies?"

Ramon piped up. "You mean these guys didn't come alone? Something followed them here, and now we got to deal with it? That's bullshit, man!"

"I mean, Michael, seriously," Cooper said. "We've got to get that ship out of here."

"It's over a hundred million metric tons and its engines are dead," Michael countered. "They've got nowhere to go."

"Well, who are these enemies? You've been talking with them, what have they said?"

Michael spread his arms out and shrugged. "It's difficult to explain."

"I've studied thermodynamics at the US Naval Academy. Try me."

Michael gleamed at her. "Cooper, I know you're smart. It's not what I was trying to say."

"Then say it!" Cooper grit her teeth and set her weapon down on a workbench. "You always do this. Just spit it out."

"I don't know! All right? Fuck!" He turned away from her and rubbed his forehead. "I can't...I can't figure it out. It doesn't even sound like science or reason. They keep saying something about the beginning and the end and all that's in between. It's the point at which it comes together, and stands above it, a nexus of some kind."

Cooper approached and placed her hand on his shoulder. "It's okay if you don't know something. You may be a genius, but you're still human."

Michael rubbed his eye. "I got my second doctorate from Johns Hopkins when I was nineteen. I learned how to communicate with an alien race in one year. The problem is, I can't understand a damn thing they say."

He turned and faced her, placing his hand on her waist.

"Please, stop touching me!" she finally blurted and he backed away.

"I'm sorry." He put his arms up. "That was wrong of me, we've been divorced—"

"It's not that."

"It's cause she's pregnant," Ramon said.

"I'm not fucking pregnant!" Cooper snapped.

Ramon stayed quiet for a moment, then whispered, "Been hormonal all day."

"I was...." she trailed off.

"What is it, Cooper?"

"The auroras appeared today, when I was with Alyssa and Devon at the pool, right before I got the call to come in."

Michael crossed his arms and blew out a breath.

"Ever since then, I've been so sensitive."

"What do you mean?"

Cooper closed her eyes and let out a breath. She felt more comfortable saying it to him at least. They'd made love, had two children, been married for years, and he was a doctor. If she couldn't tell him, she couldn't tell anyone.

"I feel like I'm on the cusp of an orgasm, like constantly. My skin is hypersensitive even to the movement of my clothes. And yes, it's like being hormonal but ten times more intense."

"Have a seat," Michael offered up a table and he grabbed some of his instruments.

He checked her eyes, ears, took her heart beat with a stethoscope.

"You're heart is racing. You're sweating, and you're definitely producing hormones. Your skin is also flushed."

"Yeah, I'm radiant, I know."

He chuckled, but then cleared his throat. "You're not the first person to be touched by the aurora, but this is the first I've heard of this kind of reaction."

"Well, tell your eyphors I don't appreciate them molesting me. I need to call and check on Alyssa. It moved across her too."

Michael looked at her, his eyes staring deep. Cooper couldn't tell if that was fear or something else.

"Cooper," he started. "I think she's fine."

"Why? You haven't even examined her."

"The aurora isn't part of the eyphor's hive structure. It's something else. Something they brought with them."

"What then? Tell me, Michael, please. I've never been this scared. Will my body ever turn to normal? Will it wear off? Am I dying?"

"No," he said quickly. "You're not dying, sweetheart. If anything, you're coming alive."

"Speak sense, dammit!" she snapped. "I'm tired of this mystery shit, I want to know what's wrong with me."

"Nothing's wrong, Cooper. That's what I'm saying. You see, I think, you've been chosen."

"Chosen by what?"

"Yeah, doc," Ramon chimed in.

"Well," Michael began. "You see—"

The door to the lab slid open before he could finish. Cooper looked over her shoulder to see Scotty Chambers waltz in with three others behind him. He looked at her rump sitting on the table.

"Now if only I could see that ass every time I walk into a room," he said with a chuckle, "I'd get through all of life's problems."

"You are one of life's problems," Cooper said.

He continued looking at her, then past her to Michael, then back to her. "We'll be setting up shop here. We can hook the PA system up to our comms, it's secure and centrally located. We'll bring all the personnel we find to this location for extraction."

Cooper stood off the table, careful to stand between Scotty and Michael. She'd never told him, even in their closest of times, what Scotty did to her. Cooper knew Michael didn't feel his threatening presence the way she did, and certainly didn't want to mention it now.

"You get to the emergency power room?" Scotty asked her.

"Sorry, boss, been too busy worrying my lovely ass off over Lenny. Poor guy."

She smiled aggressively, but he didn't budge in his smirk. "You and Ramon should head down there. I'll keep a look after your beau."

The thought chilled Cooper to her bones, but she remained still to not show it.

"We do need that conduit hook up," Michael said. "We'd appreciate any help you could give us, Commander Chambers."

"I'm here to serve," said Scotty.

"Don't worry, Michael," Cooper said, recovered her weapon, reattached it to her chest harness. "We'll get you hooked up."

She nodded to Ramon, who followed her lead. They both walked by, and Cooper gave Scotty as hard a warning look as she could.

Stay away from him, heartless prick.

Cooper fell through the ventilation grate and plummeted another twenty feet into a pool of cold water. She gasped as the chill hit, pushing off the ground beneath. Various flotsam and trash floated in the water, stinking with the smell of rot.

Confident enough she had lost the guardians and MD, she took some time for a breather. The resistance members had told her to wait for Hawkeye to find her, and this place seemed better than most. She pulled up on the brickworks and sat against the corner, then looked at her gauntlets and huffed.

What am I supposed to do with this?

"*Kill*," the voice replied.

Kill what?

The voice stayed silent.

I'm the one sitting here in wet panties, and you're speechless.

She chuckled. Cooper leaned her head back and blew out a breath. Her muscles felt like they were tightening and expanding all at once, pulsing with every breath.

"*Yes...We grow stronger. The muscles grow now as life courses through them. We rest....*"

I've got no problem with that. Cooper tilted her head one way and closed her eyes. Her body began its regeneration. Her knees had taken a pounding, but the tissues reformed into stronger, better matrices. High tension muscles all through her physique regrew as energy from somewhere within stirred. A complex biochemical reaction sent fresh particles into broken muscle structures and reformed them. Adapting. Healing.

Cooper moaned as it all went away. For the first time, these new "endowments" felt good and right. She lifted her head up and smiled, then opened her eyes to see a guardian standing full in the middle of the water.

Cooper gasped and bolted before its palm cannon swung her way. She ran at full speed with impacts trailing after her. She skipped against the walls, leapt through the corners, jumped on the brick and flipped to reverse course.

Dust filled the air. Brick became powder. Burnt, acrid smells filled the cavity. When one arm went empty, the guardian switched to his other palm cannon and led ahead of Cooper's path. The rounds slammed into her torso and pinned Cooper against the wall.

She'd never felt so much pain in all her life, this one or the last. Feeble arms tried to cover her. Impacts pinged off the black armor as if shooting a tank, but it didn't stop enough. Hits on her body felt like knife punctures, skin reforming as fast as it was hit.

"*We're not ready for a guardian!*" cried the voice.

Cooper grunted and howled against the impacts until the guardian ran out of ammunition in that arm too. The guardian charged in. A clawed hand wrapped around Cooper's neck and lifted her up.

"You are not damaged," it said.

"Glad to hear it!"

Cooper grabbed the guardian's wrist to break its grip. Her strength compared

enough. Its grip started to go. Cooper braced her feet against the wall. The guardian growled and swung its free hand towards her face. With her right arm she smacked it away.

"*We're not ready!*"

Could you please say something useful?

Bright, orange flashes plowed into the guardian's head, forming an impressive dent. The guardian let go of Cooper and she fell to the ground, hunkering low. Additional shots rang out as Cooper picked up more MD radio traffic.

"The guardian's signal's this way. Assemble on me."

The guardian jetted back into the water and leapt upward to a ledge, retreating into a dark corridor. More orange flashes chased after it, taking out chunks of brick.

Cooper turned to see a woman with sparkling brown eyes, brilliant caramel colored skin and dark hair tied back and flaring out. Bare breasts sat on either side of elegenatly laid metal panels running down the center of her chest. After a couple moments, Cooper took note of more gun metal black couplings on her arms, torso, and legs.

The woman carried twin, white MP7-like pistols in holsters on each thigh. She'd never seen shots like those. She looked at Cooper with a deep, shocked gaze.

"Who are you?" Cooper asked. "The cybernetic Lara Croft?"

"They call me Hawkeye," the woman replied. Her lips quivered. "Mom?"

The word descended into Cooper's mind like a gentle drill, setting off an emotional volcano. In an instant, she looked into those dark eyes and saw that tiny little face again, curly black strands hanging about her forehead. She danced in the gold light, the energy that "chose" her.

"Alyssa?" Cooper echoed across the gap of time. "Is that...?"

She smiled and rushed to embrace a mother that didn't look a day older than herself. Cooper returned it.

"Oh, my God, has it been that long?"

"Fifteen years, Mom," croaked Alyssa. "Fifteen years...."

"Oh, my God," Cooper repeated. "It's you. It is. I'm really holding you aren't I?"

"Yes, I'm right here," Alyssa said with a saddened, yet joyous laugh.

"I can't believe this. I can't, I can't, I can't."

"I'm here, Mom," Alyssa sobbed. "We've been waiting for you a long time."

She pulled back a little and looked at Cooper's eyes and gauntlets. "We probably shouldn't've let Prometheus do the design."

"Who?"

"Nevermind. Follow me."

Alyssa ran out the way she came in, through a narrow corridor. She stopped for a second and pulled a canister from her belt. She tossed it back in.

"Let's go!"

Cooper and the girl ran. Several times she overtook Alyssa, but had to wait for her to lead. Alyssa activated a device on one of her gauntlets and slapped a button at the top. An explosion rocked the corridor through which they had come.

"That should block them for a bit," she said between pants.

"How did they find me so damn quickly?"

"The guardians most likely," Alyssa said. "They can see through walls...and some say, walk through them. I can't believe it just ran away like that, either."

"Because of your fancy guns?"

Alyssa huffed. "They aren't afraid of my guns."

The two entered a culvert, brickworks all around them. Only a trickle of water passed through the middle. The rest was mud and trash. Alyssa slowed to a walk, checking behind her every once in a while.

"Did you come alone?" asked Cooper.

"I left one of our supply points looking for you. I move faster alone."

"What do you do? You don't look like you're from around here."

"I'm a runner. I run supplies into the city, and people out."

"Like this?" Cooper touched the locket hanging from her neck. She flicked it open and a holographic portrait of a much tinier Alyssa appeared. She stopped in her tracks.

Alyssa touched Cooper's armored wrist. "It's amazing. I can still feel warmth on it."

"And I can feel your fingers. Do you know what this is?"

"Regenerative smart matter resin, designed by the eyphors."

Cooper looked at the picture, then at the woman beyond. "You look amazing."

"And I thought when I'd grow up you wouldn't look as tall, but you're still a giant."

They laughed together. Cooper's claw nudged the edge of the locket, then a bust of Devon appeared. Cooper felt her heart crack. The emotions hit with such force, she felt the pain.

"Alyssa have you seen...?"

Her daughter visibly gulped. "I wasn't much older than you remember me, when they...separated everyone according to gender. I haven't seen him."

"Fifteen years?"

"Close to it."

Cooper closed the locket, gently placed it back. "And how do they have my memories? There's no way anyone could've videotaped what's stored in here." She tapped the gold heart.

"I can understand if you're upset. I wouldn't want people stealing my thoughts, either. But it was a precaution we had to take. Your brain was preserved the instant all function ceased, so we were able to extract your memories while stimulating your brain with electro-chemical currents."

Cooper shook her head as if to shake off the icky feeling that brought on. "Okay, and why?"

"No one's ever been brought back from the dead, Mom."

"Dead?" Cooper asked. "I was...dead?"

A pause ensued between them. Alyssa's expression seemed as surprised as Cooper felt, but at her mother's reaction rather than the actual fact of what had been said.

"When I realized how much time had passed, I thought I was in a coma, or, or...."

Alyssa shook her head. "Our worst estimates said that when you awoke, the auto-defibrillator would shock your brain so much you wouldn't remember anything. We thought that if we could extract them beforehand, we'd at least have a road map for you to become your old self. No one's seen them, not even me. I promise. I'm sorry, I thought Dad would've told you."

Cooper bit her lip as if to assuage the pain. "We didn't have much time. He couldn't really...."

"Did he say which route he'd take to get back down south?"

Cooper paused, looking out with empty eyes. *She doesn't know.*

She let the locket rest and just looked at her grown child. "He didn't say."

I can't tell her now. I just found out I was dead. She needs to.... Cooper couldn't even collect her thoughts.

"I'm just so glad to see you again," she said after a two second eternity.

Alyssa and Cooper hugged again, tighter, longer.

"I can't believe this," said Alyssa. "He must have been so happy to see you again."

Cooper thought of Michael, his gray hair, his last dying gaze. "He was. As happy as I am to see you."

Alyssa paused. "We've got to keep moving. He's probably at EndPoint, already."

Cooper just held on a little tighter when she felt Alyssa back away. "I'll kill them all if they come. Just wait a little while."

She buried her face against Alyssa's shoulder and cried into it. "They'll never take you from me again."

"Actually, they took you from me," Alyssa said. "They took my mother from me."

Cooper let go of the embrace and looked into her daughter's eyes. "Well, she's here again. And I'm not going anywhere."

They kept walking on down. Cooper examined the apparently custom metal bits comforming to her body. It formed a type of reinforcing frame, and left the rest of her bare.

"What's with this get up?" she asked.

"We call it an exo, something to give us a little parity with their biomechs and troops. You'll see, soon. We're heading over to one of our exo shops. We've been prepping people like crazy to have as many cybers as we can deploy."

"Exo's, cybers...." Cooper shook her head. "Has a woman named Kelly come through here?"

"Uh, no. Why? Who is she?"

"She's a...friend." Cooper tapped the locket. "She gave me this."

"Yeah, I sent that ahead." Alyssa shook her head. "Well, she's from the same housing unit?"

Cooper nodded.

"That could be a problem. They might be purging anyone left behind as we speak."

"Shady said she already went to ground."

"Hope she knows what she's doing then. But we have to get you out of the city. I've got a couple guys who can scout around for now."

Worry gnawed at her. She ached to see Kelly again. After what they did to her, Cooper couldn't leave her behind.

They came into a wider chamber. Crates and boxes lined the walls. Fluorescent lights gave it a little more illumination. A man walked in from the side, carrying an AA12 and boxes of ammo. A black scorpion tattooed on his forehead gleamed dark from his bald head.

"Ahhh," he mouthed. "Phoenix. You can only be Phoenix. People's already talkin' 'bout the eyes."

Cooper nodded and gave a faux smile. "They help bring out the black in my regenerative smart matter alien resin armor."

"Yeah, looks handy," he said. "I'm Scorpio. I handle this juncture, though it looks like I'll be packing up and headin' to EndPoint soon. You were probably heading that way."

"No doubt," said Alyssa. "We've got to get her to Red Eagle."

"Is Red Eagle a person or a place?" Cooper asked.

"Uh, we try not to say. But you'll find out when you reach him. It. Oh, fuck I already gave it up."

Cooper chuckled. "Watch your language, young lady."

She smiled. "I learned from the best."

Cooper cocked her head. "You were four, I never cursed around you." Then it dawned on her, and she touched the locket.

"Okay, I lied," Alyssa said. "I looked at a few."

Cooper pursed her lips and said, "I can understand. You never thought you would see me again."

"And...as you said. I was four. It was getting to the point I could barely remember you."

She touched her daughter's cheek again, and Alyssa's solemn face turned to a smile as her eye spotted the extremely close thumb claw of her mother's gauntlet.

"Wow, that looks sharp." She held her mother's hand out again and examined it closer in the better light. "I need to get me gloves like this."

"Putting them on for the first time is a bitch, but they tend to stick with you after that."

Fresh water ran through the middle of the floor. Some old mattresses with blankets laid on the tilted bank. Scorpio had boxes of rations and ammunition all over the place. It stunk like an old hamster cage. He went over to a crate, moved the corpse of a two foot leech-like thing aside and started loading twelve-gauge rounds into a big drum magazine.

"Gotta move, gotta move," he said. "Y'know?"

"Yeah," Cooper said off hand and stepped toward the leech. Like a giant centipede. Row after row of legs curled up under the belly.

"Hey, Mom," said Alyssa. "I'm gonna go get Dead Meat. See if he can find this Kelly. I'll only be a minute."

"What?" Cooper nearly panicked. "No, I just found you."

Alyssa clasped Cooper's shoulder. "No, Mom. I found you. And I'll find you again, I'm just going down a corridor. Okay?"

As Alyssa backed away, Cooper moved forward again. "No, I—"

"Mom," Alyssa put her hands up. "Just relax. Wait here."

Cooper shook her head, but couldn't say anything. Alyssa backed off and headed into another passage. Cooper needed all her will to stand there, fighting every urge to run after her. The effort nearly made her break down and cry.

"Noticed you looking at the spine tapper," Scorpio began. She barely heard him through her turmoil. "They jump by curling into a ball, like a cute widdle rollie-pollie, and then spring with these hind limbs." He pointed to two curly bits longer than the other legs.

"These stingers," he gestured to the curled up spikes all along the belly, "will stick out and inject you with a paralyzer. They don't always need to land on your back, you see. Once you're immobile they'll move there, then line up with your spinal column and lock in. After that, you're theirs."

Scorpio set down one drum mag and picked up another. "See, you gotta get 'em when they're young. They don't gots complete control. They're not very mobile, can't move so fast. MD usually does sweeps with the mantids and flame throwers down here."

Mantids? Cooper thought. *Those fucking things. Alyssa, hurry back!*

"So you don't see many mature ones," Scorpio continued. "But, hey, when they grow up, they are some nasty, beastly things."

Cooper couldn't help but notice his tone. "You seem to admire them a little."

"Well, recognize." He slapped the dead spine tapper. "This thing, some people won't admit, is Nexus's enemy number one. Hey, they's the one species that Nexus has never been able to adapt. Lookit us, after fifteen years we got neo-skins comin' outa Liang's ass, locked down in this fuckin' Ant Farm."

He ran his finger along the elongated body. "They wasn't like this when they first came here, y'know. They was like, little beetle kinda things."

"Yeah, I know. I was there."

Scorpio nodded. "So was I. I was twenty. They's evolved to take over something else and turn them into puppets, but they learned how our nervous system works. Spinal tap us. They got longer. Adapted these spiny things. In less than twenty years, they learned how we operated and adapted to us. An alien species. They's adapted to adapt, like the ultimate evolutionary weapon."

Scorpio slapped the crate and guffawed.

"These things evolve so fuckin' fast Nexus can't figure how to bend it. It's obsessed with these things, but the only way it can use it is against other species. They like to air drop these buggers into towns and shit, give a coupla weeks to take it over, then when they're all nice and slow they go kill 'em off. They're great for choking the Railroad."

He flung his arms up high. "Just like that! Why you think Nexus keeps evolving things into metal? Because of this fucker right here! Ladies and gentlemen, I give you the Master of Puppets. It only has a brain the size of a pea, but that's because it's gonna take all o' yours!"

Alyssa? Where are you? Despite Scorpio's distracting proclamations, her mind kept drifting back. *I just found you, dammit!*

"Shotguns work best against puppets. You get yourself an automatic shotgun, you're in fucking business. I's only got this one, but that Kriss over there is good."

Cooper looked to see the sub-machine gun lying on a crate. She picked it up and checked its functions.

"Look around for some gear. Got plenty lying around."

Cooper did. She found some belts to fit around her thighs and waist with ammo pouches. Several Kriss magazines loaded with .45 ACP rounds laid ready. Also a few grenades. At least it distracted her from Alyssa's absence for a few minutes.

"MD really like those. Good for puppets too. Give a good burst for the head o' neck. Don't got any of the 8mm ones, though just the forty-fives."

Alyssa returned. A wave of relief flooded Cooper's chest.

"Dead Meat thinks he knows who you're talking about. He'll find this Kelly and get her out."

Cooper smiled. "Thank you. Will he bring her here?"

"No, we got to get going."

"And meet them someplace else?"

Alyssa's gaze stiffened. "Uh, no, they're getting out on their own. We have to gear up and get out. Atom Smasher should already be breaking down the shop."

"Alyssa," Cooper said softly. "I'm not leaving without her. I can't."

Alyssa furrowed her brow. "But...you understand how important you are, right? We need to get you out of here. This is the enemy capital, Mom. You're worth a thousand lives to get you out."

"I'm not worth your life, Alyssa. It's the other way around. I'm your mother. I'd die for you, understand? And I promised Kelly that they would not hurt her again. I can't go back on that."

Alyssa's shoulders shrunk. "I'm going to catch hell for this." She scratched her forehead. "There's a waystation about ten blocks from here. It's one of the larger hubs to get groups of refugees resupplied and out of the central district. Dead Meat's going to take her there once he locates her. Or she'll be there already if she's as street smart as you say."

Cooper looked at her warmly. "Thank you."

Alyssa placed her palms on her pistols and let out a breath and a chuckle.

"Okay, follow me. Got everything you can carry, Scorp?"

Scorpio tapped the weapon slung from his chest, then picked up two heavy boxes in his muscular arms. "Set."

"Let's get suited."

Alyssa and Scorpio led Cooper further into another corridor, brickwork all around. It opened up into a large storage area filled with computers along the wall, surgical tables, power tools, and other various equipment. The smell of blood was pungent, along with sterile medical agents.

"Well, shit!" said a dark skinned man with no shirt and muscled, though wirey frame sitting at a computer. He stood up at their approach.

"You brought me a tall one. Dressed for operation. Good. No time to waste."

Alyssa held up her hands, smirked, "Easy, Atom, this is the Phoenix. I'm afraid she doesn't need your services."

The man walked up closer, eyes widening with every step and a clearer look into her eyes and gauntlets.

"N-n-no way! You're kidding!" He let out an excited cry, jumped and pumped his fist on landing. "Oh, yeah. Shit! We're in business!"

"Actually we're here to close down, remember?" Alyssa asked.

"Oh, right. Yeah, I got you. Charges are set. It'll bring the whole place down. Computers're purged, and they should be smashed by the explosion."

"Hook me up, brother!" Scorpio said and set his gear down, pulled off his shirt. A burly man, but apparent on his pale skin were numerous artificial hook ups, most circular in nature. Scorpio even went so far as to pull down his shorts.

"Uh," Cooper started, but then Alyssa spoke.

"We're cybers, Mom," Alyssa said preemptively. "Our bodies are modified and equipped to handle exoskeletons."

"I made twenty new ones just the last couple of days," said Atom Smasher. "The rest of the boys did about the same before they took off, a hundred or so now. All green though."

"Dead Meat's vets'll pump them up."

"Are you...?" Cooper began to ask Alyssa. "Bolted up too?"

"That's how all this stays on." Alyssa tapped her gauntlets and chest panels.

Atom Smasher picked up a black duffel bag and set it on one of the surgical tables.

"The princess of the Peak, she's got her own unique setup, better than most!"

Alyssa helped Scorpio and Atom Smasher set frames on their bodies, hooking into the hubs at various points on their skin. Cybernetics. Cooper only watched in silence, and curiosity, while they hooked each other up. Drills whined to screw parts into place. They were practically naked beneath the tight frames.

"Do those thin little frames stop bullets?" Cooper asked.

"About as well as your panties," Alyssa quipped. "The exo's increase strength, speed, agility, which of course assists stamina. Everything we need to get out of here is based on moving fast."

"And these'll help us carry the firepower to get use through any potential opposition," added Atom Smasher.

"And the ladies like it," concluded Scorpio.

"If you're worried about protection, since we don't have skin with enhanced electron repulsion, like you, we can carry deployable laser and plasma shields, but they're immobile."

Cooper smirked, "You ever get cold?"

"Once the reactor harness is turned on," Alyssa began, and turned a device on Atom Smasher's back, "like that, the wet wired thermal regulation system will keep us warm in howling winter winds. In those conditions we also carry capes and windbreakers to insulte against the wind. Skin is thin, no matter how warmed up it is."

Scorpio, when finished, set up his shotgun and ammo. Atom Smasher hauled up a machine gun with belts of ammo in pouches. Alyssa had already been set with her specialized pistols in their holsters.

"Well, you guys know what you're doing."

"Geared up," Alyssa said. "Ready to go?"

She nodded. "Let's do it."

Salt Lake Facility, 1350, 06/22/2024

Cooper leaned back against the elevator wall while it descended toward the transformer room beneath Michael's lab. Sweat beaded on her brow in the dull red lights. She squatted against the corner, resting the rifle between her legs.

The tightening of the fabric felt so good, so soothing as she lowered down. Ramon stood next to her.

"You really should've stayed on the Osprey."

She glared up at him. "I'm not pregnant."

He knelt next to her. His smell wafted into her nostrils, so intoxicating. Her eyes took in his smooth cheeks and warm gaze, and the veins rippling over his biceps.

"Cooper, I've been with you through your last pregnancy. Yeah, sure it's more intense than before...."

She shook her head. Cooper remembered the first day she met Ramon. BUD/S. Hell Week. For PT and swimming, the men wore small beige shorts that gave Cooper no end of splendid sights. Ramon stood in formation in front of her, the entire class sweating and

panting after their last bit of thrashing in the pool.

Being constantly wet made everything so cold. Ramon shook in front of her. The water beaded down his short buzz cut, across broad shoulders and down his golden colored back.

He had turned around, and looked at her, both of them shaking like leaves. Stepping off and ringing the bell, quitting, getting the hell out of the instructors' sadistic grasp, seemed like such an easy thing to do. But as they looked into each other's eyes, they held each other up.

"Ramon," she said. "Trust me. It's different." She moved forward and kissed him on the lips. Startled, he moved back.

"What's the matter?" she asked.

"The matter? Cooper, you're married."

She furrowed her brow. "I've been divorced two years."

"I always thought you two would get back together."

"No," she answered. "I can't. Tell me, after all we've been through, you never had feelings for me?"

"I...." Ramon trailed off.

"Never masturbated while thinking of me?"

His eyes nearly popped out of his head, mouth dropped, when Michaels' voice chimed in her headset and the elevator stopped.

"The computer shows you're there on the level," Michael said. "How are you feeling?"

"Strangely good."

"And acting very strange," Ramon added. "Got any idea what's wrong with her?"

"Well, she's not pregnant. I think that contact with the entity left behind some kind of particulate energy in her nervous system."

"Uh, a fucking horny bomb?" asked Ramon. Cooper glared at him as if to say "what?" He moved his mic from his mouth and whispered at her. "You're turning into a crazed fucking nympho!"

She flipped him off as Michael kept talking into their headsets. "It's relatively simple. If all nerves light up at once, some are clustered in more sensitive areas, like the reproductive systems. You're probably also experiencing an increase in the oxygenation in the blood stream, increasing endorphin output."

Cooper cracked her neck. "That's a lot to gleam from a cursory examination. Tell me, Michael, who has this happened to before?"

"No one," he said matter-of-factly. "You're the first to have this reaction after contact with the entity."

"What is the entity, dammit? Quit fucking around, Michael."

"I'll explain once you get back up here. But we need the power back."

"All right. Fine." She stood and readied her weapon, then nodded to Ramon to open the elevator. Cooper and Ramon followed Michael's instructions.

"You should be coming to the main circuit room," he said. "Look like any creatures down there?"

"Not yet," Cooper replied. She looked down to see the bodies lying along the walls and floor. Her flashlight illuminated the dim place. Deformed limbs laid out into pools mixing with human blood and the white slick the things bled out. “Plenty of dead ones.”

“What killed them?” asked Ramon.

“Got me. I don’t recognize any of these wounds.” She knelt near the closest one. Harpoon-like shafts stuck out of the flesh. “We have an unknown weapons discharge of some kind.”

Cooper used the barrel of her G36C to lift up a strand coming off the end of the shaft, like a stringy muscle. “Looks like arrows or harpoons with a line attached to them. Know anything about this Michael?”

“New one on me.”

“En el nombre del padre....” Ramon crossed himself.

“It’s all right, Ramon,” she said. “If it’s killing them, it might be all right.”

They continued toward the power room. A brown out in the lab meant they had to hit the breakers. If not, the techs couldn’t continue their work on the creatures. The two of them were the most qualified to enter the danger zone.

Cooper pointed her weapon straight down the hallway. Her flashlight’s gaze fell on a lab tech leaning against the wall. Veins already spread across his face. It started hobbling her way. Cooper took her time to aim in at the head.

From an adjacent hallway, impacts slammed the puppet against the wall. Something beyond the corner yanked the infested man out of her sight. Cooper and Ramon flattened themselves against the wall as the sounds came.

Cries like some kind of aquatic mammal collided with stabbing and sticking sounds. Ripping flesh rattled their nerves before the body flew back into the hallway and bent around a corner. Heavy footsteps shook through the floor. A massive figure ran across their sight.

Cooper gasped. Its pounding footsteps moved farther away.

“What was that?” asked Ramon.

“Cooper,” came Michael. “What’d you see down there?”

“Something new. Don’t know if it’s friendly.”

“Let’s just do what we came here to,” said Ramon.

Cooper headed to the UPS room door. She swiped her card, then went to put it back in her thigh belt when the doors opened. Before she could get her weapon up, two clawed hands went at her neck and pressed her into the wall.

“Cooper!” Ramon shouted.

She had never felt fear like this. Its hands clamped down like a vise and her weapon dropped to her side, hanging by her sling. She grabbed its wrists. Ramon wrapped his arm around its neck, hanging the shotgun at his side and unsheathing a knife. He pulled at it, its grip dropped to her vest.

Claws went through the fabric. She felt knuckles against her breasts as it broke through. She grabbed at the handle to the machete on her back. In that moment it surged forward. Human lips peeled back until a wide, monstrous maw of translucent fangs gaped before her.

A slimy tongue wriggled and a slug-like thing spilled out of its mouth to force Cooper’s lips apart. She would’ve screamed. It wiggled and tried to get in, but her teeth sank down. Juices squeezed over her lips. The taste nearly made her hurl. She pulled the machete free and smashed the infected man over the head.

Ramon pulled the creature off her. Its iron grip took a chunk of her armor with it.

Cooper's hands rushed to the slug in her mouth and pulled it free. With a harsh squeeze, it popped in her hand. Hot, mucus-like puss splattered on her.

Ramon wrestled the creature to the ground and killed it with his knife.

"Regrosete al infierno, puto!" He recovered his shotgun and rushed to her. "Cooper? You okay?"

She looked down at herself, realizing what had happened with the heat of the slime all over her skin. She wiped at the sticky substance, but it just smeared on her glove and fingertips. Her throat felt tightened.

Suddenly she wasn't in the facility. The walls turned into the shower rooms of her Annapolis dorm. Scotty stood above her, Lenny pinning her arms behind. The same feeling overcame her, just like that alien slug forcing its way to her throat. She shook. Paralyzed.

"Cooper!" Ramon shouted. "Come back to me, girl. Hey!"

And just like that, she snapped to. Soft brown eyes, full of fear, concern. Love. His name felt cleansing from her mouth.

"Ramon...."

VI: POWER TAP

The sound of the crashing grate shocked Cooper into moving further back into the tunnel. She looked out into the culvert, passed the guardrail of the raised sidewalk. In a blur, something dropped through the hole and landed on four legs.

A chill shot up her spine when she saw it. The memories came rushing in. At the apex of its back it stood near seven feet tall. Four legs moved it forward with a gorilla-like gait. The brown-on-brown striped patterns on its back reminded her of a tiger shark.

"Mom," Alyssa whispered. "It's a mantid. It—"

"I know what it does," Cooper hissed back. "It killed me."

Ropes followed. Watchmen slid down into the culvert.

"Target area up ahead," Cooper heard through their radios. "Follow the mantid."

"Weapons hot."

The MD troupe moved off down the waterway. Only after they had moved on did Cooper, Alyssa, Atom Smasher and Scorpio continue moving up.

"Shit!" Scorpio hissed. "That's where's we gotta go. They after the waystation."

"Will the waystation be able to repel that?" Cooper asked.

"No fucking way. Especially with a mantid leading the pack."

Cooper nodded, then looked at Alyssa. She smiled, but fear was all she felt. They headed to the waystation to find Kelly. Having a mantid near both her daughter and lover sent fire running through her limbs. "Let's go help 'em."

Alyssa smiled back and Scorpio thumped his chest. He reloaded his AA12 with high-explosive shells. Atom Smasher gave him a fist bump on the shoulder.

"Go through MD armor like nothing."

Atom Smasher carried a Mk 48 machine gun, one Cooper recognized from her SEAL days.

"Think you can take the mantid?" Atom Smasher asked Cooper.

She raised an eyebrow. "Not a clue."

Scorpio paused. "I'll take the mantid then, you take the Mack Daddies, or we'll split 'em up. Never know."

"Let's just get going," Alyssa said.

"Right."

Radio chatter mixed in her head with rattling gunfire.

"Machine gun on the ledge."

"Where's team two?"

"I got three tangos."

"Ahhh!"

"Grenade out!"

A sharp explosion rocked the ground. Cooper found a side tunnel.

"I'll go through here, see if I can't flank them," she said. "You two...." she paused, looking at Alyssa. Her tactical instincts felt the sudden temperament of her maternal ones.

"We'll get them from behind," Alyssa finished. "Hammer and anvil. Scorpio, Atom Smasher, on me."

"Got it."

They moved out before Cooper could protest. She froze. She wanted to grab Alyssa and shove her in a hole until it was done. But then said, "Shit!" and headed into the tunnel.

"Team two, respond," the Watchmen continued. Muck splashed her bare feet. She took a ladder to a level above the firefight. Weapons discharges rumbled against the concrete structure. Cooper found a grate and looked down.

Watchmen kept up fire from their positions below. They attacked a messy collection of shanty shelters backed up against a trashed train car. Resistance fighters atop the car used pistols and a machine gun to defend themselves.

The mantid held the Watchmen's front, absorbing all the bullets that hit. It kept its forefeet planted and fired tethered harpoons. Cooper gasped when it pulled one man from the shelters. Chest-mounted pincers stuck into the man, slicing him to death. The mantid gave the corpse a kick to the head when finished.

That's how I died, she thought. That's how it killed me. Alyssa's coming around now. Kelly might be down there.

Anger and terror boiled. Cooper grabbed the grate. All her rage sent waves of pleasure to every inch of her body. Heat cascaded like gentle massages. She whimpered and pulled the hundred pound slab of steel free.

With a toss, it struck flat against the leading Watchman. Cooper leapt out and landed on the grate laid atop the man.

A Watchman turned to fire when her grapples launched out and sliced into his eye sockets. Cooper knelt and aimed her Kriss at the next target.

"Unexph—" her bullets cut off his warning.

Alyssa and Scorpio attacked from behind. Scorpio's HE rounds tore apart Watchmen bodies and limbs. Her daughter's white pistols spat bright orange bursts.

"Stay in cover, Alyssa!" Cooper shouted.

"Yeah, I know, Mom!" she yelled over the din. "Not my first firefight!"

"Cybers!" Watchmen shouted. "We got cybers!" A burst from Atom Smasher silenced him mid scream.

The mantid charged Cooper. She leapt high to the side. The first harpoons flew by. She fired the Kriss in mid-air. 45-caliber shots pounded its forward body. The magazine went dry before her feet touched down.

Cooper ran and flipped around a concrete slab, taking cover to reload. More harpoons hit. Cooper reloaded, rose over and fired. Violet blood spattered at certain points. The creature squealed and kept side-stepping out of her bursts.

A harpoon ripped into the top of her shoulder. Cooper screamed. The hooks extended and the mantid pulled her through the air. When she yanked the barb free, her flesh closed and all pain vanished. The sudden absence of agony became euphoric.

Three more harpoons seared into her. Cooper reared back and screamed. A fourth harpoon shot into her lower abdomen, dead center, attached to a much thicker tether, translucent. She collapsed onto her knees.

Blue energy currents gently flowed through it. She grabbed the harpoon. The

mantid made its noises, almost cute, like a dolphin. A sharp pinch flared in her belly, as if it were digging into her womb.

"What is it doing?"

"*Taking more than it can handle,*" the voice said.

Deep down, Cooper felt something stir in her core. A fire. She pushed back to her feet. A tearing sound ripped through the air. The conduit connecting her and the mantid blazed. A light flared into the creature.

The mantid vaporized in a ferocious flash of power. The shockwave cracked against the surrounds. Dust and muck flew into the air, showering back down. Cooper removed the other harpoons. A wave of such intense ecstasy plowed into her. She fell to her knees and yelped, legs shuddering with pulsating muscles. Debris fell from the sky.

"Yeah!" shouted Scorpio. He fired bursts of high-explosive shells at the remaining Watchmen. They pulled away, running into a dank tunnel. "Get on down there. That's puppet turf!"

"Cooper?" said a gentle voice. A warm hand touched her shoulder. "Are you okay?"

She looked up into a pretty face marred by scars. Kelly smiled, and helped her up. The strength and ease with which she did caught Cooper's attention. The sound of a servo tickled her ear. A dark, rusty, t-shaped frame coupled Kelly's body, hard metal contrasted over her soft breasts. Under it, she wore a set of underwear little more substantial than her own.

"When did...?" Cooper asked.

"When did I cyber up?" Kelly chuckled. "'Bout ten hours ago. Still getting used to it. The sockets and crap itch."

"Hey, hey, still got those antihistamines I gave you?" asked Atom Smasher.

Cooper looked at him, eyes narrow, nearly erupted. "You knew?"

He looked back and forth between them, shoulders back, confused. "Oh, uh...."

"It's okay," Kelly said. "He didn't know. I found them myself and volunteered."

"I thought I might have lost you," Cooper said.

"I heard them coming. They won't take me again."

Cooper wrapped her arms around the other woman. They kissed. Kelly held onto Cooper's burning shoulders, feeling the heat pulsating in her lover. Cooper's resined fingers grabbed a handful of ass. Their kiss halted briefly to look into each other's eyes.

"I'm so glad you're okay," Cooper said. "I was so scared, I thought they might have gotten to you."

Kelly pecked her lips. "Not a chance."

"What the fuck?" Alyssa's voice ripped through the post-firefight haze.

Cooper's daughter walked up, face both scowling and confused. Her boots stamped battered, muddy ground mixed with blood and bodies. Hands rested on her pistols, sweat gleamed on the fields of skin under her exoskeleton. She looked at her mother and Kelly.

"Did I miss something?" she asked.

"Well," Cooper started, "she's my lover, too."

"You've been here three days," Alyssa said. "You always move this fast?"

Cooper shrugged. "Not always. Most times, though."

Kelly had a Kriss SMG hung over one shoulder with ammo strapped to her legs.

"Kelly," Cooper said. "This is my daughter, Alyssa."

"Hawkeye, to most," said Alyssa.

"Oh, my God, you found one of your kids?" Her smile beamed, disbelief in her eyes. "And it's...Hawkeye of all people."

"And I'll be happier if she spends the next fight in a ditch."

Alyssa glared at her mother a moment. "And does Dad know?"

Cooper kept her expression stone. *Just let it be. She needs to keep her focus. Tell her later.*

Alyssa huffed and turned to a group of heavily armed soldiers coming out of the underground tunnels. Cooper maintained her composure but was a little taken aback. None of them looked like the frightened, desperate armed citizens she'd seen all day.

Cybers, most of them, bared bodies under metal frames and actuating joints. Heavily armed. Almost equal numbers men and women. Both sets of eye candy for Cooper's gaze, rugged. She looked back at her own now cyber girlfriend, scars, wires, metal servos, all hooked into the sockets now punctuating her curvy, soft body. She liked it.

"Your shirt is filthy," Kelly noted, wiped some of the grime from her chest. "Looks like it's a sling, like one of your tits is injured."

"Oh." Cooper touched the fabric in her clawed hands, then shrugged. "Simple solution."

She took grip of the tank top in both hands and pulled apart. The wet fabric snapped like nothing and she flung it to the mud in a wet wad.

"Much improved," Kelly smirked.

Cooper concurred in her mind. The female cybers seemed to prefer toplessness out of necessity with their ramshackle exoskeletons, but then they didn't seem perturbed by it either. She felt a small tinge of liberation within her. It put a smile on her face.

A tall, pale man with long and curly hair approached Alyssa. Circuitry lines imbedded through the skin of his arms. Part of his left eye had a glint she zoomed in on, picking up an iris made of small micro circuits. He wore little more than breach cloth beneath his combat frame, a fantastic, fit physique. His reinforced hand carried a SCAR pattern rifle she recognized, though some of the doodads and camouflage pattern were alien to her.

"Dead Meat," Alyssa said. "I see you found her."

"She almost found me. She's pretty streetwise."

His eyes turned to Cooper, looked her up and down in astonishment. "This is her."

"Where at?" asked one of his following cybers, a dark man carrying a large weapon attached to a pack on his back, like some kind of flame thrower. "The Phoenix?"

Others approached, looked on her. Male and female soldiers, eyes wide, expecting to see some kind of goddess, and looking upon a tall naked woman, stained with muck and blood. But her golden eyes looked out upon them. She wore as little as they did, and seemed like one of them almost.

"If only they knew what you truly were."

And that is? Cooper asked in her thoughts, and the voice remained silent.

"Hey," Atom Smasher said and pointed to the resistance post. "Let's check these guys out."

"Weren't you with them?" Cooper asked Dead Meat.

"No, we just got here. Came through the tunnel network. Kelly and I figured you'd be where the noise was."

They walked towards the train car. A harsh stench filled their nostrils. It mixed with the burning smell of cordite and freshly spent gunpowder. Brass casings littered the ground. Blood mixed with the muddy earth.

A machine gun team at the lower level apparently bit it early on. No one had been available to clean up the bodies or take over the weapon. Cooper found a single woman kneeling next to a dead man laying on a mattress.

The woman shook, holding a single pistol. Tears rolled down her cheeks. She may have been forty.

"They're all gone. They're dead...." She sobbed and sniffed. "Phoenix beat them to hell but we're all still dead."

A bloody torrent dripped from the woman's abdomen. Her arm held a soaked, filthy rag against it. The woman looked up to see Cooper's eyes.

"I'm dead, Phoenix...." she paused, just staring up at her with a pistol shaking in her grip. "Go on. I'll hold them as long as I can."

Cooper knelt and put a hand on her shoulder. "You'll get through this, all right? Just stay strong."

The woman's arm shook, and the gun fell from her hand. "I'm...I'm glad I got to see you...."

Cooper felt the woman's shoulder slip from under her hand. She fell over lifeless. "Did they already kill everyone?"

"Most of us," Alyssa said. "Little over seven billion."

Kelly held her. "Come on, we can't stay here long."

"How many people have died for me today?" She looked at Kelly. "A couple days ago I was just another corporate grunt. Today, people are sacrificing everything for me. Why? Why are people dying for me?"

"I don't know," said Kelly. "I just know that if given a choice between me or you, I'd give them me every time."

Cooper shook her head. "I can't let this happen."

"Only one way to do that," Alyssa said, checked her pistol and put it back in its holster. "Kill all they send. Eventually, they'll stop coming."

"That's a philosophy," Kelly said quietly, so only Cooper could hear. "Before we do that, Cooper, I have to tell you something."

Cooper looked into Kelly's eyes. Saw fear there. Uncertainty. Kelly looked pale.

"What is it?" Cooper asked, concerned.

Alyssa headed back to find one of the armored Watchmen struggling to get up.

"Got a survivor," Scorpio said.

"Good," Cooper said, "when his buddies pick him up, maybe he'll give them the message of what a—"

A shot from Alyssa's pistol cut her off. The plasma bolt cracked straight through the Watchman's skull. His shattered face fell into the mud. Without so much as a blink, Alyssa holstered the weapon and strutted back toward them.

"Message sent," she said, and walked on.

Cooper stood in stunned silence. What she just saw barely registered in her head. The shot echoed in silence. Blood pooled from burnt remains to join the congealed mud and filth.

"Dead Meat," Alyssa said firmly to the commando leader, "get the word out to citizens ahead of us. We need to join up if we're going to have a chance of punching out of the city."

"It's looking like a long shot at this point," Dead Meat said.

"The more people we have, the better. Even if we lose all of them, it'll be worth it if we get her out."

Dead Meat's eyes narrowed, and Cooper's eyes widened at her daughter's brazen callousness.

"It's taken this long to build up an insurgency this size in Synchro Point," Dead Meat said.

"The purpose of which was this day," Alyssa countered back. "The Phoenix is of absolute priority and we will bear any sacrifice to ensure she fulfills her mission. To do that, we need to get her to the eyphor hive. We're all dead if she doesn't make it, so it doesn't matter how many we lose."

"And what is my mission?" Cooper asked.

Alyssa looked at her, therein she saw the cold focus of a ruthless soldier. "Only the eyphors truly know." She looked over all present. "Fall in and step!"

Kelly put her chin on Cooper's shoulder and whispered. "Wow, your daughter is vicious."

Cooper nodded. She almost couldn't believe that her insular, artistic little girl turned into the killer woman she saw. Her prideful heart swelled with dread.

"What is it you need to tell me?" Cooper asked.

"Later," Kelly replied.

Liang sat in his lab chair bathed in holograms. The device hung on an arm from the ceiling. He did his work, controls at his fingertips, switching between stations and displays. A stream of ions flowed into his eyes and filtered the nervous impulses of his brain, allowing him to work on various projects simultaneously and with max proficiency.

Linked now with the vast computing power of the Spire, Liang's intellect worked faster. Testing, refining his vision of humanity in the service of Nexus.

Despite his vigorous effort, Liang's summons chimed. Marked as urgent. The chair lowered him to the floor of his ovoid-shaped lab and he walked out into the main area.

Liang's office quarters bore much of the past in its styling of carpet and oak furnishings. Just in front of his desk, two neo-skin commanders stood in their usual manner of bared bodies bedecked only in the cybernetics criss-crossing their physiques. General Ahri-man glared at Liang with stark red eyes.

"The city stands near the point of insurrection, Overseer," said Ahri-man. "We were hoping we could pull you away from your tinkering to discuss the security situation."

"I am aware of the situation. That's why I have given broad spectrum authority to Metro Defense so that the situation can be handled."

Ahri-man looked ahead blankly.

"It doesn't seem you're fully apprised of the situation. Rapid action is needed to contain the unexphen. We have positive identification that it is a female of unknown origin. It's proven a capable combatant, and Metro Defense is not sufficient, Overseer. You've allowed them to become corrupt and ineffective."

Liang raised an eyebrow.

The other neo-skin commander, Colonel Ju-kal, whose once ebony skin had gone to a powdery blue, stepped forth with yellow eyes blazing. "Resistance fighters are covering the tracks of the unexphen. Twice now they have blocked attempts to pursue the phenomenon. Men, vehicles, gunships have been lost."

Liang took in a breath and walked over to the panoramic view of the city beneath him. He pulsed his fist.

"Must be coincidental. The urban resistance has been unable to coordinate such sensitive operations. You spoke of insurrection?" he asked.

Ahri-man answered that question. "Multiple firefights have been reported between the MD and dissident elements, most responsible for operating the Underground Railroad that filters refugees out of the city."

Liang turned and looked at them. "I'll have the MD mobilize everything."

Ahri-man ventured forth, putting up his hand. "I didn't come here to set up further embarrassments. Both Colonels Kul-man and Ju-kal command elite units that can hunt down and finish off this unexphen and any resistance they encounter."

Liang crossed his arms. "How many men?"

"Ju-kal is in command of our Hunter-Killer Operations Squadrons, while Kul-man has thirty-five hundred of our best strike team members. All are veterans of the Mass Departure, the best light 'skins available."

"Thirty five hundred?" Liang blurted. "Are you serious? Metro Defense has two hundred thousand men on the streets. That's an army."

Ahri-man sneered. "Hardly."

"Really? And why not?"

"Armies are made of soldiers, sir."

Liang froze at the comment, placed his hands behind his back, then looked outside.

"I'm well aware of the neo-skins' capabilities, General. I've reviewed your off-world records. The guardians tell me how much Nexus is pleased with you. But, I cannot let that kind of destructive power be brought on this city."

Ju-kal closed his eyes and took in a breath. "This city is a wreck. Its citizenry is stripped of all dynamics, a broken shell, hardly worthy of attaining what we have. In us is the seed of the new humanity, not those left-overs crowding rotten streets."

Liang stared at the Colonel. "Don't forget who gave you this power."

"We never do," said Ju-kal.

"Come, Overseer," said Ahri-man. "Let us cleanse this city. Only the worthy will remain."

"If the guardians wished you to be Overseer than you would be standing here instead of me!" Liang snapped. He waved his arm at the view. "Out there is the future of my vision. Many more wish to serve, and await their opportunity."

Liang scowled at the general and sat back at his desk. "To be perfect, we must embrace all the things that make us what we are, and shed off all of that which we do not need. And what we don't need is a self-imposed genocide. If the unexphen reaches the outer territories, you may deal with her as you see fit. Until then, it remains with Metro Defense. We will send what's left of the unexphen to the Depot once we're finished."

"Have you at least seen the reports?" asked Ju-kal.

Liang smirked, cocked his head. “If it will satisfy your concerns.”

He moved his hands over his desk controls, fingers interacting with holographic particles in the air. Images flashed over the ochre surface, standing like dioramas. Watchmen laid dead on the streets, in the culverts, sewers, and mud. Smoke belched. Fires burned.

A figure ran through hallways and jumped massive gaps between buildings. She fell several stories, slowed herself in the fall, as if gravity bent to her will.

“Wholly inhuman,” Ju-kal added. “She even managed to go strength for strength against a guardian.”

“It retreated,” Liang said with astonishment. He started zooming in on her face. “Has she been identified? Designated JD3605, confirmed falsified number. How...?”

He trailed off when he got a good, still close up of her face. He blinked, several times. Disbelieving.

“Impossible.”

“Sir?” General Ahri-man waited.

Jordan DeBlanc. JD. He nearly laughed at the thought. Shook his head.

Liang looked up at Ju-kal. The man’s memories were gone, but Liang had retained his own to see threats like this. If any threat would have come from the human realm, he would have intimate knowledge of it. Just like he did here.

I’m never wrong, he thought. *Ghosts from the past. How you still haunt me, Michael, wherever you are.*

“Colonel Ju-kal,” he said. “If you could, please report to your stand-by bay. I’ll have mission parameters downloaded to your unit. Surgical removal of high value threats is your forte, no?”

“Yes, sir, it is.”

Liang nodded, and Ju-kal headed away.

Memories, Liang thought. *Only some are useful. Most are meaningless. Others imperative.*

“C’mon, push this thing!” Rodman yelled at Walleye. “They sighted the damn freak, we gotta take her out. I’m sick of this revolt already.”

“We’re already maxed out,” Walleye countered, his hands firm at the controls of the tilt-rotor.

The cityscape rolled by beneath them, buildings no more than blurs. They flew rooftop level at three hundred miles an hour. The range to the distress beacon shrunk. Walleye slowed and pulled into a tight, defensive turn, not knowing what was going to be there.

Both he and Rodman looked down to see the carnage. Bodies littered the ground, Watchmen next to rebels.

“No sign of any unexplained phenomenon,” said Walleye. He slowed and put the rotors on a diagonal plane. “Going for a closer look.”

“Damn!” said Rodman. “Hey, Dispatch, we need a major ground unit up here. Mass casualties, I say again, mass casualties, fifty plus.”

Walleye looked out over some of the buildings, picking up a silhouette that set his heart racing. A single man, a long tube on his shoulder.

“RPG!” he shouted just as the rocket slammed into their frontal armor. The concussion rocked him in his seat.

"Shit! Get us out of here."

Walleye turned the tilt-rotor. A second RPG hit the side armor of the right engine. He felt the drop in power. A missile from a gunship above silenced the first team in a pall of black smoke. Walleye looked straight ahead where another RPG team set up on the roof of the building right in front of them.

He could almost make out the men's eyes. One white skinned, one a light brown. Then he realized the darker one was a woman. An anti-tank missile plowed straight between them and the two fighters vanished in a flash of heat and debris.

The tilt-rotor shuddered from the near impact. Walleye thought it rattled his brain loose for a moment. Warning lights flashed in his eyes and the buzzers went off in his ears.

"God dammit! You trying to kill us too?" Walleye shouted.

The gunship pilot responded. "I thought you were already going down."

Walleye managed to back the aircraft away from the explosion. "We need to get this bucket of bolts back to base."

He glanced at Rodmam, who only looked back with wide eyes. "They don't pay us enough for this, man!"

The early afternoon sun created a blaze of light against the surface of the canal. Cooper reached the end of the tunnel. She leaned against the concrete and fought to catch her breath. Steam huffed out of her mouth. Lungs burned. Limbs screamed.

With every inhale the burn vanished. With every exhale it returned. Pulsating energy coursed through muscle. Deep inside her abdomen came the nagging, swirling heat colliding with her inner walls. She grunted against a sting far worse than any hunger.

"*We need rest.*"

Cooper chuckled darkly, then rested her hot, sweating brow against cold concrete.

"Don't cop out on me now."

Sweat glistened over every inch of skin. Her claws dug into the side of the tunnel wall to keep her steady.

"Have I reached the limit?"

Her vision turned fuzzy, gazing into daylight from the dark tunnel. Her hands pressed against her belly.

"*It burns!...It burns!*"

Something the mantid did. It broke down a barrier of some kind. Energy kept piling through. She couldn't contain it. She needed to expend it.

"*We need rest.*"

"Rest?" Cooper thought. "Do we need rest...or...more targets?"

"*We need rest.*"

Cooper sneered. "I don't feel tired. I feel...hungry."

"*No! We cannot generate any more energy. Rest.*"

Cooper growled and slammed her fist into the wall. The hard surface cracked. Dust clouded out.

"Now you listen to me! I don't care who you are, what you're doing, or why you're here. This is my body. Mine! And you don't tell me what to do with it!"

The claws of her other hand scraped into the surface. Her muscles tensed and flexed. They writhed beneath her skin.

"*Your body...what about mine?*"

Cooper backed away from the wall and stood there, fists clenched at her sides. APC's parked on either side of the canal. Zooming her eyesight in, Watchmen came out the back. A pair of mantids joined them.

"Unexphen acquired, moving to engage. Request all available units proceed to my twenty, southwest canal zone."

"Your body?" Cooper asked the voice.

"*I never asked to be bound here with you. You never asked to be bound with me, but at least I would be alive without you. You wouldn't be alive without me.*"

"Sounds like a conundrum," she almost growled.

"*You really are clueless on what's actually transpiring here. I used to be free, but now I'm stuck with you. A bond in permanence. If you can't help contain the energy we're generating, this body will meltdown, and I'll die with you. I won't let that happen!*"

"Then work some magic, and don't let it happen."

Cooper sighed with delight at the enemy's approach. Sweat poured down her cheeks, and she shuddered. She reached above her head, stood on her toes and stretched. The movement was so pleasant she almost forgot about the situation.

"Why does everything feel so good when I'm ready to kill?"

"*That's it, ease it out.*"

A few bullets pinged her way, snapped against her skin. She readied to charge when footfalls approached from behind. Cooper looked over her shoulder to see her companions had finally caught up.

"Mom," Alyssa said between panting breaths. "What's...going on...up ahead...?"

Cooper rushed to cover her.

"Get back. We got company."

Kelly came up between them, hands on Cooper's shoulder. Alyssa narrowed her eyes at the other woman.

"You're burning up," Kelly said. "What's the matter?"

"I just...I can't contain it."

Alyssa nodded to the Watchmen outside. "You should take it out on them, then."

The first bullet struck the concrete above her head. Cooper rushed Alyssa and Kelly into the same niche. Briefly, she gazed down Kelly's creamy white body, sweat beads traveling down the contours of her sultry form locked under the metal frame. Cooper looked back up into hazel eyes brimming with determination.

"Keep me covered," she said. "I'll blaze a trail."

Cooper whirled about and charged to the first enemies with a scream. A few bullets bounced off her body, stings, before she leapt at the first. Her weight plowed into the Watchman, pressed him into a puddle of water pooled between the broken concrete. She smashed his chest with her knee, felt the bones crack beneath the armor.

She ripped the automatic shotgun from him, tore the ammo pouches from his uniform while several of his teammates poured fire onto her.

"No effect on target!" a Watchman shouted.

The pain told otherwise. Cooper leapt clear, landed in some cool water pooled against an upturned slab of concrete she used for cover. Dead Meat's cybers poured on from behind with rifles. Their directed energy weapons spewed plasma bolts that ripped conduits of smoke through the air.

"Eyphor derived weapons," Cooper noted. "Plasma based."

Cooper steamed out the burning sensation in her body. Meltdown. She had to avoid it. Repelling bullets, using her superior physiology, anything that required high energy, pushed her to that limit.

Have to conserve myself, she said, checked the shotgun's magazine, slapped it back in. *Do it the old fashioned way.*

Cooper rushed out of cover, weapon in her shoulder. Her powerful muscles at least gave her extremely enhanced stability. She aimed and fired on the move, rushing Watchmen. Explosive slugs tore into them. Cooper ducked for cover against a concrete slab. The water filling the bottom of the canal steamed against her legs.

"Push forward!" Alyssa shouted. "Rush through, violence of action!"

More cybers and armed citizens followed Cooper's lead, Kelly with them. That only urged Cooper to fight harder, forward. Faster. She reloaded, pressed onward. Legs pumped beneath her, sprinting from cover to cover. She switched out the empty shotgun for a Kriss from her next victim, she still had ammo for that weapon on her belt.

Fire. Attack. Reload. Sprint. Cover to cover. The bullets whacked against her, but she kept it at a minimum. The meltdown point receded. Her body cooled. Clouds had gathered. A light sprinkle fell into the still present sunlight, illuminating the firefight hell in an eerie golden glow.

"APC's above," Dead Meat warned. "RPG gunners, target those—"

The slam of heavy machine gun fire on concrete silenced him and sent the commando leader scrambling further into the muck.

Half a dozen mantids poured into the canal. The reign of lead from the APC's cut down swaths of Cooper's followers. The rounds hit with enough impact to rip off limbs and send a running man flipping backward onto his shoulders.

"Stop running! Get down!" she shouted, her voice high and shrill over the din of air filled with snapping bullets.

Alyssa and Dead Meat deployed two devices they had carried on their backs. Set on the ground, the devices shimmered into yellow fields of static light. Bullets sparked into the fields of heat drawn out by cascading energy.

A laser shield, Cooper realized. *Melting and softening bullets on impact.*

"*Primitive,*" the voice added.

The cybers and citizens without ample cover piled behind the shields, using it like a wall. They couldn't fire through lest the heat soften their bullets too, but popped up and down to fire at targets they could see through the light. Better than a wall in some ways.

A rebel RPG gunner launched, but the rocket hit low, flaring and dusting out the concrete slope beneath the APC's. Mantids charged in. Cooper aimed in at the closest, held the Kriss steady so the .45 rounds cut like a scalpel, aimed at the center eye cluster. The mantid fumbled and squealed, but side stepped into the maze of broken concrete and upturned earth.

Watchmen kept attacking behind the wave of mantids. Grenades crumped against the ground, spitting water upward with black debris.

A dark skinned commando shouted a foreign battlecry with a heavy plasma cannon held by both arms to his shoulder. The hot fire it spat ripped across the air and slammed against an APC on the hill. Smoking and belching flames, the APC hit reverse and pulled back.

"Good hit, Slag! Good hit!" Alyssa commended.

Kelly rushed out of cover, and slid next to Cooper, Alyssa doing the same. They took up positions on either side of her. Mantid harpoons sparked on the broken ground they used for cover.

"Hey, get those shields up over here!" Cooper shouted. "Both of you."

"I can't fire out of it," Alyssa said, aiming through and firing her plasma pistols. "And carrying it slows me down, they're better where they are."

"We're gonna get surrounded if we can't move," Kelly said. "And we don't have the muscle to push through this."

"Gunships'll be here soon," said Dead Meat. "Then we're good and dead."

Cooper looked behind her to see the bodies of slain citizens bleeding into the canal water. Rain fell on them, dropping heavier. More clouds rolling in.

"This weather'll help Nexus more than us," Alyssa said. "Every system they have available is all weather."

Kelly jumped back into cover when a mantid harpoon nearly missed her head. Two mantids took that second of opportunity and rushed. Cooper spotted them just barely in time, but her Kriss could do nothing to them at this point. Her body acted of its own accord, exploding into instinct.

"No!" she screamed, and the ground beneath the mantids bent to her will.

The two alien menaces flung up into the air. Then Cooper realized it wasn't the ground that did her bidding. The fabric of space itself bent, lifting the two hostiles over the heads of the rebel force.

"What the fuck?" Alyssa said.

"How—?" Kelly sounded.

The dark commando named Slag let out his battlecry again. Cooper suddenly recognized it as something South African. His heavy plasma cannon mashed one mantid and sent the other flying distant into the air, unbound to the earth. The Nexus teams pushed in, and Cooper felt it happen again.

Her arms tingled. She stood, palms open and aimed skyward. Bright orange lights glowed from their center.

"*Are you starting to figure it out?*"

No, Cooper thought. *Let's just make it happen.*

Gravity. The curvature of space created by the presence of mass. Everything worked on Earth because it was falling toward it. Cooper bent it back, sending the Nexus mantids and Watchmen tumbling into the air. They screamed. They cried. The sky filled with their fear. Hands and feet clawed into nothing for grip. Panic.

Cybers and citizens looked on in astonishment, utterly still while dozens of their enemies floated out of cover. Twisting. Screaming. Not a few seconds passed before everyone knew what they had to do.

"Fire!" Alyssa shouted.

Plasma. Bullets. Rockets. Some soldiers milked grenades and threw them high into the sky. Scorpio slid into the open to get a clear shot with his shotgun's explosive shells.

"Oh, yeah! Hunting on easy!"

Impacts sent even six hundred pound mantids spiraling. Cooper smiled while her troops gathered around her, charged the floating and helpless enemy. But it couldn't last. The heat built up in her limbs. Cooper felt the burn. She clenched her teeth together.

"I can't hold it," she shouted. "Get as many as you can!"

They did. Cooper held the approaching enemy in a grip of slipping gravity until her muscles felt like imploding. She tried to deliver one last blow before she let her enemies out of her grasp. Cooper propelled them as high into the air as she could. She grunted against the crunching pain of spasming muscles.

Then she let go, and her enemies rained from the sky.

Walleye suited up in front of his locker and slammed the door shut. He checked his .45 pistol and stuck it into the hip holster. He looked over his slate, double-checking the forged orders he'd put together. Then went to find his co-pilot.

"Rodman," Walleye said to the exhausted man leaning on a wall, avoiding the many bodies moving about in this emergency.

"What do you want?" he said.

"We've got a flight assignment."

"Fuck," said Rodman.

"We've got a transport ready, now."

Rodman sighed, tired. "A transport?"

"Our gunship's down. Three RPG's. Left engine's gone, man."

"All right, fuck it. Goddamn bullshit."

Walleye led his co-pilot through the locker room to the flight line. He took a shortcut which ended up in a supply closet just outside the landing deck. The two halted, frozen, at the site of the neo-skin standing inside and looking out the window.

Exposed, sinewy muscles of metal micro-fibers made up his arms and legs. A composite array of segmented spine structures ran up the middle of a bare back, skin smoky beige-blue, and terribly scarred by burns. Two rows of metal fins ran down his back, the largest at the top, getting smaller toward the bottom. Otherwise, he stood there almost naked, with a slight question mark curve in his back. Arms hung limp, but seemed ready to move at speed.

Yellow eyes gazed out through the glass until they turned Walleye's way.

"Why aren't they sending you out?" Walleye asked. "You seem qualified."

"Far more than you," the neo-skin responded. "She's killed all you sent. She continues to kill what you send."

Walleye had never seen one of the neo-skins this close. A harsh cut down the left side of his face marred his visage. Like some kind of animal gored his skin, disfiguring his upper lip.

"If you don't mind my asking, if you're the goal, the next step in our evolution, why would I want to be like you?"

Yellow eyes cut into his core. He'd never seen such utter conviction. "I have walked the frozen wastes and held fire in my hand. I've held my breath for a day in both water and vacuum. I have achieved Pure Will, and seen the depths of this universe and the next. I am Kul-Man."

Rodman chuckled. "That Mass Departure must've been something."

Walleye nodded, then continued out the door and headed for his transport. Armed Watchmen awaited behind it. The rest of the flight line thrummed with gunships responding to the unexphen as well as other crises around Synchro Point.

Walleye pulled himself into the cockpit, got the troops loaded in, and readied for the moment.

Cooper threw the Watchman against the APC like a rag doll. He flipped mid-flight, then cracked against the armor. More .45 bullets stung her waist and torso. A grapple shot out at the pistol holder, digging its bladed head into his throat.

Two more down, she thought. A mantid sprinted behind her, vanishing behind another APC. *Fuckers keep moving so fast.*

Kelly knelt next to her. "You okay?"

"Aside from the fact I feel like I'm ready to explode?"

Scorpio, Dead Meat, and Alyssa set up against another APC surrounded by dead Watchmen. Cooper had ripped out and killed their crews already. Commandos and citizens set up around them.

Alyssa smacked her arm against the armored vehicle. "Dead Meat and I know how to operate these things. Cover us."

She headed into an APC. Dead Meat took another. The turrets started moving around.

That's my girl, she thought. *Stay in there.*

The heavy machine guns chased targets around them, sending heavy slugs into approaching Watchmen.

"Where'd the mantids go?" asked Kelly. "They ran off after we started shooting."

"Mantids don't retreat!" Scorpio snapped. "Never seen 'em do it. But then I'd never seen Watchmen run like they just did neither."

"We'll have to keep ready," Cooper shouted against the din. "They move fast."

"Kelly," Cooper said. "Could you go into the APC with my daughter?"

Kelly chuckled and shook her head. "I'm staying with you. Back to back?"

"All right. Let's go."

Both women stood and pressed their backs against each other. The reactor on Kelly's shoulder blades bumped into Cooper's spine, and she giggled.

A mantid again appeared before Cooper and ground to a halt, setting its legs and readying to fire. Cooper hit it first, holding the trigger down on full auto. Explosive shells hit from Scorpio's AA12. The mantid squealed and sprinted away.

"These things can take a hit," Cooper said.

"How'd you kill the one in the gulley?" asked Kelly. "Seems the quickest way."

"Your guess is as good as mine. I think it might've killed itself."

Cooper turned her head at just the right moment to see a mantid stop and ready to fire into Kelly.

"Look out!" She shoved her body in front of her lover's. Harpoons impaled Cooper's chest and she dropped.

Kelly poured bullets into the mantid until her weapon went dry. Cooper lifted her Kriss and piled it back on as her partner reloaded. The mantid sprinted away, leaking red-violet body fluids. Kelly wrapped her arm around Cooper's waist and hauled her back up.

"You don't have to do that. Don't die for me. I'm not important enough."

"Drop that talk!" Cooper snapped and yanked a harpoon from her body. "Too many people have given their lives for me today, and I barely know what I'm here for. And I will not lose you. I promised."

"You promised they wouldn't lay a hand on me, again. That's a little different than promising I'll never meet a stray bullet. Or harpoon."

Cooper pulled her in and stole a quick kiss. "I said I'm not losing you."

Kelly nodded. "Let's kill 'em all, then."

"Down!" Scorpio shouted. The two women flattened onto the deck before he launched more HE rounds at an approaching mantid. Shells popped and exploded against its skin, finally sending it to the ground. Its legs collapsed and the torso slapped into the concrete.

Kelly and Cooper knelt. The enemies around them scattered, but a massive wave of Watchmen approached from across the canal. Alyssa and Dead Meat raked into them from the APC turrets. Puffs of concrete dust erupted through the oncoming mass of black figures.

Cooper zoomed in her vision to search for threats, and spotted an all too familiar tube shaped weapon.

"No," Cooper whispered.

But the RPG already flared, and rammed into Alyssa's APC, right near the turret, in sparks and flame.

"Alyssa!" Cooper screamed and rushed into the vehicle. There, she found Alyssa still in the turret, still firing. The intense relief washed over her like sunlight through an arctic night.

"Alyssa, they've got RPG's, get out now!"

"I felt it, don't worry," Alyssa replied. "Those relics can't penetrate this thing's armor."

"I'm not taking that chance." Cooper grabbed Alyssa's cyber frame and pulled at her. Alyssa braced herself and held against her mothers' strength.

"Stop!" Alyssa shrieked. "Listen, I know what I'm doing. I'll keep the fire on, you keep them off of us. Trust me, and let me do my job."

Cooper shook her head, searching for the words to say. Kelly entered through the back.

"I'll be fine, Mom. I've been doing this my entire life." She returned to firing. Cooper watched in silence, remembering what a delicate girl she used to be.

Kelly placed her hand on Cooper's shoulder. "Hawkeye's a legend, Cooper. We've all heard about her."

"We can't hold here, forever," Cooper said.

"I've got about two hundred rounds left...." Alyssa trailed off. "They're pressing on like madmen."

"What do we do?" Cooper asked.

Alyssa shook her head. "I don't know. Got anymore gravity tricks?"

"I nearly burned out the last time. I don't—"

An unbending sound penetrated every atom of Cooper's body, sending the others scrambling to cover their ears. An unholy cry, one of pain, of rage. It shook Cooper to her bones, rattled her skull. Even before she pulled her hands away from her ears, Alyssa's eyes filled with fear.

"What was that?" Cooper asked.

"Please don't tell me," Kelly said. "Was that a, uh, a WTF?"

Alyssa looked back into her targeting track. "We're going to have an overpowered mantid out there. Spotted!"

Cooper headed out of the APC. "Stay inside, Kelly! It's not an option!"

"But," Kelly began to protest.

Cooper held up her hand, "Stay here."

She continued on, strutted to the head of the APC, to the edge of the canal, and looked down into it. A mantid approached at the head of the others, Watchmen taking up formations behind them. The leading mantid steamed against the rain. Her vision zoomed to it.

It exuded far more heat, burning far more energy than its compatriots, far more than it seemed its body could contain. Its entire mass flared before a crushing force erupted in front of Cooper, tearing through the concrete and blasting her back.

"Singularity cannon!" a commando shouted. "Take it out!"

His body and that of several around him flashed into pink mist, torn instantaneously to a point dead center between them. Air and ground exploded into a powerful pressure wave. Debris flung into the air.

"Out of the APC's!" Alyssa shouted. "Out!"

Alyssa and Kelly darted out of theirs just in time, before it imploded in on itself, as if the invisible hand of a massive creature crumpled it up like a soda can. The pressure blast resonated through the atmosphere and flung Cooper even further back, with Alyssa and Kelly tumbling.

"What the fuck!" Cooper shouted.

Then she realized. Kelly said a WTF.

"Alyssa, what's happening to that thing?"

Her daughter scrambled to help her mother to her feet.

"Move! Get out of a hundred meter radius, that's their max range. It'll crush everything within it."

They sprinted. Dead Meat's APC raced in reverse to clear the area, but the mantid still approached, guarding its comrades. Massive gravity crushed another rebel position, taking two RPG gunners. A heavy plasma cannon fired. The impact blasted a hole in front of the mantid. Half a second later the plasma gunner vanished in a singularity.

Cooper felt the space around her change. Time stood still. She looked upon Alyssa and Kelly, unmoving. Somehow. Something...pressure. Growing. The air seemed to bend toward them in a perfectly spherical wave, racing to a point not far from her hip.

Then she realized.

Oh, shit. A singularity. I'm standing in one. Am I...? Am I dead?

From outside, the death of commandos and citizens, the crushing of APC's, looked immediate. But from inside, time slowed to a crawl. She remembered this. Gravitational time dilation.

The instant of my death, those astrophysics courses paid off.

"*I'm not ready to accept such a death*," sneered the voice.

Just like that, the gravitational stability returned and bounced outward like a blast wave that knocked Dead Meat's APC onto its side. Several rebels fell onto their asses, slamming into the ground. She, Kelly, and Alyssa were unscathed. Save for a crunching pain in her muscles that dropped Cooper to her knees.

Alyssa shook like a leaf, her bronze skin pale, eyes wide. "D-d-d...d-di...did?"

"Holy fuck," Kelly spat, shivering as if cold.

Cooper grunted and forced herself back to her feet, Kelly aiding her.

"Time to kill that thing," Cooper said. "Everyone else break contact, get back a hundred meters."

Cooper charged away from her compatriots, rushed into the canal to meet a hail of gunfire and mantid harpoons. She rolled down the sloping concrete, leapt, charged, until everything stopped again. Another singularity. It surrounded and trapped her until the gravitons cycled inward and back out again.

This time the pressure wave trounced through her enemies. Watchmen and mantids flew in every direction. She screamed through the immediate pain she knew was going to follow. The energized mantid, the WTF, stood staring her square in the face, five, dark eyes clustered together.

"What's driving you?"

Without a weapon she drove her resin encased fist into the eye cluster. The pincers sliced at her. She dodged, but it still cut her skin. Her wounds healed but at a shocking price of agony. Still, she pressed her attack.

Her fists met a barrier of sheer electrical resistance from its charged hide. Screaming, shouting, hollering with every strike. It did next to nothing. Then a pincer charged deep into her shoulder, pinned Cooper in a grip of anguish. She cried out, paralyzed. Exhaustion. Pain. Despair. All hit at once.

"*Artificial adaptations have acquired capabilities far accelerated from human norm,*" came a disembodied voice. It had to be the coldest thing Cooper ever heard. Ever felt. Ever imagined.

"*Accelerated adaptability insufficient to interfere with confirmed EndState parameters. Threat, nominal.*"

"*If it only knew,*" said the voice.

But they didn't talk to each other. Both talked to her, but they didn't hear through her. Cooper couldn't help but note the voices felt so similar. The two deepest, most terrible intelligences she'd never dreamt could exist.

"You're not the mantid," Cooper said through her quivering lips.

The other pincer came down over her head. Again and again. No hesitation. No mercy. It would strike until she died. Her other arm grabbed it, but weak. So weak. The mantid forced Cooper to her knees.

"Please...." she whispered. "Someone...something."

"*Will you cry out for a spiritual deity?*" the other voice asked. "*Such actions garner improved psychological will to push human physicality to heightened limits. Effects similar to summoned patriotism, ideological summation, memory of family, comrades.*"

It dawned on Cooper then. Her daughter remained atop the canal, Kelly at her side. Her husband was dead and unavenged. Her son's fate remained unknown to her. She would not die without knowing. The fire spread to her limbs. The arm beneath her wounded shoulder responded, grabbed the offending pincer to push it out of her flesh.

"You shouldn't give me ideas."

"Destroy this unit, the metal destiny remains in place, an outcome you cannot effect."

"*Well, he hasn't changed,*" quipped the voice.

Cooper let out a harsh cry, ripped the pincer clear from its joint, spun it about in her grip and slashed it down repeatedly into the eye cluster. It's own electrically charged and hyper-bonded blade tore through the enhancing protection. She yanked the other pincer free and slashed them down, back and forth, one savage blow after the other.

When the thing laid sprawled out and lifeless, Cooper let out a huff and tossed the pincers onto its corpse. The remaining Watchman retreated, with a phalanx of mantids standing stoic and still above the opposite end of the canal. On the friendly side, Kelly and Alyssa stood with the other rebels, looking down on her in astonishment.

She returned to them. Her eyes fixed on Kelly, the rain dripping down her shoulders and breasts to soak her black panties under the metal frame. Cooper grabbed her up and kissed her. Kelly held on to her, gripping tight to the hot skin that still turned the rain water to steam.

"Wow," a female soldier said, "you're like a, uh, a human guardian."

"Beat a mantid to death with its own pincers," Dead Meat said, "that's a fucking thing of beauty."

"I knows right?" added Scorpio. "One that gone all WTF an' shit."

"You pushed back a singularity," Alyssa added, shaking her head. "Twice."

Cooper held Kelly tight. "And I'm starting to feel the wear, guys."

Alyssa sighed, shook her head again and pointed down the canal. "APC's and Watchmen on approach." Her voice sounded near dead.

"They're massing on the far side," Dead Meat added, rechecked his weapon.

"My plasma cannon's fried," said Slag, hawking the heavy thing's power pack off his back.

"Now what do we do?" Cooper asked. "I'm almost tapped out."

Kelly shook her head against Cooper's shoulder, "I don't know."

Walleye had been a double agent for near five years now. He'd kept his cool through all kinds of strenuous situations. This time, however, he sweated like never before in his life.

"Approaching target area," said Rodman.

"Circling around," Walleye replied.

Two other transports below off-loaded their foot units to reinforce a wave that had already been butchered. Including mantids, one of them Accelerated. Reports indicated she had withstood singularity attacks. Walleye looked ahead, almost spaced out, overwhelmed by what he had been hearing on the tacnet, it strained belief.

He skirted the area. Tracers crossed through the air. A battered Metro Defense APC laid on its side near the edge of a canal. Not far away rested a crumpled heap of metal he could've only assumed was once an identical APC. Singularity craters littered the area, vastly outnumbered by dead Watchmen and citizens. Mantid corpses laid sprawled and twisted on the ground. He'd never seen so many of them dead.

Walleye banked the tilt-rotor towards a clear spot separated from the canal. The rain continued to thicken.

"Looks like a good LZ," he said.

Perfect timing.

Walleye slowed to a near stand-still, opening the side panel doors but not yet low enough to drop off the Watchmen.

Do not hesitate.

"I'm sorry, Rodman," Walleye said, then pulled the Colt .45 from his holster and pressed it against the man's helmet. Before a word escaped, the pistol cracked and Rodman's cranium splattered against the side display.

He dropped the gun. His cargo bay cameras showed the men had unbuckled and stood at the ready. Walleye yanked back on the stick, and watched with wide eyes, teeth grit together, as the whole squad fell forty feet to their deaths.

"Holy shit!" Kelly shouted. "Did you see that?"

"What?" asked Cooper. They awaited behind the overturned APC for the next wave of Watchmen.

"That transport just dumped its whole load." She pointed to the dark machine that just barreled over them. "Just...dumped them."

Cooper locked eyes on it, zooming her view in to see its dark design, the sharp angles and tough, menacing appearance. The side panels to the cargo compartment still hung open.

"It's coming around," she said.

"Who that?" Scorpio said. "It drop all its boys and now it's coming for us? You shittin' me, right?"

The panels along its forward flanks opened and an array of barrels gaped at approaching Watchmen. A cascade of destructive energy lanced into the next wave. Bright blue light surrounded a column of pitch black in each shot.

"Yeah!" Scorpio shouted. "Eat some plasma you's fucks!"

"Is that for us?" asked Cooper, before she grabbed her stomach and keeled into the bulkhead.

"Mom!" Alyssa shouted and clutched her up. "You all right?"

"What's with that gunship?"

"I don't know." They looked outside the back to see the transport lower its gear, then flip a one-eighty and present its cargo compartment.

"Everyone get on board!" Cooper shouted.

"Wait," Alyssa said. "I need to identify the pilot."

Another horrendous howl bore through the field. The sound conquered even the rumbling engine.

Shit, it's like mass doesn't even stop it, Cooper noted. The sound penetrated straight through her core.

"All right!" Alyssa screamed when the sound faded. "Fuck it, get the Phoenix on board! Dead Meat, hold them off!"

"No," Cooper countered, "everyone on board. Go!"

Cooper stood up and waved the troops forward, watching them pass on before moving toward it. Alyssa grabbed her arm.

"Mom, we came for you. Get on the damn plane!"

"Since when do you think you can give me orders?"

Cooper twisted her arm out of Alyssa's grip, grabbed her by the exoskeleton frame, then snagged Kelly by hers. She tugged her daughter and lover to the tilt-rotor.

Alyssa rushed to the front and pressed the pilot comm button.

"This is Hawkeye, who's flying this thing?"

"Name's Walleye."

"Holy shit, you do exist," Alyssa spat.

"I always did."

The side panels closed down as all got aboard.

"Well," Cooper said and fell to her knees. Kelly rushed to her side. "We're in his hands now."

"Yeah, and you're in mine," Kelly said. She placed her hand on Cooper's back. She felt the movements of muscles beneath, spasming and contracting. "Hopefully, you'll be okay."

"We're going low and fast," Walleye announced. "I've scrambled the radio serials, so we have some time before they realize which transport just bailed on them."

"I hope you're right," said Alyssa.

Citizens and commandos crowded the cargo compartment. Cooper could barely keep herself up, lying flat on Kelly who held her tight.

"Easy, Coop. Easy, baby. We're getting out of here."

Cooper laid her head on Kelly's breasts, skin sticky with sweat and rain water, but so soft and pleasantly warm. Kelly wrapped a leg around her to hold the embrace even tighter.

"There was that thing you wanted to tell me," Cooper whispered against a soft mound.

"Later," Kelly said, smelled her hair and laid on a gentle kiss.

VII: RAILROAD'S END

06/22/2024, 1425 "*... eerrr ... eerrr ... This is the Emergency Broadcast System. All residents of St. Louis are advised to seek shelter or evacuate. An Unexplained Phenomenon has appeared northwest of the city. Seismic activity has been reported as well as severe wind patterns. Wind gusts of up to one hundred miles an hour have been observed near the phenomenon's epicenter. Evacuation is strongly advised.*"

Salt Lake Facility, 1420, 06/22/2024

Cooper washed the gunk from her face and hands. She splashed the water against her, sudding up with hand soap as much as she could. She raided the locker rooms to find any Scope and Listerine, then washed it through her mouth to wipe out the taste of the gunk. She pulled out her field hygiene kit and brushed her teeth furiously for several minutes, scrubbed at every crevice.

Then she wiped the drying slime from beneath the tear in her armor, pulling it out from her exposed breasts. Exhaustion and fear rattled her nerves. The sense of violation brought up a moment she didn't want to bring up. Not now.

Focus. Focus, she thought. But then couldn't. Lenny wasn't dead, just injured. Scotty still leered at her whenever he could, and he wasn't hiding it like he used to. And so close to Michael.

She looked into the mirror at her worn out eyes, then marveled at how her body still felt in the throes of arousal, pulsating like a broken power line bouncing in a puddle.

Ramon cracked open the door to the women's locker room and knocked. "You all right, Cooper?"

She hesitated. Hearing his voice made her skin flush with warmth. "Come in."

He stepped inside. Cooper fought from looking down the front of his rather tight suit. Like hers, it didn't hide much, designed to act like a wet suit as well as body armor.

He gestured at her headset, left on the sink. "You probably didn't hear. Scotty's picked up signals from two employees over in D-Lab. He wants us to go find out what they're doing."

Cooper nodded. She didn't say much. Just looked along his strong, muscled arm as it flexed to hold up his AA12.

"Y'know, you never did take me to that strip club."

"What?" he asked.

"Like you said you would in Afghanistan, once we got back. Remember?"

Ramon sighed and set his shotgun on top of the sink, then removed his headset and set it next to the weapon.

"Cooper, we have to—"

She stepped forward and touched his bicep, felt the hard muscle under soft, smooth skin. His body heat rushed into her fingertips, the sweaty texture of his flesh so enticing. She wanted to be naked beneath him, to feel every inch.

"Hey, easy, girl," he said. "There's not much—"

She interrupted him with a kiss, grasping his waist. He feebly pushed against her shoulders. But the harder he pushed, the stronger she pressed.

"Coop—"

"Shut the fuck up!" she growled. Her body shoved his against the wall. He received her kiss, breasts pressing against his chest.

"Ramon," she moaned, legs pinning him there, boiling over with heat. "Touch me. Please."

"We can't do this. Not here."

"We might not get another chance." She unclipped the collar latch of her suit, shoulder fabric loosening. "I might not get another chance at you."

She kissed him harder, licking at his neck, then grabbed his hand. He resisted weakly as she guided him between her legs. Even from beneath his suit she felt him grow against her. Cooper rubbed his aroused state, so amazingly firm against her hand. She worked the fasteners of his suit around him.

"No, Cooper, wait. Not here, I can't—"

She freed his penis into her gentle fingers. One hand on him while the other pulled his armor loose from his shoulders, yanking it down to his waist, then to his thighs. Cooper reveled in his amazing body, big pectoral muscles, rippling abdomen. She pulled her suit free and pressed her soft breasts against his virile power. Her porcelain skin glowed against his bronze.

His strong arms gripped around her body, their nakedness pressing together. She twisted about in his arms and pushed her butt against him. Her muscles clenched deep within, desperate for something to fill the wanting gap.

His fingers reached down between her legs, and all his resistance faded. Fear of death, fear of those creatures disappeared for that brief moment. The pulsating energy in her blood now blazed like flash fires in her veins. Even such a simple touch sent her legs shivering, thighs shaking off loose beads of sweat.

Cooper took his hand and led him down to the floor, laying him on his back. She straddled over him, reversed, and dropped to her knees. He rose into her. She quivered at his press. Her cry reverberated against the locker room walls. Cooper pressed her elbows onto his shins, gyrated up and down in fast, hungry movements.

"Cooper," Ramon pleaded softly. "Slow down or...."

"No! Don't, not yet," Cooper said. "Stay hard for me, baby!"

Ramon tried to stay her bucking, but didn't have the will. He held for her. Over and over, Cooper shivered into a squealing climax. They came on almost rapid fire, each more powerful than the last. Nothing like it had ever happened before in her life.

She chased each orgasm with a faster and faster rhythm, her body demanding more. Her loins ignited and she gripped onto him, lowering until he filled every last bit of her. Legs and hips trembled out of her control, letting out short quakes of sound from her throat. The sweat dripped from her tiny bangs onto her face. She tasted the salt when it dropped to her lips.

Then she rode on. Crying out. "Fuck...fuck...fuck!"

"Cooper...." Ramon groaned. "I can't."

"Wait!" Cooper screamed when she realized he couldn't hold out any longer.

She lifted up and spun around. Her lips slipped onto him, tongue working to the dance of her lust, in time with his furious pumping. She pushed down farther than she had ever tried on any man, neck straining. Her hands felt onto his slick skin, fingers gripping onto his sweaty surface.

Cooper moaned, lips sealed but still unable to hold it all. His essence seemed to clear out the violating feel of the alien creature that had tried to jam its way past her teeth. Ramon poured out from beneath her lips. She looked up into his eyes. Their gloved hands interlocked fingers at his waist. Cooper finished, lifted up and took in a deep breath. Ramon leaned back, eyes closed.

"Cooper...." he whispered.

She put her hand to her mouth, headed back over to the sink. She leaned onto it, feeling the waning strength in her legs, but kept herself up. Breath after breath, she calmed. Every heartbeat felt like a sledge hammer trying to burst out from under her sternum.

Such an immense satisfaction ran through her veins, like a cold mountain breeze relieving the intensity of a burning hot day. Burning. Like her body had been doing ever since morning. A wildfire quenched by winter's embrace. Still, it lingered, like the taste.

Cooper cracked her neck and picked up her toothbrush, turned the water back on. Ramon just watched her, eyes on her gleaming, porcelain backside. Beads of sweat roamed down her curves. He still couldn't fathom what just happened.

"Will you marry me?" he asked.

"Huh?" She looked back at him, toothpaste foaming at her lips, then casually replied, "No," and got back to brushing. She rinsed and spat, then rinsed and spat again.

"Oh," Ramon resigned. "Okay."

Cooper turned back around, licked behind her lips, then gently toed his leg. "C'mon, work to do. Two employees over in D-Lab."

She got dressed in her ripped suit, and Ramon pulled his back up to over his shoulders. In silence, they steadied themselves, prepped weapons and gear. With every second, the event passed as if it had never happened. Cooper moved so casually, professionally, energized.

"You would've been a pretty good dancer," Ramon said finally. "I'm sorry I never got around to it."

She smiled and pecked his lips. "Thank you."

"Are you...focused?"

"Yeah. Yeah...I feel...well, you know."

"Right." He smiled slightly, then fumbled his weapon and nearly fell onto the sink counter. Cooper steadied him, and patted his stomach.

"Come on, shake it off."

"What, like you did?"

She replaced her headset and got back on the net, reset her weapon, and readied her magazines with all remaining rounds from her pack.

"Did you shake that demon, or whatever?" he asked.

She smiled wide. "I wouldn't say it was a demon."

"Right," he said. "The demon would be you."

She laughed. "Shall we get going?"

He nodded. She and Ramon ran to the location. The pumping of her legs and increasing heart rate brought the feelings riling back, but under a more tempered, controlled manner. Cooper accepted and ignored it, trying not to give it more thought.

"Looks like this is it," said Ramon at an airlock door. "Guess the labs are the only secure area."

"Right." Cooper pulled her access card and swiped it. A red light flashed. Access Denied.

"What?" Ramon snapped. "That's bullshit!"

She swiped it again. Same result. Ramon swiped his. Access Denied. Cooper pressed the talk button.

"This is Triple-R, identify yourselves," she demanded.

"Who?" came back a tinny voice.

"Triple-R. We're here to evacuate any survivors."

"Never 'eard of you."

Cooper rolled her eyes. "It's not my fault you never paid attention at the security brief. I know they made you sit through it. The least you could do is open the fucking airlock."

"If you're 'ere to evacuate us," Cooper now noted a thick British accent, "we'll have to decline. Something important has happened."

"Important?" Ramon said off the comm. "Disastrous would be a better term."

"Or Royal fucked," Cooper added, then pushed the talk button again. "All right, but let us in. We need positive identification."

"You really think I'm falling for that one, love?" The talk panel went dead.

"What the—?"

"Little Limey shit," Ramon snapped.

Cooper kicked the door, losing her patience.

"Hey, these labs are air tight," Ramon said. "But they still need ventilation."

She went down the hallway and found the proper vent. A little tight and high up, but enough room for her to get into. "Well, hold this, Ramon."

Cooper handed over her G36 and pack, then he helped her up to the vent. She removed the grate with her multi-tool, and Ramon pushed her up into the chute.

Fuck, it's cold! she thought. *Damn it feels great!*

The cold air bit at her skin, taking away the heat radiating through her pores. She broke through the air lock's secure ventilation system and found the vent overlooking the lab. A man moved around beneath, rolling from console to console on his chair.

Cooper pulled the multi-tool from her thigh harness and started at the screws. When it fell, Cooper followed. The man jumped at the noise. Papers flew up and coffee spilled to the floor. Cooper strode towards him, pulled out the MP7 from her thigh holster for emphasis.

She hiked one boot up onto his desk. "So, what's so important that you can't be bothered? Or, before you answer, how about you unfuck the codes and let my partner in?"

The lab tech had dark, scraggly college hair, looked in his mid-thirties. His name tag read Alistair McKeon, BAE.

"British Aerospace?" Cooper asked.

McKeon stood. "Kitty-cat Club?"

"I think I preferDéjà Vu. Thousands of pretty girls, and three ugly ones."

"I've been there. It's the other way around." He strode over to the airlock and allowed access. "I'm more into the school-girl look, not so much the six foot 'spandex mercenary come rescue me', thing. Seriously, empowered women drive me nuts."

"Trust me, empowered's not how I feel at the moment." Cooper stood straight, hand on her hip. Ramon came through and handed back her weapon and pack.

"Thought there were supposed to be two of them?" Ramon asked.

McKeon closed the airlock. "My 'assistant' is down in the computer core a level below."

"What's so important, then?" Cooper asked.

"Only a massive, oncoming calamity of post-Biblical proportions."

"Less hyperbole. More facts."

An airlock door at another side of the lab opened. In walked a man covered head to toe in an environmentally sealed suit. He removed his helmet and revealed Asiatic features framed by close-cropped hair. Cooper recognized him from her Triple-R orientation.

"President Liang?" she asked.

"Yes," he said dismissively, then looked over at McKeon. "The resonance has already started."

"What?" McKeon shot up from his seat. "Where?"

"Satellites detected it north of St. Louis. It's about half the size of a football field, but it's growing at a steady rate."

McKeon slumped down in his chair. "We're finished."

"Anyone want to explain what the fuck is going on?" Cooper snapped.

Liang fixed her a solid stare. He always had a kind of permanently fixed smirk. "A gateway between universes is opening in Missouri."

Cooper blinked and cocked her head, "You mean the Mormons were right?"

"It's growing. We've been trying to interrupt it's coming, but all we've done is shift its position away."

"If we'd pushed it to the moon, we might've been all right," said McKeon. "But Missouri?"

"Wait," Cooper started. "You said it's a gateway. What's coming through it?"

"The eyphor's enemies," said Liang. "I assume that these creatures are part of their repertoire of weapons. Others might be coming."

"Or already here," McKeon said, then rubbed his forehead. "I saw a report about a day ago. Strange crossings on I-70 out of Denver. They thought they were deer or something, but they put the pictures up on the news. I don't know how old the resonance is, but it looks like they've already infiltrated across four states to get here."

"Hey, Cooper," Ramon said. "That thing we saw, killing the creatures."

She shook her head. "Why would it be killing the creatures if it's on their side?"

"Biological weapons are notoriously difficult to control," Liang groaned. He tossed the suit's helmet onto a workstation. "I suspect operations of this magnitude might be too complicated for a woman of such a savage ilk to understand."

Cooper cocked her eyebrow at him. "Are we going have difficulties, Mister President?"

He merely smirked and sniffed. "A woman. A base animal without the benefits of higher intellect, typical of the gender."

Cooper held her hand up, and turned about. "I don't have time for this."

"I saw you two," Liang continued. "I have cameras everywhere, even in places the corporation forbids. Motion sensors told me you were there, and I saw the whole proceedings."

"Uh," McKeon sounded, "what proceedings?"

Liang shook his head. "You two fucking in the locker room like swamp rats. Uncontrollable. You," he looked at Ramon, "letting this bitch in heat jump you like that. Men are supposed to be made of stronger stuff."

Ramon looked at him with narrowed eyes and spoke low, "Hey, that's none of your business, man. You know nothing about her or me."

"Know one woman you know them all," Liang continued. "There hasn't been one great civilization that hasn't been sunk by their weight. If they could only fulfill their purpose and breed, and stay out of the way of everything else. Like your husband, how you almost sunk his career with your emotional antics."

Cooper readied to lay into him, but her ex-husband chimed in her ear. "Cooper, you copy?"

She hoped to hear something good. "Yeah. What's up?"

"I'm...uh, I'm..."

"Spit it out, beau. It sounds like things aren't going well."

"Damn right, they're not. Have Alistair and Robert filled you in on the resonance?"

"Yes, it's here, it's growing, some bad shit coming through it."

"That's it. I think we only have one chance to fight this. I've talked to your boss, Scotty, and he agrees."

Cooper felt a cold chill at what was coming. "What's that?"

"He's calling in everyone. Rangewood's going to escort myself and a few other engineers to the core reactor of the facility. We're going to redirect power into the eyphor's main drives."

Cooper's eyes shifted in thought. "And what's that going to do?"

"Honey, there's a crap load of war machines in that thing's belly. All they need is some juice."

Cooper saw everything through a haze. Voices echoed in her head. Every inch of her body felt on fire, feverish. She broke through it. A cold wind washed over her. Kelly knelt and smiled, filling her vision. Cooper looked up to her glory beneath the cyber exoskeleton, soft skin of her tummy heaving against the stillness of metal with every breath. Her hazel eyes carried a worried look.

"Are you all right?" her voice bounced around with a metallic tinge. "Cooper?"

Cooper lifted up onto one arm. She looked straight into Kelly's milky white breasts. Pink nipples beckoned her lips.

"I could wake up to you every morning."

"Hopeless romantic." She smiled. "Glad you're back."

"I don't know if I am."

She sat up and felt grass against her skin, also noting her gauntlets were gone. The rear end of the tilt rotor faced her, surrounded by large evergreens. A smell of fresh pine

filled her nostrils.

"So this is the outside," Kelly nearly whispered. "It's beautiful. It smells so good."

Cooper breathed out pleasantly. Naked in the wild, like ancestral times past. A feeling so natural overcame her.

"I hope your son is out here, and not back there."

"I know," Cooper said. She found Alyssa about ten feet away, laying on her belly, dressed in exoskeleton and little else, drawing in a leather bound sketchbook. She smiled at Cooper with a quick glance, and then got back to her drawing.

She marveled at the sight, almost didn't believe it. The ruthless soldier she'd experienced the last day was gone. There, laying on her front, ankles crossed and kicking innocently back and forth, Cooper looked upon the four year old girl she remembered seeing not even a week ago.

Kelly held Cooper's head up and kissed her. "At least you're not too hot to touch now."

"Just hot to the touch?"

Cooper ran her fingers through Kelly's hair and stroked her face. They hugged and held each other for a moment in the much cooler mountain air. Alyssa cleared her throat loudly as they did, though not taking her eyes off her drawing.

Kelly pressed her cheek against Cooper's and whispered. "I don't think she likes me."

Cooper nodded and rubbed Kelly's back. "It'll be okay. Leave us for a couple minutes?"

"Okay." She kissed Cooper's cheek and headed back towards the transport.

Cooper walked over and knelt next to Alyssa, looking at her drawing of an emblem. A highly stylized bird with sweeping blades for feathers, wings spread high.

"A phoenix?" Cooper asked.

"Sure," said Alyssa. "I'd deliver supplies to Dad, and while resting up to go back, he'd teach me how to draw."

"You hardly ever needed a teacher. You were a natural." Cooper knew that was an embellishment, but Alyssa smiled at her anyway.

"Thanks." She closed up the sketchbook and rose up to her knees.

"You ever get cold?" Cooper asked. "I'm...registering a chill."

"Exo's don't get along well with clothes, fabrics block off the linkages, unless you want to cut and rip a hole in every spot, and I'd prefer this to rags. And considering most rigs are custom, makes uniform development a little rough. Our manufacturing base for those types of items are a little insufficient at the moment."

Alyssa ran fingers along her arm. "Conductive epidermal wiring heats and cools, distributes thermal energy or dissipates it. I'm good in most local extremes, use thermal blankets to sleep. And you?"

"I haven't felt too hot or cold as far the environment's concerned. I guess my body's even better adapted than yours. So," Cooper smirked, "best we save the clothes we find for people who need them, right?"

"Or are you just showing off for your new girlfriend?"

Cooper's eyes widened. "I take it you don't approve of our relationship then?"

"Approval is not so much at the heart of it. I'm damn surprised for sure. Is this new? Does Dad know?"

Cooper's throat tightened, and she felt sick at the mention of Michael from Alyssa's lips again. She clearly thought he was still alive. She would have to tell her, but the words wouldn't come up. They felt weighted down, chained to multi-ton boulders in her lungs.

"When was the last you heard from him, Alyssa?" Cooper could only ask.

"Three days ago we received a scrambled communiqué reporting the return of full brain function, and integration was complete. He said you were going to be rising any minute, once your internal defibrillator restarted your heart."

"I have...." Cooper touched her chest and felt her heartbeat, but the thought of an internal defibrillator was the least of her problems right now. "Integration?"

Alyssa took in a breath and pressed her lips together. "With the bio-energy source we implanted in your uterus."

Cooper's eyes nearly popped out of her head.

"You've been bonded with an eyphor designed biogenetic weapons system, specially calibrated to counter Nexus technology."

Cooper blew out a breath. "Sooo...I'm pregnant with an alien?"

Alyssa shrugged. "That's one way of looking at it."

"Well, then," she said through grit teeth. "I guess my attraction to women is no concern of yours, or your father's, or anyone else's. Looks like you've all done enough work on me. And, by the way, it's nothing new. I've known I liked girls since I was eight. It's part of me, more a part than whatever it was you put in my body."

A silence ensued between them. Alyssa looked away. "You...wouldn't be alive without it. I'm sorry, Mom. I felt that if I, that if we could bring you back...."

"What, honey?"

"That we'd find Devon and we could be a family again. That's what I've always wanted, ever since Dad explained to me what he was doing, when I was old enough to understand. Please forgive me, if we did certain...things. I don't know if Devon will forgive me when we find him, but I don't want you to be mad at me too."

Cooper placed her hand on Alyssa's shoulder. "What would Devon need to forgive you for?"

She shook her head, slapping the sketchbook on her leg. "Devon fought them so I could get away. I can't shake the feeling that they have him. I don't know what to do when I think about it."

"Don't worry. We'll find him. Why would he need to forgive you?"

"I ran away," Alyssa snapped. "And they took him. If I had fought...I'm so sorry."

"No, honey. I don't know how it happened, but if all the armies of the world couldn't stop them, you have no reason to blame yourself. We'll find him, I promise."

She drew her daughter into a hug and Alyssa rested her arms around Cooper's shoulders.

"*Tell her, you coward.*" Cooper shook at the sound of the voice. "*Tell your daughter her father's dead.*"

Stay out of my business, bitch.

"I'm going to go check on the boys," said Cooper. "Get to know them."

"And the girls," Alyssa said, "about six of them. Try not to get to know them too well. You seem to have tendencies."

Cooper snorted and headed over to Kelly, looking out into the distance. The Spire stood straight into the sky like a streak of light, fiber thin at this distance. Cooper looked down from that along to Kelly's backside, gulped at the shapely form, one hand on her hip. Black panties delved into a sharp v-shape on the perfect curves of her buttocks.

Cooper slowly strode forward, quiet, then grabbed a handful past the servo frames. Kelly looked over her shoulder and smiled, they kissed quickly.

"Staring at the Spire?" Cooper asked.

Kelly looked back to the horizon. "It makes me angry how pretty it is, and the...it doesn't even look like anything real. Like a laser light more than a building. Seems impossible how something like that can even stand."

"It must go deep," Cooper said. "The base has to be at least half the height, miles underground. Maybe even further."

"Heard some rumors say each Spire goes all the way to the core, that they meet in the middle. Wonder what they do down there."

"Nothing good," Cooper said, patted Kelly's butt and said, "c'mon, let's go meet our new friends before the shooting starts again."

They headed to the tilt-rotor, heard the sounds of drills and welding inside the cargo bay. Cooper led the way and Kelly followed. There, a man laid on a make shift work bench made of packs and ammo boxes. Atom Smasher stood over him with drill in hand. Cooper cocked her eyebrow approvingly at the naked form laid out in front of her.

Slim and muscled, well endowed, good skin tone. Sweat beaded over him, dripped across those ripples. She circled him while Atom Smasher worked. His eyes stayed closed, probably anesthetized for the cyberization process, but she recognized him.

"Jamison," she said.

"We call him Walleye," Atom Smasher said. "Most of us never thought he existed.

"He dropped his crew and flew us out of there," Cooper said with awe.

"Not wasting too many resources on him, are we?" Kelly asked.

"Wasting?" Cooper asked. "The guy who saved all our asses?"

"I'm using mostly parts I'm tearing out of this transport," Atom Smasher said.

Walleye. Cooper found him as beautiful as his deeds. He stirred while laying there with his eyes closed, and she cocked an eyebrow at it, wondering how good it would feel in her gentle grip.

From the look of it, Atom Smasher was almost complete with the cyberization, the wetwiring and anchor points.

"How can you wire humans together like that with just those regular tools? A drill and a screwdriver make a cyborg?"

Atom Smasher chuckled, not looking up from his work, except stealing a glance at Kelly. "I, uh, helped design most of these systems to be self-contained and self-installing. The wetwires are coated with nanofilaments that follow the build of the body to get to where they need to be, lead by a tiny motor that drags it from the front."

"It's kind of a weird feeling," Kelly said, "like little worms crawling through your skin, but they settle and then it's like they're not there."

She smiled at Cooper, then looked at Atom Smasher doing his work. Kelly seemed to have an effect on him.

"The other incisions, the anchor points, burrow themselves through muscle tissue and hook into bone. They're also coated with nano-fibers that rebuild the muscle and bone

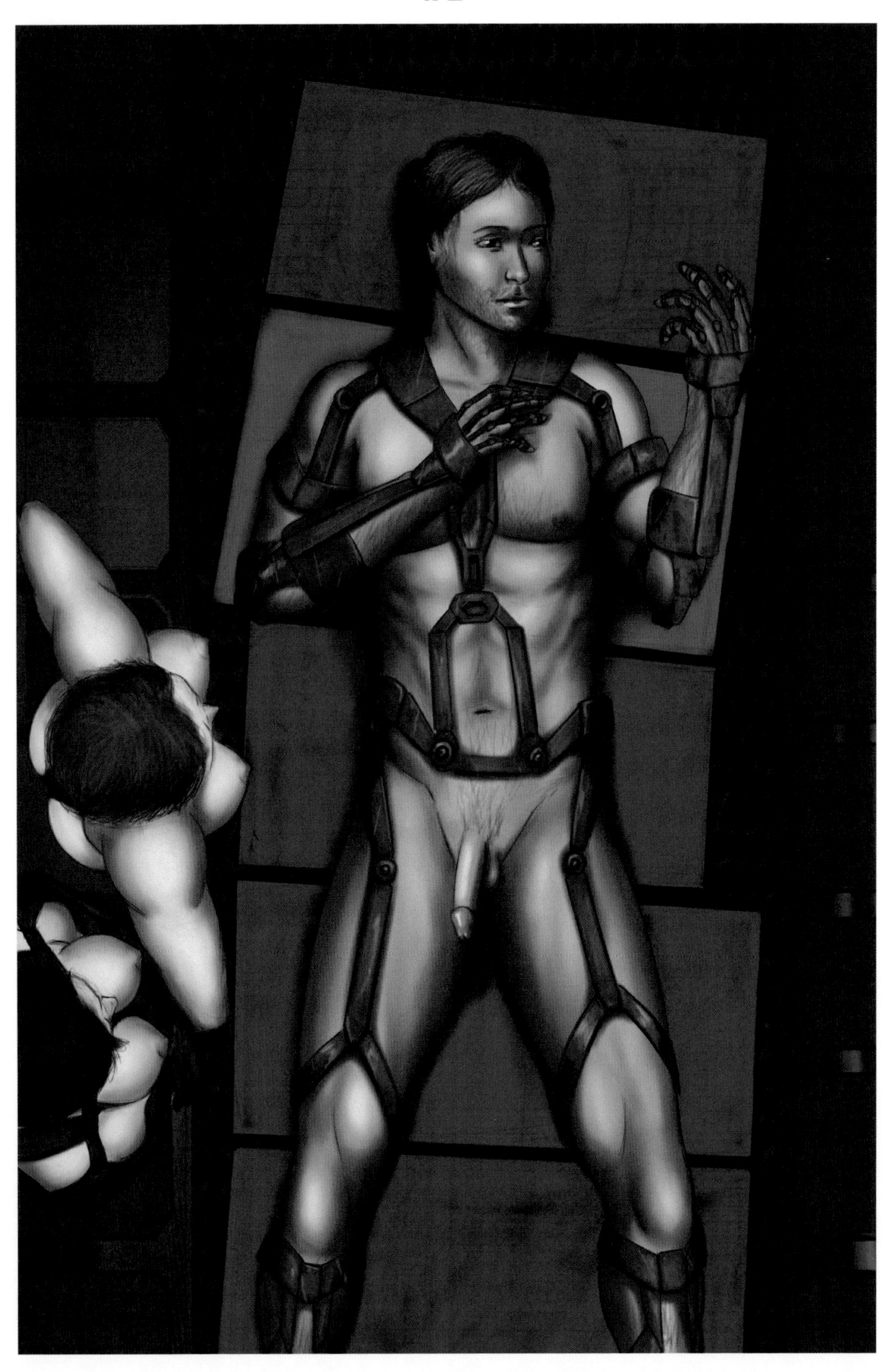

around them, reinforcing the anchor points. The rest is just drilling the exoskeleton into the anchor, setting it in. And voila, hydraulic joints to strengthen the body, on which we can attach all of kinds of lovely gear."

Atom Smasher connected Walleye's IV to a hand-held apparatus. "Time to wake up, smell the roses."

Walleye stirred, in more ways than one.

"Mm," Cooper sounded through a barely contained giggle, looked at Kelly, whose stern face was not amused.

"Something?" she asked.

Kelly shrugged. Walleye groaned and sat up. Atom Smasher gave him a slap on the shoulder, held up a pill bottle.

"Two of these should take the edge off. I put the last of my thermalplast around the incision areas, but it should hold you. If it itches, don't scratch! It'll make it worse."

Walleye groaned and held out his hand to let Atom Smasher put the pills in his palm, then downed them.

"Taste like shit."

"Well, I ain't a chef," Atom Smasher said, then stood up with a brief whir of his own cyber harness. "I'll be packing up."

"How you feeling?" Cooper asked him.

Walleye looked himself over, curled up one arm that flexed a rock of a bicep, the kind of arms Cooper liked to wrap herself in.

"Strange feeling," he said, "it's like I'm not even using my own limbs, it does everything."

"Nice," Cooper said.

He looked at her, she moved her head sideways, hands on hips. His reaction to her bare breasted form was immediate and impressive.

"Hey," Kelly said, "pack it up Mack Daddy, she's out of your league."

"Don't hate," Cooper teased her.

"Shorts, my man!" Atom Smasher said and tossed the fabric over to Walleye.

"Awww," Cooper sounded.

"Don't like him too much," Kelly whispered to her. "He's still Nexus, I'd bet my life on it."

"I can hear you, y'know," Walleye said.

"Good, then you know I'm watching."

Atom Smasher gathered up his gear, laughed uncomfortably at the exchange, and said, "I'll be outside guys."

Walleye finished dressing, followed Cooper and the suspicious Kelly outside. Alyssa walked over to the tilt-rotor. They had landed near a dirt road.

"So how's our ride there, Walleye?" asked Alyssa. Cooper was taken aback by her hostile tone.

Does she not trust him either?

"No way I can repair that engine out here. They shot through the main shaft assembly. The rotor's come loose."

"What happened?" Cooper asked.

"We were almost clear of the city. Got jumped by a pair of gunships. They did a number on the starboard engine before we got clear of them. Right now, looks like, we're near Montezuma."

"Montezuma?"

"Yeah, they bounced us over Mount Evans." He glared over at Alyssa. "So, it's up to you now."

"You've taken me off my route." She cocked a challenging eyebrow. "Never had a gunship take me most of the way."

"It's a transport," he corrected in a low whisper.

"Is there something going on between you two?" Cooper asked.

Alyssa rested her hands on her twin pistols. "I just want to know what kind of man can spend so many years in the Mack Daddies and not get his hands dirty."

"I managed to skirt most of it." He looked to Cooper, then Kelly, who backed away and circled around the other woman, backing her up.

"Don't worry," said Walleye. "I'm used to people keeping their distance."

He strode over, kicked the lid off an ammo crate and loaded up an auto shotgun and bullpup-style assault rifle.

Alyssa paced away, keeping one eye on him.

"Thanks for saving our asses, Walleye," Cooper said. Both the other women turned to her, disbelieving. "He saved our lives, ladies, now get over it."

"No," Kelly said, holding onto Cooper's shoulder. "They do this all the time. They act all nice, and then set their trap."

"Did any of those acts before involve dropping a squad of Watchmen to their deaths?"

"You can also see my co-pilot in the cockpit," Walleye added. "I worked with that man for three years, but it didn't change anything."

"And he's been doing spy stuff presumably for your side," Cooper said to Alyssa. "He's definitely been working on *my* side."

Kelly sighed and backed away. "Fine. But I'm not taking my eyes off of him."

"Hey, looks like me and Kelly can get along just fine," Alyssa grinned.

"I can understand her reasoning," Cooper countered her daughter. "The things the Watchmen did to her, just seeing the uniform's color could set her off."

Cooper looked over to Kelly, smiled softly at her. "But at least she'll never have to see their faces again. Not like I did."

"What's that?" Alyssa asked, and Walleye perked up from his weapons prep to hear her as well.

Cooper didn't know why she blurted it out. She feared something about her daughter, so cold behind the eyes. She needed to brave that cold to see what was there.

"I was raped in the Naval Academy," Cooper said. "Attacked by two men who were supposed to be my comrades."

Kelly stepped up behind her and touched her arm, gently holding it there. Cooper kept her eyes locked on Alyssa's, waiting for something to happen. Her daughter stepped forward, brow down a little. Was it curiosity?

"How long ago?" she asked. "Before...you know...?"

"Around twelve years before Salt Lake, so six years before you were born. I never got justice for it. They escaped, and followed me throughout my career. I even think one of them betrayed us to Nexus, with Robert Liang."

"Never got justice?" Alyssa asked, then looked at Kelly. "Well, par for the course I guess."

Cooper then narrowed her gaze, her throat stunned into barely making a sound.

"Our best estimates state around seven out of ten women in Synchro Point have been sexually assaulted," Alyssa said. "Happens every day. Small wonder if it's because guys like Liang and your old enemies are in charge of the place. The whole thing is like one long trip down the mind of Robert Liang."

A stunned chill held Cooper still, lips and jaw tight. Alyssa gazed off to the streak of white that was the Spire rising into the sky.

"They escaped justice too," Alyssa said. "Or maybe there was no justice to escape from. Maybe that's why you care for those people so much, cause you're just like them. A victim."

Cooper stepped forward, looked Alyssa in the eye. "I cared for those following us, because they won't follow us if we don't. If they're willing to die for me, I need to be willing to die for them. I take it you haven't been assaulted the way me and Kelly were, or the seven out of ten?"

"I've been shot twice," Alyssa said in a tone that couldn't have been more blasé. "Suppose that counts for rapid onset penetration in an unwilling fashion."

Cooper shook her head. "What happened to you?"

Alyssa huffed, her bright brown eyes turning to chilled stone. "What happened to me?" she almost hissed. "Seven billion people died, that's what happened to me. And all I know is that you're the thing that can end the spiral to extinction."

"If you're so worried about extinction you should value every human life."

"Like the Watchmen? They're human too, you know. They're not even sterilized like most of the remainder are. Every one of them we kill is a greater blow to the survival of our species than most of our losses, but you think that's going to stop me from blowing their brains out? So long as there'll be enough of us at the end, we can suffer a few more deaths so long as it gets you to where you need to be."

Cooper put up her hands. "And where do I need to be, then?"

"With the eyphors. That's all I know. That's all they'll tell us. Letting a human know why is too great a risk, so they kept it from us. Except for Dad. They told him. They trust him, so I'm going to trust them. And that is all any of us need to know."

Cooper shook her head. "The Navy would have loved you."

Up the nearby dirt path, a car approached, big V8 growling. Her eyes zoomed in to see Dead Meat and Scorpio in the front. It thundered on up to the stricken tilt-rotor.

"Woo-hoo!" Scorpio whooped as he climbed out. "Some serious meat on this baby!"

Cooper recognized the make, Dodge Charger, late model. The white paint had chipped away, stained with rust. A solid, air hogging vent replaced the normal aluminum cross beams. A giant blower stood on top of the engine, quite obviously since it had no hood. No roof either, but it did have a one foot tall spoiler.

"Oh, hey," Dead Meat said. "We just got word. Red Eagle's at EndPoint. We've got to get you there, now."

"Yeah," Scorpio added. "We got a big trunk, get all dem guns in it. Brought a couple from Montezuma too."

"The citizens we picked up are huddling with the folks back in the town. Most of them are in too bad a shape to follow us."

"Oh, and they sent us a bunch of flowers," Dead Meat said, pulling out a box of various, colorful, picked things. "For luck I guess."

"Show their appreciation, I'm sure," Cooper said.

Dead Meat set in on the hood, then called the rest of his commandos in from their defensive perimeter. A second vehicle came in from Montezuma, a heavy off road gun truck in green camouflage scheme, badly scarred. Two commandos got out and distributed spare ammunition and weapons to the others, along with some quick bites of food.

The troupe spent the next few minutes setting up the cars and their gear. In the middle of it, Walleye offered an assault rifle to Kelly.

"Want a SCAR?" he asked.

Kelly glared at him, turning white. "What the fuck is that supposed to mean? Some Watchman joke?"

He noticed his mistake, but remained stoic, one hand up slowly. "Special-ops Capable Assault Rifle." Walleye pointed to the letters etched on the side of it.

"So?"

"It spells SCAR. I'm sorry if I upset you. I wasn't referring to anything."

"Here," Dead Meat said to Kelly and handed over a modified, blacked out Kriss. "Eight millimeter, high velocity. Better than those forty-five models."

"Thanks," Kelly said and took up the SMG.

Cooper nodded to Walleye, and he handed over the SCAR.

"This is different," she said.

"Nexus modified," said Walleye. "Uses a 7.62 tracker round. It can adjust in mid-flight to compensate for drag, drift, and torque. Just lock onto a target through the scope with the thumb trigger, then let fly."

"Has it been hacked?" Atom Smasher asked from a ways off.

"Hacked?" Cooper asked.

"Forces weapons have encryption keys locking their mechanisms in place," Dead Meat explained. "Atom Smasher hasn't found one he couldn't hack yet."

"We's got a fews, oh, techy man," said Scorpio, hauling a few out of the trunk. "Have at 'em."

Cooper checked through the scope of hers, looked at the crosshairs. "Interesting," she said, then loaded up her waist belt with 7.62.x51mm tracker rounds, as many as they had.

"How'd you learn to shoot?" Dead Meat asked Kelly.

"Uh," she started, looked at Cooper for a moment. Their eyes met, and then Kelly looked back to her weapon. "My Daddy taught me before he...before they took him."

Cooper felt something wrong deep down in her gut. It didn't seem like mourning in Kelly. Regret? Shame? Something to do with her father. It darkened her a little, and Cooper strode over to the box of flowers. She pulled out one, brilliant red, a symmetric cascade of what seemed a thousand small petals. It almost formed a ball.

"A dahlia," Cooper said. "Pretty."

"What is?" Kelly asked, then joined up with Cooper.

Cooper proffered the flower to Kelly, touched it to her pouty lips, then rubbed it down her chin, neck, breasts, then belly.

"Everyone has a call sign except you." Cooper set the flower stem into Kelly's chest harness, a big blossom. "Dahlia. Dark, mysterious, and lovely."

"I like it," Kelly said, smiled.

"I managed to snag myself an A1," Walleye said and lifted up the bullpup. "Fully Nexus built and designed, 4.8mm APEDS. Armor Piercing Explosive, Discarding Sabot. Only kinetic weapon guaranteed to penetrate their soldiers' armor."

"Could use a few more of those," Cooper said.

"We'll have to kill a few of them to take theirs. Otherwise, not exactly on the market."

"Those things can take a minute to hack too," Atom Smasher said, tablets hooked into the two other weapons with elaborate wire sets.

"Is that the short minute or long minute?" asked Dead Meat.

"Depends on if I get my coffee or not."

Walleye smiled at the car, circled around the vehicle for the driver's side door. Dead Meat stopped him cold with a hand on his chest piece.

"I think you've driven far enough today." The tall rebel slipped in through the door. Walleye's jaw quivered.

Cooper stepped up to him, so close their bodies almost bumped. She nearly startled him.

"Hey, VIP's ride in the back," she said, then pulled the back door open for him. Walleye chuckled and they piled in.

"Crowded ride," Alyssa said from the front passenger seat.

"We can squeeze it in," Cooper said as she wrapped up in a single seat with Kelly. Walleye sat next to them. Their eyes locked, Kelly's beaming her hostility, Cooper gently nudged her chin. "Why are you even worried? I'm here."

Kelly smirked, gave Cooper a little peck on the nose. "Still not taking my eye off of him."

"Strap in," Dead Meat mumbled. He mashed on the gas. The HEMI roared to life. The Charger pulled a 180 and skirted back onto the dirt trail.

Eight heavy bio-carrier transports flew low through the valleys in two columns. Each carried a squad of sixteen light neo-skins, members of Colonel Ju-kal's hunter-killer unit. Like most biomechs, the bio-carriers originated as living creatures, now long detached from their origins. Its hollowed out, bulbous body served to carry others of its ilk wherever Nexus needed them, providing protection with its thick, spined hide. Plasma-ion compulsion engines powered by Nexus's unique energy source meant it could stay aloft almost indefinitely and provide flexible support to its troops.

Ju-kal himself sat in the lead bio-carrier, stone still in a revetment of its inner ribbed "stomach." His mind looked at the networked video feed from the Phase-1 neo-skins on the ground. He saw all they saw, uploaded to his brain.

Approaching coordinates. Stolen tilt-rotor in sight.

Ju-kal hadn't been a Phase-1 neo-skin, or "soldier," in almost thirty years. He wasn't used to how slow they moved, only slightly faster than a normal human, though they could maintain that movement almost indefinitely. Many were also fresh, not veterans of the Mass

Departure. A mantid ran ahead of them. Its clicks and warped sounds came through into Ju-kal's mind as language.

Tracks. Treads. Tires. Carbon emissions – the mantid reported.

Good – Ju-kal noted. *Ascertain direction.*

North, north-west, sir – responded the soldiers.

The tilt-rotor is compromised. One casualty. Investigate for further intelligence. Post guard. Be wary of traps left behind by the rebels.

Ju-kal switched to a verbal carrier and reported back to the Spire. "Stolen tilt-rotor found. Unexphen unaccounted for. Direction estimated to north, north-west in ground vehicle. Continuing pursuit."

He received confirmation. The lead mantid pressed on down the dirt road. It's incredibly sensitive nose picked up a scent. Ju-kal nearly twitched at the memory it recalled. Jordan DeBlanc. A sweet scent. The best he'd ever tasted. Sweet smell of the woman who haunted his dreams.

No. Not his dreams. The dreams of who he was before.

Recall tactical knowledge, Jordan 'Cooper' DeBlanc. Training. Skill sets. Personal weaknesses. Points of acumen. Collate with known capabilities of enhanced adaptations.

It produced a formidable picture. Years and years of combined memory, joint training exercises. Though while the neo-skin he was today tried to accumulate combat data, the memories of the man he used to be kept leering at those curves. The sway of her hips. Swell of her rump. Shake of her breasts. Scent of her hair. Feel of her skin.

Personal relationship analysis...competitive allies, untrustworthy. Professional hostility. Pheromones of subject indicate no attraction toward this past unit.

Ju-kal broke into a sweat. Heart rate increased. A reproductive stirring, though not for its intended purpose.

Look at her, he thought. *The way she struts, that exuberant confidence. Broad shoulders, those fucking lips. So thick and full.*

He twitched. *Maintain mission parameters.*

"What do you think, Lenny?" he asked through memory.

The clean shaven, muscled young cadet looked at him with both fear and excitement.

"I don't know, man. I mean, she's good and all, but I don't think she's really that big a problem for us."

"You don't just want to put that bitch down a little? Not like it'll hurt her all that much, some of the stories I here. She lines up upper classman and blows 'em in line, like she practically made a drill manual for it."

Lenny shifted in his seat. His lips flared shortly, sniffed. "Think she does DP?"

Scotty smiled. "We'll find out."

"Yeah," Lenny said low from across the mess hall table. "She wants to fuck her way to the top, then...."

"We'll have to fuck her back to the bottom."

Maintain mission parameters.

Ju-kal came out of the memory drenched in sweat. He moved slightly more than the utterly still neo-skins. He looked upon one. LK1705. That unit had followed him all throughout the Mass Departure. Even despite the memory lockdown, somehow, they had

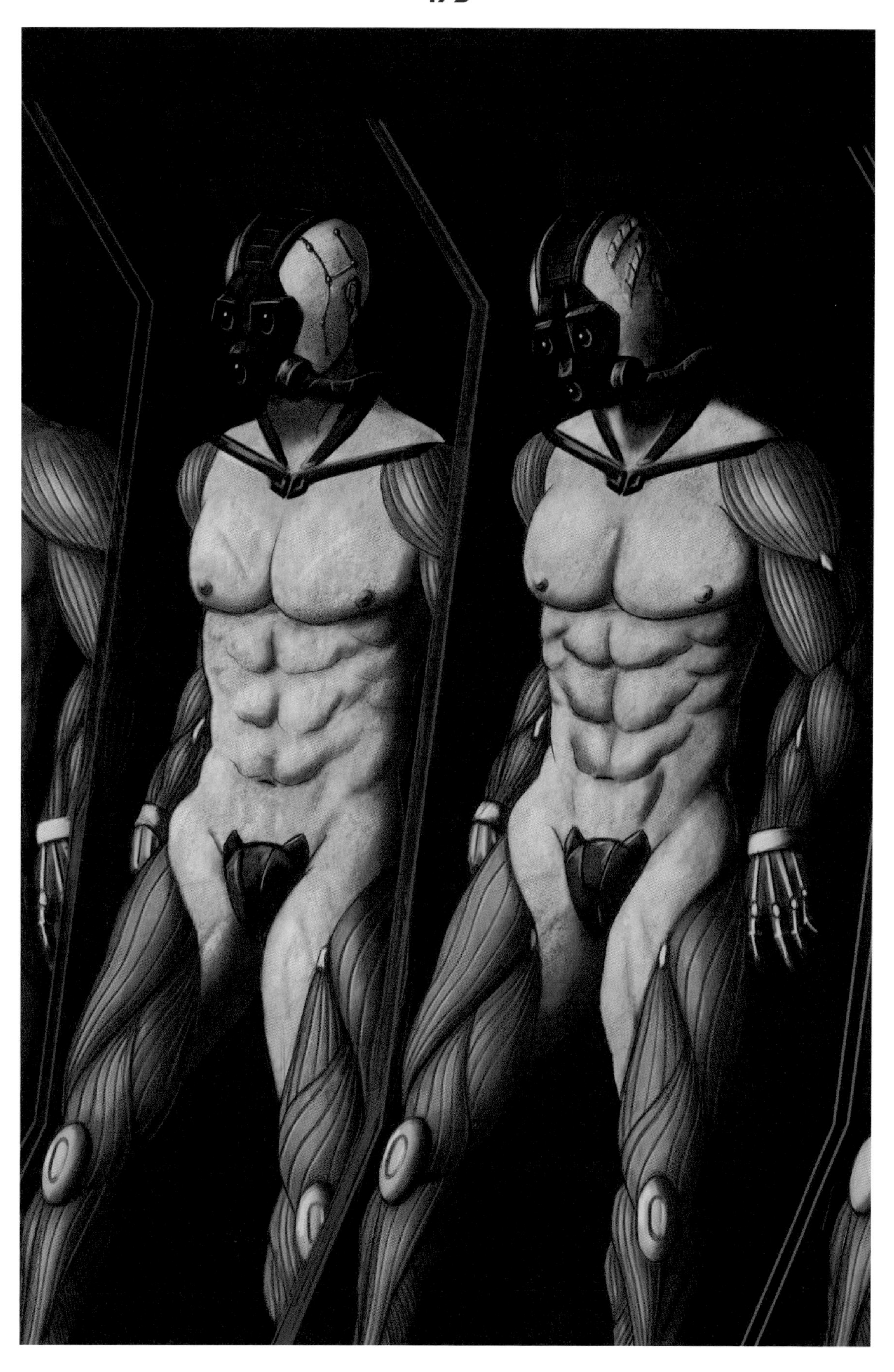

stuck together. Instinct.

Now he realized. "LK1705. Lenny Knox."

Continue combat data collation – he ordered to his internal processors. *Provide full report with strategic....*

He lost concentration, grabbed his head with a synthetic hand.

"Fucking bitch!" he breathed hard. "Gonna find you...gonna...look so good...look so good, baby."

He stilled. *Maintain mission parameters.*

The Charger rumbled down the dirt trail. Dead Meat didn't pull any punches, making liberal use of the air-brake to swing around the curves. Cooper held onto the roll cage and Kelly kept hold of her. Their second vehicle of commandos could barely keep up. Sometimes she looked back to see them well behind their dust.

Hulks of vehicles, wreckage, burnt-out buildings, even bodies littered the side of the road. Some seemed more fresh than others, but it all carried the stench of death. It reminded her more of Afghanistan than Colorado.

Then Dead Meat slammed on the brakes and pulled up next to an old store sitting by the road.

"What the hell, Allan?" asked Alyssa.

Dead Meat pointed ahead to a freshly burning set of vehicles a hundred meters away. "Auto-cannon."

"Oh, shit!" Alyssa spat, then ripped out of her seatbelt and out of the car.

The second vehicle came to a dead halt just behind them, set up on an opposite angle and the troops deployed.

"Auto-cannon ahead, Slag!" Dead Meat called out.

"Roger!" Slaghead replied.

Cooper followed everyone else as they rushed out. She knelt next to her daughter.

"What's the matter?"

"An automated gravpulse gun. An area-denial weapon. There haven't been any this close to EndPoint, but they've been pressing forward. Doesn't help they've had a typhoid outbreak up there."

"Looks like the rock face is blocking it off," said Dead Meat. "There's a radio tower behind there, atop the hill. Would be a good place to put the gun."

"We gotta take it out, and quick," Alyssa said.

"Hey, I'm game," said Scorpio. "Would you be good, Phoenix? You weren't so hot a while ago."

Cooper huffed and flexed her arm a couple times. The armor formed, pouring over her skin like liquid and solidifying. The act caused a slight discomfort in her abdomen, a pulsating type of pain, but she could deal with it.

"Feel all right."

"Those eyes is something," said Scorpio.

"I got a satchel charge," Slag added. "Plus an RPG-17 with two rounds."

"Relic weapon," Dead Meat said. "Still, could maybe disable the cannon if it came down to it."

Walleye stepped forward and leaned against the corner of the building. "What's likely to be our opposition?"

Dead Meat glared at him for a second. "Phase-1 soldiers, most likely. Probably six of them. Maybe mantid support. Hopefully there aren't any camps nearby."

"That's a lot of hopes and probablies," Walleye said.

"We don't have the luxury of piling on any time we have a problem. There's no Metro Defense this side of Mount Evans. Just us and the skins."

"Shut up," Cooper spat. "His gun's pointing the same way as ours. He's saved my life three times already and he's saved all of us."

"Hey, I always thought he's cool," said Scorpio. He wagged his finger between him and Alyssa. "And I don't know why you two's ain't gettin' along. You's the eyes. The eye from outside, the eye from inside."

Kelly huffed, leaning over them on the store's porch rail. "The eyes on the wall, and the eyes in the sky. But I also thought walleyed meant you couldn't see straight. Your vision is curved? Crooked?"

"That'll be enough from you, too," Cooper said. "If he's not one of us, than I'm not one of you."

"Mom!"

"Enough, dear."

"No, Cooper," Kelly said. "How can you say that? As to what he did before, if losing a few Watchmen, who are fucking undesirables anyway, can get you taken out, I'm sure they'd do it."

"He's had plenty of opportunities already, Kelly," Cooper countered. "He had us all in the same cargo hold where he killed the others."

Walleye took in a breath as more theories rushed at him.

"They're using him to infiltrate EndPoint, then," said Dead Meat. "Maybe there's a bomb implanted in him. That way they get the Phoenix, the northernmost defense, our scientists—"

"Stop!" Cooper snapped. "If the Planetary Army wants me to do this whole Phoenix thing, we're going to do it my way."

Slag nodded approvingly. "I got your back."

He pointed his fist toward her, and she gave it a bump back.

"Cute, Slag, but you've been here three days, Mom." Alyssa shook her head. "Listen to me. I'm right, so's Kelly."

"Glad you two are getting along then. It was starting to get awkward."

"Never knew you to be such a sarcastically stubborn bitch," Alyssa said.

"You were only four. I held back. Now, enough of this bullshit. Get ready to move."

Cooper checked her SCAR and headed toward the woods. Walleye got up and followed her, quickly matched by Kelly. The fourteen headed into the hills. A steady rumble rattled the ground.

"Is that the gun?" she asked.

"Big gravpulse," Scorpio answered. "Like they's gots on the transports, but a lot bigger. Use a gravity well to hurl plasma...nasty stuff."

"Almost like a singularity gun," added Slag. "But instead of imploding you, it'll explode you."

Atom Smasher joined the group. He carried a duffel bag and his Mk48 light machine gun. "Guys need tech support?"

"Going after an auto-cannon," said Slag. "What you think?"

They slapped hands together. "I got ways."

Kelly looked at him, "Hey, I'll trade ya."

Atom looked at her, got dough-eyed all of a sudden and nearly did so.

"Hey," Slag said and thumped a meaty fist on Atom's chest. "No time for that, switching weapons, gear, ammo. Deal. Let's go."

"Dammit," Kelly said, "it's a nice looking gun."

Cooper propelled herself forward. She followed the sound. After a couple minutes of moving, she looked over her shoulder to see the rest of the troupe nearly a hundred feet behind. Sharper ears picked up their pants and gasps for air. She could smell their sweat on the wind.

This must be what a wolf sees.

"Leave the others," the voice chimed in her head.

No soldier goes solo, moron.

"They cannot follow. We will regret."

Cooper ignored it and moved forward. A silhouette near the ridge stopped her cold in her tracks. She flattened herself against a rock, then zoomed in to see a soldier walking along, holding a SCAR like hers.

Dull, beige-green patterns of ballistic padding covered his limbs and torso. A rebreather mask concealed his mouth and nose. He wore no helmet. His bald head shined in the sunlight.

Radio tower antennas reached to the sky. A natural ramp of dirt skirted up the ridge. Cooper ran to the top and headed for a small brick wall surrounding a complex of three old buildings.

Some kind of chatter entered her mind, not unlike the Watchmen's radios. Except she couldn't understand it.

"Reee-prrrr-zzz-trreee-jiiiinnnn...."

She shook her head of it. Then thought, *Where'd the soldiers go?*

Alyssa and Dead Meat moved around the corner, heading for one of the small buildings. The ground shook again as the gun fired somewhere up ahead.

"I'll cover you," Walleye told Cooper. She nodded and smiled. Walleye and Scorpio kept to the wall, while Kelly moved to the second building.

On the way, a soldier appeared on the roof ahead of them. His pale face and red eyes filled Cooper with a surprised dread, and then the crack of his SCAR shattered the mountain silence. Cooper dropped into the prone, belly against the dirt.

Kelly dove for a pile of rubble that barely covered her. Cooper aimed her own SCAR at the soldier and triple tapped him in the chest. Dust puffed off his armor, but he didn't fall. He knelt and disappeared behind the building.

Oh, shit, she thought.

"We will regret."

Shut up!

A second soldier appeared from the wall in front of them. The black Kriss in his hands piled several shots of 8mm HVP (High Velocity Pistol) into Cooper's body. She grunted against the pain and fired back. Walleye shot a pair of small shells out of the un-

der-slung shotcannon on his A1. Impacts flared against the soldier's body and forced him to the ground.

"C'mon." She grabbed Kelly by the shoulder and got her to her feet. They ran for the next building.

Two Nexus soldiers came over the small wall ahead of them. Cooper and Kelly fired before they could. Alyssa's white-orange pistol shots came in from the side. One of the soldiers fell to the ground, limp and unmoving, while the other escaped around the side of a building.

A fusillade of fire went over their heads, Atom Smasher laying down rounds from a distance with the Mk48. 7.62mm bullets whip-cracked in rapid succession like firecrackers in the air.

Walleye and Scorpio ran up to the buildings under his covering fire. One commando attempted to follow, but a pink mist jetted out the back of his head, scalp and skull flinging limply from a flap of skin before he hit the ground.

"Look out!" Scorpio warned, pushing Kelly into cover. He held the trigger of his AA12 down on a soldier coming from behind. Kelly landed next to Cooper's feet.

Scorpio unloaded a drum magazine of buckshot into the trooper, forcing him to a knee. Blood spurted from his upraised hand and scalp, but he didn't go down.

As the drum went dry, Scorpio let it hang from the sling, then shoved a pistol into the man's eye socket. A single pop and the soldier finally went down. Then a burst of bullets ripped through Scorpio's leg. He screamed and fell.

Cooper aimed in at the soldier kneeling behind the wall. Her shots sent him scrambling for cover.

"Neo-skin!" Walleye shouted and aimed up.

Cooper followed his aim and glimpsed a man with the skin of his arms and legs removed. His heavily muscled torso seemed bare, angled panels of metal cascaded down the natural shape of his body, a three monocle mask on his face, A1 in his hands, muzzle flaring.

She pushed Walleye away and took the hits. Screams escaped her lungs. Explosive bullets cut skin. They stung like nothing else she'd ever felt. The aching fire in her womb flared. Her skin closed back up. Despite it, she aimed back and fired. The tungsten rounds sparked against him. The neo-skin turned and bolted down the roof, launching into a leap that took him clear outside the compound.

"Dammit!" when her gaze drifted back, a pair of metal orbs rolled off the roof.

"Grenades!" she screamed. She looked to see Kelly getting back to her feet, then bolted to cover her.

"Get down!"

The blast forced Cooper into her lover. Shrapnel cut into her back and legs. She growled against the burn. The pain didn't go away as quickly as before, and her abdomen roared in agony.

"*We will regret.*"

"All right," she groaned. When she pushed up, Cooper looked around to see Kelly between her and a mantid.

Harpoons struck into Kelly's chest and belly. She landed in front of Cooper, blood gargling on her voice, hands hovering over the shafts.

Cooper froze. Rage and terror numbed her limbs. Everything moved as slow as a glacier. Time rusted to a halt. She perceived the tendrils spinning and tightening, readying to drag Kelly's body toward mantid pincers. Cooper's grapples launched forward and cut the lines. She piled into the six hundred pound killing machine.

"I hate you things!" she howled, claws digging into its underside. "I hate you! I hate you! I hate you!" Red-violet gore spilled onto her, jetting from its cut innards. She hurled it into one of the concrete façades.

She rushed back to Kelly. The girl's body panted and heaved as she lay in the same spot. Blood pooled out. Fear filled Kelly's eyes. Cooper knelt and cradled her head.

"Kelly! Kelly! Hang in there, okay?"

Scorpio grunted and applied a dressing to his leg. "This is bad fuckin' ju-ju."

"Atom Smasher!" Walleye called out. "Wounded!"

"I'm up! Cover me!" he said.

Slag shouted something ferocious and unintelligible while firing his AA12 into the woods.

"Slag!" Atom Smasher shouted, and in Slag's brief moment of attention, threw him a fully loaded Mk48. Slag cut loose with it, pushing back a group of his attackers but killing none.

The mountain air crackled with passing rounds. Alyssa and Dead Meat kept up fire from their building. Yet, Kelly filled Cooper's vision. She looked into her eyes. The girl pleaded for help.

"Just stay with me."

Kelly gargled. Blood filled her throat. Cooper cradled her cheeks.

"Don't try to say anything."

Atom Smasher slid next to them, on his knees and reaching into his med pack. Her skin went pale. Eyes blanking out.

"No, Kelly. Kelly! Stay with me."

"Need to tell you...."

"Shh-shhh-sh," Cooper tried. "Don't say anything, just stay awake."

"My name...."

"Yeah, yeah, Kelly. That's your name. You're with me. I love you, stay with me."

"My name...Kelly...Kelly Knox...."

The last word thundered in Cooper's ears.

"Watch out, Cooper," Atom Smasher said, pulling out chords and hooking them up to points on her cyber harness. Then he aligned a syringe with a long, thick needle to a slot in the small plate on her chest, and drove it in.

Kelly let out a pained hiss, and she sweated over pale skin stained red with blood.

"We got to get her out," he said. "I can't work here, you can't cover me forever."

Neither could Slag's ferocity hold back bullets. A fierce salvo ripped through various parts of his body, dropping him to the ground to silence his war cries.

Subtle memory played back in Cooper's mind. When she said the names of the men who had brutalized her, the name of Lenny Knox, Kelly's eyes changed. Her skin turned as pale as it was now on the dirt. Now, she knew why.

"*We regret.*"

"Yes, we do," she admitted.

Walleye knelt next to Scorpio and fired his shot-cannon. "Neo-skin's over there!"

The mini-shells patched next to the neo-skin's feet. He ran with a fast, slithery stride. His upper body hardly moved as legs pumped beneath him. He dove into the nearest building.

She looked down at Kelly, still panting like crazy, spitting up blood. "I'll get you an opening, get her out of here."

"I'll take care of her," Atom said. "I will."

Cooper shoved off the ground and sprinted after the neo-skin. With a single kick, the door flew off the hinges. The neo-skin sprayed 4.8mm APEDS from his A1. A flurry of small explosive shells sent Cooper to the ground.

She screamed against the pain, but pushed ahead. As her body repaired itself, anguish in her abdomen increased. Only rage remained. A rage her strength couldn't answer.

She rushed him. He side-stepped and Cooper ran into the wall, bending it beneath her momentum. The neo-skin sped forward, knocked her back against the wall with a butt-stroke across the face. He kicked her in the gut, sent her through the building to the outside.

The ground flattened against her back. She shook her head of it. The neo-skin leapt out of the building.

Walleye sprayed him with his A1. The neo-skin put up his hand and started running. Cooper bolted to her feet and plowed into him. He landed on his back. The grapples scraped at him. Vision nearing black, Cooper slammed her fist into his chest, over and over.

His exposed skin seemed to repel her punches the harder she struck but that only drove her instinct to punch even harder. The titanium ribs within bent under her blows. Her fists worked like pile drivers. Pained grunts and moans escaped his voicemitter. Cooper stopped. Sweat drenched her clothes. Her muscles felt ready to squeeze her bones to the breaking point.

"They're moving to the flanks!" Alyssa shouted. "They're going to assault!"

"Break contact!" Walleye shouted. "We'll get the auto-cannon. Wounded to the vehicles."

He rushed to Cooper's side.

"Are you all right?" Walleye asked.

"I can't even remember what that is." She fought from sneering. Light-headed. Drowsy. "Kelly...."

"I have a daughter," Lenny's voice rumbled distantly in her mind. "She's almost two years old now...Her name's Kelly. Kelly Knox...."

"...I'll tell her the kind of man her father is...."

Walleye's gloved hand touched her shoulder. He shouted and pulled back. The rubber on his glove had melted. Walleye ripped it from his hand. The woman barely cared as she pushed up, away from the dead neo-skin at her feet.

She walked over to see Kelly's body, but only found a streak of her lover's crimson life trailed across the ground. Blood pooled into the hard soil. All that remained was her Kriss, laid next to the dahlia she'd put on her exoskeleton, both surrounded by brass casings.

"I never understood until I had a daughter..." Lenny repeated over and over in her head. "I never understood until I had a daughter...."

Cooper picked up the flower, but just by touch it burned. It turned black in her hot fingers, then ignited. She dropped it, and it fell a puff of ash and flame.

Alyssa ran toward her, Dead Meat firing for cover. Two of his commandos ran back

under covering fire, bullets ripped through their bodies. Alyssa looked at her mother.

"I promised I would protect you," Cooper said, gritting her teeth. Tears rushed down her cheeks. "God dammit! I promised!"

"She thought the mantid would hurt you," Alyssa said, barely above a whisper.

Walleye came up from behind. "She got between you and it. I guess, she thought—

"I didn't need her to!" Cooper erupted and looked at them both. "I've been taking bullets all fucking day. Don't get between me and them! None of you!"

Her eyes drilled into Alyssa's. "*None* of you."

Alyssa shook her head. "I'm a soldier in the Planetary Armed Forces—"

Cooper clamped Alyssa's shoulder armor and pulled her closer, their faces looking at each other over Kelly's blood. "No, Alyssa. You're my daughter. I will be between you and them. Understand?"

"I never understood until I had a daughter...I never understood until I had a daughter...."

Alyssa met her golden gaze. Cooper admired the woman before her as much as she lamented the loss of the child, and feared the terrible cold rage within that woman. She released her grip on Alyssa's shoulder guard. The metal simmered and gleamed red with the print of her hand.

"She's with Atom, now," Alyssa said. "If there's anyone who can save her...."

The ground rumbled with another firing of the auto-cannon, not far away. The air crackled with incoming bullets.

"Mom," Alyssa said. "Let's take care of the cannon. Atom will take care of Kelly. Ready?"

Cooper barely heard her, but she looked at her daughter then, then back at Walleye. He knelt behind her, his cool brown eyes not unlike Ramon's.

"C'mon," he said. "We can do this."

"*Take them,*" the voice said. "*Watch them die too.*"

Cooper reeled her head back. Teeth ground against each other, but then contained the scream she wanted to unleash at the sky. The ground shook again, the auto-cannon firing.

"More soldiers inbound!" shouted Dead Meat. He helped Scorpio to the wall.

"Get out of here!" Walleye said, then to Alyssa and Cooper, "Follow me."

He ran off. Cooper tried to follow, but stopped as she adjusted to the massive cramps in her legs. They came to a trench dug out in the earth, braced by dark metal panels. Three conduits ran through the trench, about a foot deep.

"These are the power coils," Walleye said. "They'll lead us to it."

Cooper pushed through another two hundred feet. They got to the end of the trench. A drop-off looked over the valley for two miles. White smoke wafted up from the three barrels sticking out of the end of a turret the size of a Volkswagen.

"I never understood until I had a daughter...."

A tingling sensation filled Cooper's limbs. It started as a light tickle, but grew uncomfortable.

"What is this?" she asked.

Walleye furrowed his brow. "What's what?"

"You don't feel it?"

"Feel what?" asked Alyssa.

Steam rose from her shoulders and back.

"*Don't touch it!*" the voice screamed in her head. The sound came so loud, she screamed and grasped her head. She fell to her knees.

"Cooper!" Walleye shouted and placed his hand on her shoulder, recoiling. "Ah! You're like...like, uh, boiling kettle."

"*Don't touch it!*"

"Shut up! Shut up! Get out of my head!"

"Mom?"

"*I'm not in your head, you stupid primate!*"

The tingling got worse. It felt like neurotoxin boiling in her veins. Her eyes then saw differently. A new spectrum flushed over her vision. Swirling blue light flowed through the conduits leading to the gun. Incandescent strands of yellow cascaded over it, churning in an eternal dance.

"*We cannot take the energy. Don't touch it!*"

"If you can't explain it, shut your goddamned mouth."

Walleye and Alyssa backed away, half-tempted to point their weapons her way. Cooper reached for the light with her left hand. Some jumped at her like lightning. It hurt at first, but then pure delight wafted through her arm. In her pained state, everything felt so much better.

"Yeah, more of that."

"Cooper," Walleye finally said. "What's going on with you?"

"I'm taking this gun down!" Cooper dove forward and braced both hands against the conduit. All the blue-white power in her vision flowed up her arms, funneling straight to her abdomen. The pleasure she expected turned to utter anguish.

"*Too much! Too much!*"

"Stop!" Cooper tried to let go, but her hands locked onto the metal. Grass at her feet curled into black cinders. Sand fused to glass at her toes. Walleye and Alyssa ran farther away, and the guns melted. Sparks flew from them.

"Help!" Cooper cried.

Walleye shot mini-shells into the conduits further up, but it didn't change anything.

"Push through it!" Alyssa shouted.

"Got it," Walleye answered.

Walleye and Alyssa charged before the air got too hot around Cooper. Walleye swung his rifle like a club, breaking Cooper off of the auto-cannon. Cooper fell to the ground and the reaction stopped. All went black.

"I never understood until I had a daughter...."

06/22/2024, 1133. Weather Channel excerpt. "*The light is just tremendous. It's somewhere in Missouri but we can see it reaching over the horizon all the way here in western Kansas. Good Lord, what is going on? Standing out here, the wind feels like we're on the cusp of a hurricane. Dust is flying everywhere. I think it's expand— (unintelligible)*" Transmission Ends

Salt Lake Facility, 1200, 06/22/2024

Cooper and Ramon ran down the storage area in the ship's belly. She tried to keep her weapon level, but found it hard to keep her eyes off the mass of alien technology around her. Various types of war machines sat recessed in stacked revetments like a bee hive. A gentle blue light bathed everything. She'd never been this deep inside the ship.

"They automated or what?" panted Ramon.

"How the hell would I know?"

The machines had such an organic look about them. Every line seemed so smooth. Every joint natural and even. Yet the obviously mechanical intakes, scoops, thruster vents, left an undoubtedly artificial appearance.

"Cooper," Michael chimed in her headset. "Where are you?"

"We're in some kind of hangar...lotta machines."

"Liang's escort hasn't reported in for a while. He should be with Scotty."

"Scotty should be up ahead," said Ramon.

Cooper grunted at the prospect. "We'll know in a minute."

Cooper and Ramon slowed down to go tactical, weapons in their shoulders. The rest of their team should've been less than a hundred feet ahead.

"Any sign yet, Cooper?" Michael asked.

"No, nothing." They halted and held their positions. The waypoint marked in their visors was right at their feet. "Dammit, they were supposed to be right here."

"Contact!" Ramon shouted. He fired his assault shotgun at something moving fast between parked eyphor machines.

"What do you see?"

"It's one of those four-legged things. They after us now?"

"Cooper, what's happening?" asked Michael.

"Get back to you, baby."

Her flashlight glimpsed the movement of some kind of gray-green body. Cooper answered with a burst from her G36. The chamber filled with strange noises, like the songs of aquatic mammals.

"There!" Ramon snapped. The flashlight of his shotgun blazed on the creature. His AA12 spat a flurry of buckshot, sparking out some shards from its skin. It quickly side-stepped the barrage.

Harpoons slashed into his legs and sent him to the ground screaming.

"No!" Cooper shouted and poured on. The tendrils pulled Ramon to the beast. He struggled against it with a knife. Its chest-mounted pincers snapped at his flesh.

Cooper's magazine went dry. She pressed the release and let it fall, pulling another from her thigh pouch and snapping it in. She fired a couple more sprays into the alien before a heavy force bumped her from behind. Cooper fell forward, dropping her weapon.

Twin pincers pierced into her back and came through her belly. It lifted Cooper up to pull the pincers free. The pain shocked her body, but she had no breath to scream.

"Cooper! No!" Ramon screamed. His attacker jabbed sharp hooks into his chest. Blood spurted from the impacts, ripping through the memory molecule layers. Pincers grabbed between his ribs and ripped his chest open, until he lay silent seconds later.

The two aliens ran off into the dark of the eyphor hangar.

"Cooper," came Michael. "What's happened? Are you all right?"

She could only grunt into the mike. Gasping for air.

"Stay there. I'm coming for you."

"No," she finally said. "Stay away...."

"Like hell. Hang on, baby. I'm coming for you."